John Fairfax is the pen name of William Brodrick, who practised as a barrister before becoming a full-time novelist. Under his own name he is a previous winner of the Crime Writers' Association Golden Dagger Award.

'John Fairfax is a master of the courtroom drama and these Benson and de Vere stories are unputdownable. [Benson is] fearless, which makes him scary, not only to the criminals, but also his legal colleagues. A five-star bravura performance. This writer gets better and better'

A.N. Wilson, *The Tablet*

'If you love legal thrillers don't miss Fairfax, our answer to John Grisham. This is the fourth outing for William Benson, a defence barrister who fights for the innocent with little chance of clearing their name. But, he could be on a loser defending Karmen Naylor who's on a murder charge. It doesn't help her case that her estranged father's a London crime boss. Getting involved puts Benson in grave danger. Meanwhile sidekick lawyer Tess de Vere has learned a dangerous secret involving the Troubles in Northern Ireland'

Peterborough Telegraph

Fatal Proof

John Fairfax

abacus
books

ABACUS

First published in the United Kingdom in 2023 by Abacus
This paperback edition published in 2023

1 3 5 7 9 10 8 6 4 2

A CIP catalogue record for this book is available from the British Library.

ISBN: 978-0-3491-4352-1

Printed and bound in Great Britain by Clays Ltd, Elcograf S.p.A.

Papers used by Abacus are from well-managed forests
and other responsible sources.

Abacus
An imprint of
Little, Brown Book Group
Carmelite House
50 Victoria Embankment
London EC4Y 0DZ

An Hachette UK Company
www.hachette.co.uk

www.littlebrown.co.uk

For my children
Benedict, Jerome and Myriam

Murder, like talent, seems occasionally to run in families

The Physiology of Common Life,
George Henry Lewes

Wednesday 13th January 2010

Hollingtons Solicitors
Covent Garden, London

'According to his wife, he's ready to name names. Point the finger. We're talking state-sponsored murder. Sanctioned from the top. In Northern Ireland during the seventies. A death squad. British soldiers operating outside the law. Targeting PIRA personnel. That's the Provisional Irish Republican Army. The volunteers.'

Tess was amazed. Not so much at the allegation as at Julia Hollington's exceptional talent for saying the same thing more than once. To repeat an idea . . . *God, I've just done it myself.*

'He's ill. The wife says there's not much time left. We're talking urgency.'

We're talking. That was another piece of litter. Julia dropped it everywhere.

'I think it's best if *you* go and see *them*. Rather than *them* coming to see *you*. Take a full statement. Get a complete account on the record. Peter will lead on this. You're to assist him, Tess.'

Julia was the managing partner at Hollingtons, a City firm founded by her grandfather and given an international footprint by her father. She'd withdrawn from practice years ago, but as the childless guardian of a family tradition, she refused to actually retire. And it was to Julia, compassionate and

1

attentive, that a former British soldier's wife had turned for help. She'd gone to the top, refusing to talk to anyone else.

'If this chap is reliable, if he can prove what he says, then we're talking murder trials against individual soldiers and Cabinet ministers, not to mention civil actions for damages in the High Court, and proceedings in the International Criminal Court, the International Court of Justice and the European Court of Human Rights. We're talking judgments in London, The Hague and Strasbourg. This could be a very significant case.'

Most of that analysis, uttered with steely calm, was inaccurate. Julia had been an air transport lawyer with a niche practice grounded – an appropriate term – in the Guadalajara Convention of 1961.

'You report directly to me. No one else. For now, keep the investigation between ourselves.'

They were sitting in Julia's spacious office. It was here, in this sunlit room, that Tess had been interviewed for a place in the firm. That had been seven years ago. The first-class degree from Oxford had been taken for granted. So had the dazzling results, recently obtained, from the Law Society. Something else had mattered far more than academic brilliance. Julia, being Julia, had told Tess the answer she was looking for before she'd asked the question.

'We're an old-fashioned firm. Not modern.'

'I understand that.'

'We prize integrity above all. Personal and professional. Do you?'

'Absolutely.'

There had been three others on the panel. A woman and two men. They'd closed their eyes in unison as Julia had lowered her voice.

'If there was ever a conflict between the requirements of the law and your own best interests, to which voice would you listen? The shout or the whisper?'

Of course, Julia hadn't specified which voice came from where. But Tess had guessed the law never raised its voice.

'The whisper,' she'd said quietly.

'I thought as much,' Julia had replied, and without a glance at her colleagues she extended her hand. 'Welcome to Hollingtons.'

Throughout the years that had followed, whenever Julia had caught Tess's eye, she'd given a surreptitious nod, as if to say, 'You are the Chosen One.' The future guardian of the firm's moral compass. A woman after her own heart . . .

Peter gave a light cough.

'Why the secrecy?' There was something in his whisper that sounded flippant. 'We're talking ancient history.'

Julia smiled endearingly.

'Peter, I appreciate that, as an American, your national memory doesn't extend much beyond two hundred years, but here, in the land of Stonehenge, we don't talk of political assassination a few decades ago in the same breath as the Ides of March. These crimes are still within the reach of the courts, and the client insists on secrecy because those involved are still alive. He considers them to be dangerous and—'

'Julia, these former soldiers are pensioners. Some of them will be over eighty. Maybe incontinent. They're harmless.'

'I'll let the client be the judge of that. In any event, he's concerned interested parties could destroy whatever evidence they might possess. Which is likely to happen if it becomes known that Hollingtons is investigating a group of former soldiers who threw the rule book out of the window.'

Peter gave the brisk nod of a no-nonsense sergeant major.

'We'll report to you,' he said, adding, after a pause, 'and no one else.'

* * *

'I don't know how she can lead the firm.'

'She doesn't. The partners have nudged her into administration. We can do what we want.'

He sipped his black coffee, looking at Tess through a swirl of steam.

'She seems to think being moral is being clever . . .' he began, but then left the idea hanging.

Aged thirty-five, Peter had built a reputation as a ruthless strategist, only fighting cases he knew he could win. Based in the New York office, he'd been offered a post in London to enhance his experience of human rights litigation. And so, two years ago, he'd walked into Tess's life. And then, about eight months later, they'd become a couple. They'd never worked together until now.

'We'll interview this guy, but it would be better if he'd quietly die. Leave this world. Move on.' Peter put his cup down. 'We have to let the killers go. Whether they're Brits or Provos or Loyalists. The price of peace is always injustice. We've all got to accept it. Especially the victims.'

Tess looked down. Peter had knitted his fingers with hers, as if to pull her towards his thinking, but she was tumbling away, towards a dingy holding cell beneath the courts of the Old Bailey, where as a teenage student she'd sat opposite William Benson, shortly after he'd been convicted of murder. She'd wanted to reach over and touch him, but she'd stopped herself. 'I'm innocent,' he'd murmured. Two weeks later, on the day he'd been sentenced to life, he'd revealed what he planned to do when he was released on licence. Against the odds, he'd come to the Bar. There, answerable to no one, he'd ask the question 'Why?' On behalf of those who had no voice, or were too scared to speak or didn't know how to express themselves.

Tess blinked as if she had dust in her eyes. In those days, she'd never have accepted any kind of injustice. Even those that purchased peace. She looked at Peter's clean and tidy nails. And with the strange ache of someone unsure of her bearings, she drew back her hand.

PART ONE

January 2019
Four days before trial

1

'Rizla, listen to me. Please listen.'

'Archie, if I've said it once, I've said it a dozen times: you can't call me Rizla any more. That's my prison name. I left the can ten years ago. So did you.'

'Sorry, when I get worried, it slips out. But you've got to—'

'There's nothing to worry about.'

'These crime families live by different rules. Violence is all they know.'

'I've got you to look after me, Arch. Remember that scooby with a Millwall brick? He—'

'You have to return this case.'

After a few months inside, Benson had started work on a handbook for newcomers detained at Her Majesty's pleasure. Knowing he faced an eleven-year tariff, it had been something to do, apart from the puzzles and the smoking; and the law degree.

scooby (n) *offens.* someone who's too friendly with the screws (see **screw**).

Millwall brick (n) *Antiq.* a newspaper (*orig.* tabloid) tightly rolled and folded lengthwise for use as a weapon (*hist.* devised by football hooligans wondering what else to do with it).

The handbook – *Benson's Guide to the Underworld* – had worked its way from D Wing of HMP Kensal Green to every penitentiary in the UK. Twenty years later, it was still in circulation. A copy of the latest revised edition had arrived last week from HMP Denton Fields, rousing memories of sound and sensation. Benson had been beaten senseless there. By a screw with no sense of humour.

screw (n) **1** *Zool.* a species of lizard having a long tongue and the power of changing its personality. **2** someone you can never trust. **3** a prison guard.

'There are two gangs,' said Archie. 'One of 'em takes a whack at the other. In the middle is Karmen Naylor. Our client. She says she's been framed. Me? I don't give a hoot. Do you want to know why?'

'Why, Archie?'

'Because she's still dangerous.'

He brought his heavy frame forward, as if peering into the crimson mist from Denton Fields.

'Anyone connected with her is dangerous. Representing her is dangerous. You need to bail out.'

Six years into his sentence, Benson had taken on an editorial assistant – a one-eyed bitty from Wigan called Doyle, who'd just earned a nine-month tariff for arson. When asked for his first name, Doyle had turned around, dropped his trousers and tugged off his underpants.

bitty (n) **1** a drug addict. **2** a volatile person.

Benson had stared at the large tattooed backside. On each buttock there'd been a large B. 'Fill in the blank,' Doyle had said, pleased with himself. Hardly original. But it showed playfulness. Qualities that Bob would need in plenty, because fourteen years later he was still slopping out.

'I've something important to say,' said Archie. 'Tess de Vere's getting married.'

Benson lurched out of the fog.

'Married? Who the hell to?'

'I'm winding you up. Now concentrate. Do you need a burn, or what?'

burn (n) **1** a lethal herb which, when lit and inhaled, shortens the life of a prisoner while killing time to reduce a sentence. **2** an approved toxin capable of lowering the prison population and government expenditure thereon without the need for spending cuts. **3** tobacco. **4** a cigarette.

'No, Arch, I'm fine.'

'Do I now have your attention?'

'You do.'

'Let's talk Tess, then. For two years she sends you no work. Nowt. And then, out of the blue, you get a peach. A high-profile, headline-grabbing, top-drawer earner. Agreed?'

'Agreed.'

It had been a real peach, too. Multiple law-enforcement agencies, following a tip-off, had intercepted a Ford transit van on the M1 driven by a known drug dealer, Steven Bucklow. The police – all tooled up and filmed from a helicopter for Sky News – had found three million smackers in three suit-cases. Investigators believed the money was being transported south as part of a money-laundering operation. But that remained surmise because Bucklow, like a good villain, hadn't said a word to his captors. Except to say he'd wanted Benson and de Vere. Unfortunately, he'd soon changed his mind.

'Why do you think Bucklow sacked you?'

'We both know, Archie.'

'We do. It's called terror.'

A month or so after taking on *R-v-Bucklow*, Tess had been instructed to defend the Hither Green Butcher, otherwise known as Karmen Naylor, the estranged daughter of Tony Naylor, a south London crime boss, who was accused of slaying her father's right-hand man. She, like Bucklow, had insisted on having Benson as her brief in court.

'Look at the facts, Rizla. Bucklow is as happy as Larry until he finds out you're also acting for a Naylor. The mention of the name was all it took. He crapped himself. This is a hardcore crook sending you a hardcore message. You don't want to get anywhere near the Naylors. You might end up in a ditch.'

'There aren't many ditches in London, Arch. I think you mean the foundations of a flyover.'

The 'warning' sent by Bucklow had been confirmed by the Tuesday Club, a group of ex-cons who carried out research for Benson. They'd delivered their report on the victim, Billy Hudson. Anyone who'd crossed him had either been hospitalised or was dead. Then came the disclosure of a police intelligence statement about the Naylor Family Crime Group. After reading it Archie had twiddled his signet ring and suggested breakfast at the Chip-net, a café behind Kentish Town railway station, founded by an ex-con to employ ex-cons.

Chip-net (n) the safety net strung between landings to prevent suicide by jumping. No jokes about that one.

'Rizla, you've got your last conference with her this morning. Pull out . . . I don't want you to get hurt.'

'No one's going to get hurt, Archie.'

'Wrong. The Naylors expect you to win, and if you don't, they'll cut your throat and dump you God knows where. And then there's the opposition. The Ronsons. They want you to lose. And if you don't . . . Rizla, they set dogs onto people. Five-stone pit bulls. Not chihuahuas. Win or lose' – Archie pointed out of the window, presumably towards a flyover – 'there'll be consequences. You have to drop this case.'

For the greater part of his sixty-seven years, Archie had sustained himself on the honey of all-day breakfasts. And meat pies. And cream cakes. And various real ales. And pork scratchings. And nuts. Somehow or other he bulged out of his baggy jumper and vast corduroy trousers, communicating good health. In HMP Lindley, where he'd been two'd up with Benson, no one had crossed Archie, with or without a Millwall brick.

Two-up (v) to share a cell with someone, hence, **two'd up** *usu.* a form of salvation or damnation.

With judicial exactness, Benson pushed his plate forward.

'I've listened, Mr Congreve. Here's what I think. First, Karmen Naylor is innocent. Second, the case against her is shameful. Those are reasons enough to take the case. In fact, they don't apply because, third, and most important of all, it doesn't matter what I think. It doesn't matter that the Naylors are sharpening knives or the Ronsons sharpening teeth. We defend anyone who claims to be innocent. It's called the cab-rank rule. We take whoever's standing on the kerb.'

'Well, you're going to pay for this.'

'No, Archie, you are. Breakfast was your idea. Application dismissed.'

Benson strode along Camden Road, pushed forward by the memory of clanging iron, the scrape of a lock turning, a flash of meaningless graffiti beside a filthy toilet, the sickening smell of blood, and its taste, all of it sediment raised from the seabed by the landing of that damned guidebook on his desk. By the time he turned into Blackstock Road, his emotions had settled. And yet his thoughts didn't turn to Karmen Naylor and the last pre-trial conference. His mind was on Tess. He'd not forgotten a single freckle.

2

The wind funnelled down a side street off Blackstock Road, chasing cigarette butts stained red with lipstick and plastic wrappers from cheap sweets. A scrunched paper cup spun and bounced off the pavement, striking Tess on the ankle. She watched it skip off, and then turned her attention to the dark blue figure scurrying close to the wall, hooded, his hands in his duffel coat pockets. She knew that walk. As expected, he'd come without the trial brief or a notebook. Every last case detail would be in his memory, from dates of birth to time of death. Whatever he was told would be retained, word for word. As he approached her, he jerked his head towards the cliff of pockmarked brick.

'I hate these places.'

Towering beside them was HMP Drayton Park. It had been built in the nineteenth century to hold women only, providing, too often, their next residence after the poorhouse. It now held Karmen Naylor on remand. It was where she'd stay if the jury found her guilty.

'They give me the jitters.'

He hadn't even stopped. Going straight towards a battered iron door, he poked a button in the wall. A savage buzzer screamed back, as if the Luftwaffe had been spotted over Islington. Tess gawped at him from behind. There'd been no greeting. No glance of reproof. Just a sudden blast of familiarity.

'Let's try and change Karmen's mind,' he said. 'We need her in the witness box.'

* * *

Benson sat in the interview room, massaging his hands as if they were cold. He breathed deeply and he stared at the worn linoleum. He was just this side of outright sweating. And then, when the guard clanged open the door – Tess was in an agony of expectation, knowing yet doubting – he stood up, cool and calm, holding out his hand:

'Karmen, how are you?'

Tess breathed out. In a prison visit, there was always a fear that Benson would fall to pieces in front of a trembling client, and Tess would have to sweep him up off the floor, saying, with a wink, don't worry, he'll be fine in court. Before she could suppress another reaction, it was there, warm in her stomach: she'd missed this. She'd missed him.

'Same as last time, Mr Benson,' said Karmen huskily.

'Hell?'

'Absolute hell. You can't imagine what it's like.'

'No,' said Benson wistfully. 'I can't.'

This, then, was the Hither Green Butcher: a petite waitress swamped in a maroon tracksuit. Black hair, parted in the middle, fell in natural curls to her shoulders. High cheekbones underlined darting eyes, reddened by months of sleeplessness. Tight lips suggested someone who'd learned to keep quiet. But not with everyone. With Benson she was an open book. That's what Georgina, her assistant, had said.

'I used to think hell was all about fire and pain,' she said. 'You know: deserved, endless agony. But it's not. It's much simpler. It's about waiting and staring at a wall. I can't take it much longer.'

'Well, you have to, because it's going to get an awful lot worse.'

'How?'

'When the trial begins, you'll come back here and realise you might not be leaving. That wall you've been staring at starts closing in. You'll find it difficult to breathe and you'll be two'd up with a junkie who's freaking out and the slop in the toilet will—'

'I want to go home, Mr Benson.'

'And I want to take you there. But you have to help me.'

'I'm sorry, Mr Benson, I won't let them question me.'

This had been Karmen's unfailing refrain from the day Tess had first met her. She was terrified the prosecution would trip her up, even though she had nothing to hide. According to Georgina, Benson hadn't tried to dissuade her. Now, though, with the trial at hand, it was time to spell out the implications of silence.

'You need to give evidence, Karmen,' said Benson. 'Because—'

'I know, I know, the judge will comment on it. The prosecution will comment on it. They'll say I could have explained myself, but I've said all I've got to say. It's in the interviews, and—'

'Karmen. Hold it there.'

Benson waited, as if to let water come off the boil. Then he said:

'I'm urging you to speak because you know something that no one else could even begin to imagine. And the jury needs to hear it. Everyone in court will be aware of who you are and where you've come from. They're going to look at you and think of your father and wonder if you, too, could do the sort of thing that he has done. Fact. If you say nothing, they can't possibly know what you are really like. But if you speak, we can use any prejudice to our advantage.'

'Advantage?'

'Yes, advantage.'

'How?'

'Tell them what it's been like to be Karmen Naylor. What you endured at school, university, the workplace. Your whole life. How you've never been able to be yourself. How you've been tarred with innuendo and myth and false accusations.

16

How you haven't got a friend in the world because they're all terrified of your surname. That you stayed away from home from the moment you went to university, but everyone knew who you were. You started work, but had to keep moving . . . from Newcastle to Leeds to Manchester because, in the end, someone made the connection: you're Tony Naylor's daughter . . . This is the best way to convince the jury you're completely different from what they expected. This is the best way to get them on your side.'

The constant rumble of the prison reached them like distant waves tossing iron and humanity onto a beach of scrapped expectations. The shouting was as loud as it was pointless.

'You can't sit back and risk being convicted. We can change your life, Karmen, for good, in the last place you'd think possible, the Old Bailey. But you have to step forward and—'

'I can't, Mr Benson.'

'I'll guide you all the way.'

'No.'

'I'm the one who'll ask the questions. The prosecution will have nothing to contradict your answers. By the time we're finished—'

'I said I can't.'

'But why?'

'I've never told my father what it's been like. He thinks I became a waitress because I was working my way up, planning to run my own restaurants . . . that he'd pay for, and that I would never have accepted. I couldn't tell him the truth. It would finish him off. That's why I never changed my name.'

'Do you want to stay in here?'

'No.'

'Then recognise your needs are more important than his feelings.'

'Not on this issue.'

'But his feelings are based on a total misunderstanding of your life.'

'That's as may be. Anyway, there's another reason. In fact, it's the main reason.'

'What is it?'

'To do as you ask involves condemning him, for who he is and what he's done. I've never done that; and I never would. Not after all he has done for me . . . Mr Benson, my father has done a lot of bad things. But with me he tried to do something good. He thinks he succeeded. I'm not going to take that away from him.'

Tess felt a rush of sympathy and identification. Karmen was a woman drowning in her own blood.

'That's sentimental crap,' snapped Benson. 'It's what he's done that's put you in here. You owe him nothing. You owe yourself everything. Now think again. Clearly.'

Tess tensed, willing Karmen to capitulate, but instead she smiled with appreciation.

'This is why I wanted you to represent me, Mr Benson. Because you care. Because you speak the truth without hesitation. But you're going to have to find another way of getting me out of this hellhole. The judge and the prosecutor can say what they like, but I will not deny my father.'

Benson was very still for a moment. And then, as if opening up the brief that wasn't there, and taking out the pen he didn't have, for the notebook he hadn't brought, he said:

'Okay. Let's talk about Billy Hudson.'

3

At the mention of that name, Karmen's smile vanished. And while Tess didn't move an inch, she withdrew deep inside herself. There, as if crouched in a hide, she watched, motionless and intent.

'Imagine we've never spoken of him before. Imagine you're in court, and the jury are listening to the prosecutor give an outline of his life, and how you came to know him.'

'It makes no difference, Mr Benson. I know very little about him.'

'You're born in the same year as Billy. 1988.'

'I know that much.'

'Aged eleven, he's working as a runner for one of your father's lieutenants, Lewis Derby. Delivering messages, keeping a lookout, following people. Did you know that?'

'I've already told you. No.'

'Aged twenty – in 2008 – he becomes your father's personal enforcer, driver and bodyguard. Wherever your father went, Billy went. And wherever Billy went, he went with the authority of your father. Is this news as well?'

'Yes. Because in 2006 I went to university and never lived at home again.'

'Aged twenty-two – we're now in 2010 – Billy takes over the management of Hither Green Tyres Ltd. A family business run by Jack Kilgour, who was forced to sell it to your father for peanuts. It became Hudson's HQ. It's where he sat behind a desk and made sure everyone stayed in line. Kilgour still worked there, by the way, with his two sons. For more peanuts. Which was good for your father, because they're the only ones who knew anything about changing tyres. Is this more news? Not just the peanuts, the—'

'Absolutely. All of it. I was living in Newcastle, for God's sake, working at a Thai restaurant. I'd graduated the year before . . . how would I know anything about Billy's status? I've told you a thousand times: as a kid, I was protected from what was going on. From the age of eighteen, I just wasn't there.'

'January 2017. Your father is charged with the murder of Jim "the Kite" Fitzgerald. A cousin of Stuart Ronson, head of the Ronsons. They're from north of the Thames, with pretensions over the south. Unknown to your father there's an informer in his ranks. A covert human intelligence source. A CHIS. Codenamed Q. And Q has gone to the police and told them everything. He's told them the Kite came south and knocked a Naylor girl about. So your father went north, strung up the Kite by his ankles and cut his throat. His body was dumped at sea. Now, before Q can give evidence—'

'I know, Mr Benson. My father had a stroke and the case was dropped.'

'In April 2017. And it's at this point, aged twenty-nine, you leave Manchester and come home.'

'My father needed help. Remember, my mother had died. There was no one else.'

'Two months later, that June, you went to the offices of Ruth Mowbray, the family solicitor. She slides some paperwork over the table. You signed it and that made you a director of HGT Ltd.'

'That's right.'

'But you had no knowledge of the tyre-fitting business.'

'I understood I was replacing my father.'

'What do you think that means to someone investigating the Naylor family?'

Karmen let the question sink in.

'Don't be ridiculous. My brother Ryan runs the show, with his team, not me. The police know that.'

'But you're company secretary.'

'So what?'

'Company secretaries are responsible for the smooth running of a business. They ensure compliance with the law. And when it comes to the Naylors, compliance takes on a whole new meaning. And that was your job. Billy Hudson was answerable to you. Not Ryan.'

'On paper.'

'In fact.'

'Look, I thought it was legitimate. I thought the Kilgours were employees. My dream was to get Billy to move out and then develop the business. Make it grow. Rival Kwik Fit. I'd gone crazy.'

'What about any meetings with Ryan and his boys?'

'Never happened. Not when I was there. If they did, it was a Friday night.'

'Just like yours?'

'No . . . that's different.'

'You met Billy regularly. Why?'

'I didn't. I spent time with the Kilgours, learning the ropes. Then I helped out in reception. And yes, I'd talk to Billy. I was working up to asking him to leave. That's why I was there the night he was killed. I asked him to find another base, and he agreed. I thought my dream was coming true.'

'When did you last see him, prior to that meeting on Friday the eighteenth of May 2018?'

'The Wednesday before.'

'That's the sixteenth.'

'Yes. I saw him in the morning and asked if I could see him, and he said he was heading to Manchester and would be back on Friday.'

'Why arrange a meeting at nine in the evening?'

'He suggested the time, and it suited me because I wanted to get him when there was no one around.'

'You mean witnesses?'

'No, no.'

'Because – conveniently enough – there weren't any, and – as you say – that's the night Billy was murdered.'

'But not by me. I didn't even go into his office . . . we met in Mr Kilgour's, by the entrance. For quarter of an hour. If that.'

'Why did you leave driving like a maniac?'

'Because I was excited. Billy had said he'd find other premises.'

'Not because you were hyper-stressed at having just killed him?'

'No, I saw him alive, walking back to his office.'

'But you're the only person known to have been with him at about the time he was killed.'

'I've been set up. You know it. I know it.'

'After Billy arrived, he turned off the CCTV system. This was usual practice. To protect the identity of anyone who came for a meeting. But it also meant you could remove his body without being seen.'

'If I was going to kill Billy and put his body in the boot of my car, I'd have avoided the other CCTV camera on the street, both arriving and leaving, but I didn't. So what was I doing?'

'Being smart. Behaving as if you were innocent. Speaking of your car, some of Hudson's blood was found on the rear bumper.'

'Someone put it there.'

'When?'

'How do I know?'

'Who?'

'Someone working for Stuart Ronson. There's no other possible explanation.'

'Blood and fibres were found on the jetty at *Allhallows Rest*. The cottage you own on the Hoo Peninsula. Paid for by your father.'

'It was his. He put it in my name, that's all.'

'It was where you went after leaving Billy on the night he died. More blood and a button were found on a boat. *Little Winner*. Named after you, and that you own.'

'Yes, I know, and paid for by my father, but it's the same arrangement. It's meaningless, it's—'

'A boat you took to sea the day after the killing—'

'I always sail on a Saturday. To get away from everything.'

'—to dispose of the body. It doesn't look good.'

'I don't care what it looks like, Mr Benson. I'm innocent. We both know what happened. My father killed a Ronson big cheese who happened to be a relative of the boss. So the boss kills a big cheese of my father's and framed his relative. It's tit for tat. I'm in this situation simply because I'm Tony Naylor's daughter.'

'That's our case, Karmen. But to get that argument before the jury, we have to tell them all about the Kite, and your father and Q. And this is the rub: once that information is before the jury, the prosecution can use it, too. And they will. I already know what they're going to say.'

'Well I don't. I can't imagine how they'd twist my life to fit the picture of someone who'd end up killing Billy Hudson.'

'How about this: there was more to your leaving the north than compassion. Little Winner finally got sick of doing menial jobs in Newcastle and Leeds and Manchester, so she came home and signed on the dotted line. And after that, she was learning the ropes. From Billy Hudson, the man your father trusted with his life.'

'Then why would I kill him?'

'You were stepping up to the plate.'

'But why? Billy had done nothing wrong . . . not that I knew of.'

'Because the family were still looking for Q. And they'd come to believe it was Billy.'

'I don't know what the family were thinking, but I certainly didn't. And anyway, the police said he wasn't Q.'

'That was after he was dead, Karmen. Before that, you weren't to know. I'm only showing you what the jury might think, with a little help from the prosecutor.'

'Then I'm finished.'

'You're not. But I need a little help, too. And you'd be in a hell of a lot better position if you'd give evidence and distance yourself from your father. Show them – as you did to me, just now – that you knew nothing about his world. Help me, Karmen. Help me get you out of this place.'

Tess seemed to creep back into the grey interview room, hearing once more the distant rumble of voices and the booming of iron on iron. Benson was watching Karmen intently, begging her with his eyes to capitulate. Tess had to speak:

'Mr Benson is right, Karmen. You need to tell your story.'

After a long, painful pause, Karmen stood up.

'Then I better start getting used to this.' She tilted her head towards the din and the expectation of harm. 'Because I will not deny my father.'

4

'Whoever called a gangland enforcer a big cheese?' said Benson.

They were standing on the pavement again, beside the soaring mottled cliff. He thrust his hands into the pockets of his duffel coat, but in his mind his fingers made their way into Tess's long sandy hair. He could almost feel her skin, and the warm nape of her neck.

'I don't understand her,' he said. 'She's agreed to have no contact with her father or her brother. She's agreed to keeping them away from court during the trial. She's agreed to me putting the murder of the Kite before the jury . . . but she won't separate herself from the man accused of killing him. I just don't get it. She's . . .' – Benson thumped a packet

of Camels against his other hand. He bit one and lit up –
'. . . she's naive, because she let her name be nailed to a
cottage and a boat she never wanted; bought with money
she'd never have touched. She's contradictory, because she
went and used them after she came home. She's blind because
she thought the Kilgours were ordinary employees. She's
stubborn. She's foolish—'

'She's a girl who still needs her father,' added Tess.
'Regardless of what he's done.'

Benson blew smoke out of the side of his mouth.

'Are you okay?'

'Yeah, I'm fine. I'm only thinking of the stories Karmen
must have told herself. We can all relate to that.' She pointed
at Benson's hand. 'I thought you'd given up?'

'That was years back.'

He almost added 'when we worked together'. Instead,
Benson stuck to his game plan: the friendliness that follows
amnesia.

'I've arranged a meeting with Jack Kilgour for Monday. At
HGT Ltd. I want to examine the premises.'

'And me? I sense a last-minute mission.'

'More a last-ditch plea for help.'

Benson was doing his level best to keep his eyes off Tess's
tumbling hair and the soft, fine skin of an earlobe.

'From whom?'

'Let's go through this in stages. Tony Naylor whacks one
of the Ronsons. An informer, Q, goes to the police. Now, Q
was either there or knew someone who was. Or overheard a
conversation afterwards. You know the various possibilities.
Whoever Q might be, they're unlikely to be someone who
felt for the Kite. The most obvious explanation is that Q
wants to do anything that would harm the Naylors. He did
then, and he does now.'

From the corner of his eye, Benson caught Tess's nod.

'In their turn, the Ronsons whack a Naylor. Rather than bringing on the pit bulls, they kill Hudson in a way associated with the Naylors. That's how they frame Karmen. But the Ronsons could only pull that off by knowing everything about their targets. They knew Karmen was meeting Hudson that Friday night. They knew she planned to go to Allhallows the next day. They knew she went sailing every Saturday. They knew she owned the cottage, and they knew what position she held in HGT Ltd. Q is someone very close to the inner workings of the Naylors, a family they want to destroy.'

Tess completed Benson's argument:

'So it was Q, or someone very like Q, who fed that information to the Ronsons.'

'I'd say it's Q. There's a philosopher called—'

'Occam, yes, I know. My father bangs on about him. Keep things simple. But we've looked into this, Will. We tried to locate the informant. The Tuesday Club found nothing. They spoke to players on both sides, and no one is prepared to say anything. We have to forget Q. Q is out of reach. Always was.'

'Tess, there's Q. And there's people who know Q. And there's people who know people who know Q. There's always a thread. We have to find the other end. Because if we land that fish, Little Winner walks free.'

'Look, Will, I'll be frank. I always thought finding Q was a waste of bloody time. We don't even know if it's Q who gave information to the Ronsons. And even if he did, why would Q help Karmen? Karmen in the dock is what he wanted. To help her, Q would have to admit his role in Hudson's killing, which puts *him* in the dock . . . for conspiracy to murder. It ain't going to happen.'

'And I, to be frank, always thought that was a second-order problem. First off, we find Q. Or someone he knows.'

'Which is why we questioned everyone we could. There are no names left on the board.'

'There's one.'

'Who?'

'Nina Osabede.'

Tess laughed.

'Osabede? You're joking. She told us where to go. She told the police where to go.'

'She's the mother of Hudson's child. Doorstep her.'

'But why? They barely knew each other.'

'We don't know what she knows until we ask her.'

Tess shrugged. Benson shrugged back. And they both knew. The whole discussion had been out of step because Tess had kept away from Benson. She'd contented herself with a read-over of notes drawn up by Georgina. The zing of argument hadn't happened. Tess twisted a button on her coat as if it were a bottle top.

'Will, this isn't easy, but there's something I should say.'

But she didn't. The effect of indecision set loose Benson's affection. She was about to apologise for having cut him off. To spare them both the embarrassment of half-truths, Benson spoke, just as the button came loose in Tess's hand:

'There isn't much hope, I know. But wasn't it ever thus? Even for me? We meet in chambers on Monday night.'

The few inches between them felt like a mile. Benson caught a glimpse of a 1964 cherry red Mini parked on the other side of the road. It belonged to Tess. And it brought to mind once more her reappearance in his life.

'There's just one more thing,' he said, his breath catching.

He'd worked on a parting line for hours. He'd savoured it on first seeing her, and he'd felt it beating in his veins while he'd grilled Karmen Naylor, and now he could barely get it out; but when he did, he filled it with every ounce of possible meaning:

'It's great to see you again, Tess. Have a good weekend.'

5

'He'll do it again. You always said he was a genius, Tess,' said Orla, pouring coffee but spilling some on the tablecloth.

'For God's sake be careful,' said Laurence. He lurched forward to dab the stain with a napkin, but hit the cup, spilling a lot more. He glared at the pool. 'Damn it. You're infectious.'

'It's okay, Dad,' mumbled Tess.

'It isn't. This is borrowed linen.'

'Relax. It's not wine.'

'Coffee stains, too. And I don't want a bad review on Airbnb.'

Tess had joined her parents for Sunday lunch at the flat they'd rented in Hammersmith. Orla was moving gingerly around the table, cup and saucer in hand, laying it down before her husband.

'I'm sorry, Larry. Truly.' She threw Tess an everything-is-all-right smile. 'You said Benson was a genius, darling. That he wins cases that you'd think can't be won . . . So, sure, he'll do it again.'

That lilting Irish accent had once captivated Tess's very English father. But not now. And Tess had no idea why. Well into their retirement, they'd come to London for a month, arriving last week, and from the moment she'd met them at the airport an unaccustomed viciousness had kept breaking into the simplest of exchanges.

'Winning has bugger all to do with justice, Orla. Maybe he should damn well lose. For Christ's sake, this woman . . . what's her name, Tess?'

'Karmen Naylor.'

'This Naylor woman's criminal royalty. She's Tony Naylor's only daughter. And the bloke she killed was one of Tony's hard men. It's internal dirty business.'

'You read the wrong papers, Dad.'

'She's as ruthless as her father. Has to be.'

'Really?' muttered Tess, watching her mother fidget with a napkin.

'Yes. They're a family business. It's as simple as that. You know, there comes a time in the animal kingdom when the cub makes its first kill. It's part of growing into the pack. And it's the same with these gangs. The day comes when you, too, pull the trigger. Take the Hell's Angels. You want to ride the bike? Well, you have to bite the head off a chicken.'

'This is why Benson might lose,' said Tess, addressing her mother.

'What do you mean?' said Laurence.

'Dad, you've got a PhD in history.'

'So what?'

'You've spent thirty-odd years assessing competing narratives . . . and after all that, given half a chance, you trot out tweets and headlines and nonsense.'

'Nonsense?'

'You know nothing about the animal kingdom. Or criminal gang culture. Or the Hell's Angels. And somehow you've not only linked all three, which is something of an intellectual feat, you've used the resulting drivel to condemn a woman about whom you know absolutely nothing, save how she's been presented by the press. If the jury thinks like you, Karmen Naylor is going down before she even enters the dock.'

'Tess, just hold it.'

'There isn't even a gun in the case, never mind a chicken.'

'I was keeping things simple. For your mother.'

'How thoughtful.'

'I'm not stupid, Larry.'

'I never said you were.'

Tess quickly drew the line of fire towards herself:

'Well, whatever you kept simple was simple prejudice.'

Laurence hitched up the sleeves of his tweed jacket and propped his elbows on the table. It was a characteristic posture captured in numerous photographs taken at the University of Galway, from the day he began his career to his final appearance as senior lecturer. It was an attitude he'd assumed at home whenever squaring up to argue with Tess, their eyes glinting with anticipation. They'd loved wrestling with ideas.

'This woman visits her father's henchman at his place of work. It's late on a Friday evening. Afterwards she goes to a cottage by the sea. Which was bought for her by her father. Come Monday morning, the associate's gone missing and his blood is found all over the floor, and traces of blood are found at this woman's cottage and on the boat. My reasoned conclusion is that this woman bled him dry and then fed him to the fish. Now, I know there was a previous killing, with blood all over the floor—'

'Dad, enough.'

'Why?'

'Because I'm not at work today.'

'Fair enough. But I wasn't spouting prejudice or nonsense.'

'Okay.'

'The point is, people will think these two killings must be linked. Because they share certain similarities. But that, I submit, would be a mistake. Why? Because the simplest explanation is usually the right one – I learned that from a chap called Occam – and in this case, why go and—'

'Dad.'

'Yes?'

'Stop.'

Tess closed her eyes, feeling a pain in her heart. As a young girl she'd held his hand in Barna Woods, listening to the birdsong, bound to him by a silence that never needed to be broken. Glances were enough to communicate complete mutual understanding. But now they needed words, and they didn't work very well. She felt sad, and clutched her own hand, as if grasping his. She wanted to lead him through the trees, towards the burst of morning sunlight where, stumbling into high nettles, they'd laughed, shocked by the magical sound of redwings.

'What's wrong, Tess?'

'Nothing . . . really.'

She wanted to run ahead, pulling him after her, along the winding trail, the bracken crunching underfoot. She wanted to dash home, to the weathered stone farmhouse on Galway Bay, where the wind rattled her bedroom window and the heating was never on, and the curtains were never drawn, and where her mother looked out to sea, humming like one of those birds in the forest, high in the branches, ever present, ever watchful, always swooping down when Tess broke through the door, arms spread like tiny wings.

'Tess, what is it? Tell me . . .'

Orla was speaking from the other side of the room, far, far away. Tess could barely hear the Gaelic, the language of childhood comfort. She was only aware of the rolling itch on her cheeks. The tears had just risen, like water spilling over the edge of the sink, from a tap left running because someone had gone off to do something more important.

'Please don't cry,' said Orla, keeping her distance.

Tess wanted her parents back, as they were. When her father had told her stories from his wild days in the merchant navy; of storms around the Cape of Good Hope. And pirates. Even her mother had listened, open-mouthed. Her father was on the move, coming closer.

'Is it something I've said? Or done?'

Tess let out a short crying laugh. In a sudden shift of inner light she saw Julia Hollington at her desk, twelve years ago.

We're talking state-sponsored murder. Sanctioned from the top. In Northern Ireland during the seventies.

'Tell me everything, Tess.' Her father was on his knees by her chair, his hands holding hers. 'Tell me what's on your mind.'

Tess looked at the blurred figure, a wash of aged forest green and silver. What could she say?

'Everything,' he repeated.

She couldn't tell him anything. He squeezed harder, thinking he was holding on to that little girl who used to swing from his arm on the way home. But that bird had flown.

'I'm just apprehensive about the coming trial,' she lied. 'We've no evidence whatsoever. Even our client refuses to go into the witness box. She's scared and I can't persuade her to change her mind.'

'Don't worry, my love,' came the gentle, distant Gaelic. 'Your man Benson is a genius. Everything will be fine.'

Tess turned to her mother. She had the cavernous eyes of a ballet dancer, along with the bodily grace and seeming weightlessness, but her expression disclosed an immense sorrow, and guilt. Tess couldn't understand why. You of all people have kept your innocence, she screamed silently. You, betrayed, exploited and deceived, have nothing to regret. How could you possibly accuse yourself of anything? Tess pulled away from her father.

'I'm sorry, I really must go,' she said. 'Sally's expecting me.'

Once out of the flat, Tess began to run, taking the footpath that skirted the Thames towards Chiswick Mall, avoiding the racket on the Great West Road. But this time she found herself exposed to an even greater noise than any onslaught of trucks and cars. Her father's gentle voice crashed into his biting asides; she seemed to hear gunshots, one after the other, loud, shocking reports, flashes in the night, while her mother knocked over pots and pans. Tess gave up. She slowed, and walked to the river wall. Watched by a child who'd strayed from her parents, she vomited. Pretty much her whole lunch came up, as if it had been poison.

6

Her dark brown hair had been wound into a bun. She was dressed in torn blue jeans and a red fisherman's smock. And she was staring at Benson with horror.

'What the hell are you doing here?'

Benson had only met the woman once before. But he knew everything about her. She ran the Etterby Gallery in Chelsea. She was forty years old and considered herself a catch that had never been caught. Her favourite tipple was a corpse reviver. She lived in a mullion-windowed Georgian house on Chiswick Mall facing a gentle bend in the Thames – the house whose shiny front door now stood open. More particularly, she'd been responsible, with Tess, for proving Benson's innocence. She was Tess's best friend. Her name was Sally Martindale.

'I never thanked you properly,' he said.

There was a peculiar familiarity between them. The kind that springs between two people who know a third person, and that third person has spoken endlessly about the exploits of the other. As a result, Benson could recall Sally's arrest in Vienna as if he'd been there. He could see her dragging a restaurant table through Montmartre on her way back to London. He saw her hunched in the rain, dogged and insistent, chasing leads the police had left unexplored.

'I never thanked you properly,' repeated Benson.

They were seated in armchairs at opposite ends of the sitting room.

'There's no bloody point,' said Sally. 'You abandoned your appeal against conviction.'

'Yes, I did.'

'You put in the paperwork.'

'Sort of. It's an online procedure.'

'You had a famous QC lined up to represent you. Janet Forde.'

'Not quite. Janet volunteered and I accepted.'

'But then, at the last moment, you withdrew the application.'

'I did.'

'You waited until the judges were on the bench.'

'No, I made my mind up when they appeared. They looked at me, and I looked at them . . . and, bang, I just couldn't—'

'Bah. The whole charade shocked me. As a result, you remain a convicted murderer.'

'On paper.'

'You remain convicted.'

'I do.'

'To what end?'

'I'm sending a message.'

'To whom? Those with ears to hear?'

'You could say that.'

'Speaking as someone who tried to save you, I'm deaf as a post. See that brick?'

Sally was pointing, so Benson looked across the room to an antique glass dome that had probably once held a stuffed bird. Maybe an eagle. Something daunting. Benson studied it.

'I'd call that a half-brick,' he said.

'Call it what you bloody like. It came through Tess's window and could have stoved my head in.'

'I'm sorry about that.'

34

'And so you should be. I was only there because we were trying to find out who'd killed Paul Harbeton. To get your case before the Court of Appeal.'

'I'm truly grateful.'

'Not so grateful as to finish the job. And what about compensation? Without a quashed conviction, you get nothing.'

'Without a quashed conviction you cannot *apply*. My conviction has not been—'

'Fine, fine, so you abandoned the right to apply?'

'No, I haven't acquired the right. I think you mean *chance*. But yes, I get the point.'

'Okay, you *chose* not have the *chance* to exercise the *right*?'

'That's it. Spot on.'

'Because? Wait, hold it . . . only those with eyes to see and ears to hear will understand?'

'Almost certainly. But look, it's very difficult to explain. I hardly understand it myself. But there are people inside who shouldn't be there. People who will never be freed because the truth will never come to light. Some have been failed by the system, others have been failed by themselves or their families or witnesses who were too frightened to come forward. Whatever the reason, it's the system that keeps them behind bars, it has to, but these people were my friends. We supported each other. I identify with them. I just can't leave them behind . . .'

Sally's expression softened, suddenly; but there was more she wanted to say:

'You got millions anyhow. And yet you gave them away.'

Those millions had been given to Benson by the person who'd helped put him in prison in the full knowledge that he was innocent. Without thinking it through, he'd accepted the money. And for a short while he'd listened to the clatter of pounds, shillings and pence.

'I thought you were going to set up a trust,' Sally went on, 'the More than One Chance Fund.'

'Foundation.'

'All right, damn it, Foundation. But you changed your mind. At the last moment. Again.'

'I'd drawn up the deed. I'd picked the trustees. We were about to sign and—'

'Let me guess. They were all smiling and one of them opened his mouth and . . . bang, you just couldn't do it?'

'God, it's as if you were there. That's exactly right. Unfortunately, I only see things clearly when—'

'Fascinating. And what did you see?'

'That I'd been bought off. So I rang Save the Children.'

'And what a call that must have been.'

'It was.'

'Tell me, Mr Benson, what was the point of it all? Why did we spend years looking for evidence? Why, when we finally found it, did we confront the person responsible for your tragedy? Why didn't we just leave you where Tess had found you?'

'Because you discovered the truth. Because Maureen Harbeton now knows what happened to her son. Because I've been freed, even though I refuse to acknowledge the Court of Appeal.'

They looked at each other in silence across a length of Persian carpet. The weight of all that might have been said over the years was pressing down upon them.

'Why are you here, Mr Benson?' said Sally. 'You didn't come to thank me.'

A scattering of lamps created pools of clarity, sharp marble edges, glinting frames, a copper shine on ridges of old oil paint. But Benson sat in a shadow. Sally had made tea, placed the tray on a table and then retreated to a window facing the river.

'Within weeks of proving me innocent, Tess walked out of my life. She didn't instruct me again for two years. Not until six months back. But only because the client insisted.'

'Why are you telling me this?'

'Because it doesn't make sense. Not after everything we'd been through. She's there, in court, when I was sentenced. She's there by my side after I come to the Bar. We'd become Benson and de Vere. I'm proved to be innocent. The same day, she kissed me. And it wasn't just a kiss: something happened to us. We'd arrived. I know it. And then, all of a sudden, it's over. There has to be an explanation.'

'I don't know what it is. And if I did, I wouldn't tell you.'

'I'm quite sure she's told you nothing.'

'Good. You see, I can't help you, Mr Benson.'

'Then help Tess.'

'Is she in trouble?'

'I'm not sure. But something's not quite right.'

'How do you know?'

'Because I've done to her what she did to me.'

Benson moved to the edge of his seat.

'Tess began her career at Hollingtons in 2003.'

'I know.'

'She was there for seven years. Then, in 2010, she says she went to Strasbourg. To work with the Council of Europe Directorate General for Human Rights and the Rule of Law. That's quite a mouthful. But you needn't swallow it.'

'Why not?'

'She didn't take the job.'

'Oh yes she did.'

'No, Sally. She lasted a week and then disappeared.'

'What have you been doing?'

'Something happened while she was at Hollingtons. She was working with Peter Farsely on a human rights case. And maybe it's this—'

'You've begun an investigation into Tess?'

'Yes.'

'But you've no right.'

'Tess had no right either. And neither did you.'

Sally frowned and began edging away from the window towards the door. Benson's eyes tracked her.

'Everyone thinks Tess left Hollingtons and went abroad because her relationship with Peter Farsely went off the rails. That's not true.'

'Yes, it is.'

'It isn't. That's a cover story. And I found the hole in it. During a visit to a hypnotist.'

'I think you'd better leave.'

'Sally, hear me out. Tess is hiding something from both of us. Probably from everyone.'

'That's her choice.'

'Friends have a choice, too, especially when they've been told a lie. Tell me, did you visit Tess when she was abroad? Did you ever go to Strasbourg?'

Sally tiptoed out of the room, as if she didn't want anyone to know she was there. Moments later, Benson caught the soft scrape of the front door on the mat, and he felt the breeze off the river, and he heard a clipped, inviting voice:

'Goodbye.'

When Benson was outside, at the bottom of the short steps, Sally spoke as from a mountaintop:

'Out of respect for your good intentions, I will say nothing to Tess of this unwanted visit or your unwanted disclosures. Take my advice, Mr Benson. Walk right up the Great West Road, don't turn around, and get on with your life.'

7

Reaching Chiswick Mall, Tess glanced to her right and saw a long figure turn on to the Great West Road. There was something vaguely familiar about the shape, but she was still in the grip of other distractions. The echo of imagined gunshots, the smell of burning paper in the kitchen sink, the sharp taste of acid in her mouth. When Sally opened the front door she swept inside, her teeth clenched, hoping the smell of bile wouldn't escape her lips. After rinsing her mouth out in the bathroom, she threw herself on the sofa.

'You've had a visitor,' she said, nodding at two cups of undrunk tea.

'A prophet preaching Armageddon.'

'You let him in?'

'And I kicked him out. It's good to see you, Tess.'

'You, too.'

'You've been a stranger. You should have called me sooner.'

Tess had been avoiding Sally for much the same reason she'd been avoiding Benson. And for much the same reason, she couldn't explain. An alliance that had begun during freshers' week at Oxford had inevitably suffered. There'd been far fewer midweek cocktails. And hardly any Sunday afternoon teas. Today was an exception, and it felt like one. But with her parents staying nearby, Tess had thought of her old friend and simply couldn't keep away. She'd sent the text before she could stop her fingers.

'They've been married for forty years,' she said. 'They leaned on each other, like an arch, and I grew up in the space beneath. And now they're like two columns in a ruin.'

'Who are?'

'My bloody parents, who else?'

They both laughed uneasily.

'A few months back, they were looking forward to coming to London. All was fine. And now they're here they can't even stand near each other in the same room. My mother has this look that she's responsible for something . . . but for what, I don't know; and he speaks to her with . . .'

Hatred, she thought. But she didn't want to say so, as if in the uttering she might breathe more life into the word.

'There's something good in this,' said Sally.

'Good?'

'Yes. They're being honest. And while you may not like it, this is the real deal. For them and for you. And maybe you can help.'

The real deal? Absolute mutual honesty? Who in their right mind wanted that? Not her father. And certainly not Tess. God knows what her mother would think if she knew the truth about her husband. Or indeed her daughter. Tess sighed and Sally's face lit up.

'I've got an idea.'

'Yes?'

'Let's talk about someone else's crap life. That always works.'

'Who are you thinking of?'

'The Hither Green Butcher. She's neck deep in shite.'

'Picture this,' said Tess, cradling a tumbler of scotch, 'Tony Naylor sires a nasty piece of work who happily grunts his way into the business – that's Ryan; he's done what was expected of him – but then along comes this girl who wants to be the Virgin Mary in the nativity. Brings an apple for the teacher. She stops Tony in his tracks, and something glimmers in the sewer of his mind and he thinks, Christ, I could have been different, and maybe she can be different, so he does everything in his power to give her a different kind of life. Private school. Skiing in Verbier. University. The lot. Whereas for Ryan it was the local comp. Until he did the decent thing and got expelled.

'She grabs every opportunity. But no one trusts her. She can't escape her name.'

'So where did it lead?'

'Pretty much nowhere. She waits tables, where no one asks any questions, and where no one would think you're connected to a crime boss. But even that didn't work. She had to keep starting over.'

'How old is she?'

'Thirty-one.'

'That's a long time to feel misunderstood. She can't be normal. Not with her background.'

'But she is. In a way, that's what this trial is all about. Because she's Tony Naylor's daughter people think she can't be that different. And at the end of that short road, you meet people like my father who think she must be capable of murder. And she isn't.'

'Then why's she in the dock?'

'She's been framed.'

'Who by?'

'The most likely candidate is another gang. Poor woman is a victim of circumstance. She only returned to London because her father had a stroke; and as soon as she got home she became a target.'

Sally swished the whisky around her glass; when it was still again, she said:

'Who did you instruct for the defence?'

'Benson.' Tess hesitated but then went on, quickly, 'Karmen wouldn't have anyone else. So it's him and me again. Which is embarrassing.'

'It's also a winning combination.'

Tess had handled the preliminary conferences, but left those involving Benson to Georgina, hoping that Karmen might eventually plead. But now the trial was upon them. Which is why she'd gone to HMP Drayton Park. Prior to seeing Benson, skirting by that wall, her recollection of him was an amalgam of two totally contradictory images. First, his court presence, rising like an assassin out of the sea – not quite Daniel Craig as Bond in his trunks, but just as intimidating – and second, on Ludgate Hill in his duffel coat, looking for matches. The menace had gone. He'd sunk back into the water. She loved him for it. Only . . . Sally was staring at her with an expression somewhere between pity and confusion.

'What is all this nonsense, Tess? For years you wondered if you loved him, and when you finally got together you dropped him. What happened? I've told you before: I don't understand.'

Tess groaned. First her parents, and now Sally. She swung her feet onto the carpet with an accidental stamp.

'You asked me that two years ago and I said I didn't know, and two years later I still don't know. I thought I wanted something, but I didn't. It's a given. Like back pain the doctor doesn't understand. Sometimes, Sally, there's no point in asking questions, even of yourself. I'm happy. That's all that matters.'

Tess had pushed her argument too far. She'd made a claim that wasn't true, and which Sally knew wasn't true.

'I'm sort-of happy,' she said, touching her necklace. 'You can't ask for more. It's the human condition.'

'Well that's all right then.'

The riposte struck Tess like a slap. She'd broken faith and was still breaking faith. She'd been evading emotional honesty for a very long time. Ever since Benson was proved innocent; ever since . . . She watched Sally, uneasily. She was carefully placing the two undrunk cups of tea on a tray, on either side of the pot, trying to get the balance right. She began walking cautiously trying to keep the tea in the cups. With her back to Tess, she said:

'You've not been honest with me since you left Hollingtons.'

'What do you mean?'

You never told me why you went to Strasbourg. You went away hurt and you came back hurt.' Sally moved warily out of sight. 'You're still hurt. You're not "sort-of happy". And you've no intention of saying why. That's our real deal.'

Her voice became loud, without anger, raised to carry from the kitchen.

'Which is fine. But keep the existentialist crap to yourself. Along with the medical mystery. I deserve better.'

8

Hither Green Tyres Ltd was comfortably wedged on a triangle of land between Southbrook Road and the railway line. The premises had once been part of a small brewery, built in the nineteenth century from the magenta brick used for mills and factories and prisons. The main buildings had been destroyed during the Blitz, showing just how low the Nazis could stoop – targeting beer production rather than munitions. All that remained was the original storage block, where the kegs had once been lined up, ready for delivery to pubs throughout south London. Albert Kilgour, a former drayman and Jack's father, had bought the ruins and opened a garage.

'I joined the trade and so did my boys.'

They were standing on Southbrook Road, facing the main entrance. Jack Kilgour shook his head, eyeing the wide gate and the surrounding wall.

'HGT was my life, once.'

Acting for the company, Ryan Naylor had sold the property to a developer. In due course it would be demolished.

'My dad wishes the place had got flattened during the war.'

'And you?'

He shrugged.

'And the boys?'

Another shrug.

Benson felt for Albert Kilgour: he'd lived to see his child and grandchildren dispossessed. And he felt for Jack, who'd been emasculated in front of his sons, when they were still young enough to think no one could push their dad around.

'Where are they working now?'

Jack's laugh rattled in his throat.

'They're on the dole. People are scared of them.'

Aged sixty, Jack looked much older. His limp hair was white. There were hollows of yellow skin around his eyes and drooping mouth. A decade of comfort eating, begun after Tony Naylor had come round to discuss the purchase of his business, had made him large and cumbersome. He waddled and sweated. He wheezed heavily, sucking on a burn between hasty puffs of his inhaler. Swapping the inhaler for a fob key, he pointed it at the gate. It rumbled open, sliding to one side on a rail.

'There's only two CCTV cameras,' said Jack, halting on the forecourt. 'One's directed at the workshop, the other at the loading bay and the reception area, where I worked with Miss Naylor.'

Benson noted they were not overlooked by adjacent buildings. And while the surrounding wall could be easily scaled, once the gate was closed and those cameras were turned off, HGT Ltd was like a desert island. Which was no doubt why Tony Naylor had taken it from the Kilgours.

'That's the workshop,' said Jack, pointing his burn at the large shuttered entrance to his right. 'That's where the tyres were delivered.' His arm had drifted to the left, indicating the loading bay – another shuttered opening, only this time it began a metre or so off the ground. 'And that's the reception area . . . my office.' He nodded at a wheelchair ramp and a dirty white door just along from the loading bay. 'There's no other way into the building.'

'Take me there, Jack.'

As the lights flickered into brightness, Benson saw the grubby counter and the dusty order books and files of receipts and diaries, and, on the back wall, posters advertising Pirelli and Dunlop, and, framed on a shelf, a family photograph. This is where Jack had worked.

'That's me,' he said, pointing at a thin, muscular man with his arms around two youths. 'With my boys, Pete and Greg. That's my mum and dad behind. The wife took the photo.'

Benson took in the smiles and the clean blue overalls.

'Does she wish the place had been flattened during the war?'

'I wouldn't know.'

'Why?'

'We're divorced.'

'I'm sorry.'

'She got out. After I sold up to Mr Naylor.'

'You mean Tony?'

'Yes.'

Benson pointed towards a small room, more of a closet:

'And that's Karmen's office?'

'Yep.'

There was nothing of significance. Just a small table, a chair and an empty filing cabinet. No posters, no photographs. Not even a telephone or a wastepaper basket. It was somewhere to sit and feel you had a stake in what was going on.

Benson turned around.

'After Karmen met Billy on the night he was killed, she says she came and went using the door to reception. So if anyone else turned up—'

'This is the entrance they'll have used,' said Jack, 'because the workshop was closed.'

'And the loading bay?'

'Yeah, of course. I shut them myself.'

'At six thirty?'

Jack nodded, stubbing out the cigarette with his boot. He took out another from a shoulder pocket. He struggled with a failing lighter, so Benson struck a match.

'Relax, Jack. When you left, you put the alarm on?'

'Pete did. If he'd forgotten, God knows what would have happened to him.'

'So that's about six forty?'

'Yeah.'

The next person to enter the building, then, at 8.14 p.m., had been Billy. He'd come for the planned meeting with Karmen. He'd turned the alarm off, along with the CCTV cameras.

'Okay, Jack?'

'Yeah, I'm fine.'

'Ever tried patches?'

'Nah.'

'Hypnosis?'

'Nah.'

'Why not?'

'Because I like it, Mr Benson. If I didn't have my fags . . .'

'Me, too, Jack. Me too.'

'I mean, you've only got one life.'

'You said it. Only one.'

The CCTV camera at the mouth of Southbrook Road – some twenty yards from the entrance to HGT Ltd – had captured Karmen's second-hand VW Golf at 8.58 p.m. By her own account, she'd entered the premises through Jack's office. Thereafter there was no agreement on what had happened. According to the police, Karmen had made her way into the workshop.

'Take me there, Jack.'

Using his shoulder, Jack jolted open a door behind the counter, and they stepped into a cold, spacious darkness. He slapped a switch and, again, the lights struggled, finally bursting into life with a glare.

'This is where my boys changed the tyres.'

'The hand tools?'

'Along that wall, in cabinets. Mr Naylor sold them all. And the rest of the gear. Everything's gone.'

'Do you mean Ryan Naylor?'

'Yeah.'

'Did you get anything from the sale?'

'Nah. Nowt. Not a penny.'

According to the prosecution, Karmen had selected a large wrench. She'd then ascended the small staircase that led to the door of Billy's office. On the plan in the trial brief, the door was marked D1. Benson, having reached it, examined the left-side jamb. A red circle had been drawn around a deep indentation in the wood. The damage had been captured in photograph 36 of bundle A.

'This is where they say it began,' mumbled Benson to himself.

'Yeah.'

Jack had hauled himself up the stairs and was leaning on the banister, panting.

'He'd come out to meet her,' continued Benson, 'and as he turned around she whacked him.'

The wrench had glanced off his skull and hit the jamb of D1. Said the Crown. Billy had stumbled into the room, knocking papers and pens off his desk, and a cup of coffee, and a lamp, before collapsing near the doorway that opened onto the loading bay. That door had been marked D2 on the plan.

'And that's where he lay, helpless,' said Benson, in a meditation.

'Yeah.

'It's where she took out a knife and cut one of his veins.'

Benson quickly turned to look at Jack, and caught – as expected – the look of satisfaction. Billy Hudson's murder had been no tragedy. Not for the Kilgours. But it had been horrific; and Jack was staring at the ground where a pool of blood and vomit had been found by Greg the next morning. Smudge marks trailed across the concrete floor to the mouth of the loading bay from where – so the theory went – Billy's body had been rolled into the boot of Karmen's Golf. CCTV footage from the entrance to Southbrook Road showed the vehicle seconds after it had left the premises, moving at high speed. The time: 9.17 p.m.

'Did you like her?' said Benson.

'Who?'

'Karmen.'

Jack thought for a while; then he chanced it.

'She's a Naylor, Mr Benson. What else can I say?'

'Whether or not you liked her.'

'I said she's a Naylor.'

Karmen's account of the evening was very different. Billy had met her by the entrance, she said. They'd stayed in the reception area. There'd been little to discuss. Billy had agreed to move. He'd said there were plenty of other places he could use. And anyway, he couldn't stomach the sight of Kilgour and his gutless sons.

'What the hell is that?'

Looking through a glass fire-escape door, Benson had recognised a couple of large bins against the rear wall, with a line of trees on the other side – background detail that he'd examined in a photograph taken by the police. But Benson had just seen something new, through a gap in the branches: a man. He was walking along what seemed to be a path. A path that didn't appear on the plan in the trial brief. Jack came closer, shaking his inhaler, nodding at the fire escape.

'That's a way out, Mr Benson, not a way in.'

Benson kept his eyes on the break in the trees, his imagination stirring, his attention rapt.

'Thanks, Jack. I've got what I wanted. You can go home now.'

9

'I'm here on serious business,' said Tess, dropping into the padded chair.

'Just tell me what you want.'

'Turn me into Louise Brooks.'

Anina Omilacha Osabede, dob 04.03.1992, commonly known as Nina, lived in Peckham and worked at Snip-Snap on Lewisham High Street. She'd met Billy Hudson briefly in January 2017. A pregnancy ensued. At the time of Hudson's murder, she'd been visiting her father, who lived in sheltered accommodation, also in Peckham. Such were the details given during a voluntary interview with the police, after which – citing health concerns – she'd refused to cooperate.

'Who's that?' said Nina, smiling.

'A film star from the twenties.'

Nina tapped the name into her phone.

'Wow. A flapper . . . a sex symbol . . . a dancer . . .' – Nina had a sing-song laugh, and it rang out as she read, scrolling down the screen – '. . . an actress . . . an escort . . . and a drinker with suicidal tendencies. She's some girl. You're sure?'

'I just want the hair.'

'It's a shingled bob. Seriously vintage. I'll tell you what: how about I give it a modern spin? Super-short with a punk twist?'

'Get chopping.'

When left down, Tess's hair reached well below her shoulders. This short style would see most of it lying on the floor.

To the sound of snipping, Tess looked into the mirror, studying Nina's wonderfully oval face and frizzy copper hair, the pastel rose lipstick and the bold black eyeliner. With the tight red trousers and green nail varnish, she could easily have joined Tess and Sally when they hit the town. There was no anxiety in her features; no tension in her movements. Once Nina had cut enough hair to make stopping impossible, Tess made her play.

'This isn't the serious business I was talking about.'

'Really?'

'Yes. I'm hoping—'

At that moment, Nina's mobile rang. She looked at the screen and apologised. Then, turning her back on Tess, she took the call, speaking quietly.

'I can't stay on, I'm working . . . Yes, I'm fine. You? . . . Great . . .'

Her tone was warm and assured. Excited, even.

'I'm okay, honest. Relax . . . I've got to go . . . Yes . . . Okay. See you soon.'

Nina pocketed her mobile and snipped her scissors in the air.

'Sorry about that. You were saying?'

'That I was hoping.'

'What for?'

'Your help. In the defence of Karmen Naylor. My name's Tess de Vere. I'm her solicitor.'

Nina froze. For a long while they stared at each other's reflection, like cats before a fight, before that awful whine fills the sharp night air. Tess continued:

'The trial opens tomorrow. Karmen says she's innocent.'

'So what?'

'We're trying to trace someone who might be involved in the killing. A police informer.'

'I can't help you.'

'We know this informer had been ready to give evidence against Tony Naylor.'

'I'm not interested.'

'The case folded because Tony had a stroke.'

'Not interested.'

'The informer then takes matters into their own hands. We think. They give information to the Ronsons, so they can hit Billy and frame Karmen.'

'Why tell me all this?'

'Nina . . . Karmen is facing a life sentence because she had the misfortune to be born into the crime world. Just like you had the misfortune to meet a criminal. She's a victim. You're a victim. You can't turn back the clock, but you've got a future. Karmen's been damned since the day she was born. Even if she's acquitted, she'll never escape her name. Can't you spare me a few minutes, before you turn me into a flapper?'

'I don't know anything.'

'You met Billy after Tony Naylor was arrested for the murder of James Fitzgerald.'

'And?'

'Everyone in the Naylor business must have been wondering who the hell the informer might be. Did Billy say anything to you about—'

'Are you serious? During a one-night stand?'

'Well, before or afterwards.'

'We just smoked. On both occasions. Look, I didn't even know Billy was involved with the Naylors. I thought he ran a tyre-fitting business.'

This was exactly what Tess had expected to hear. But she pushed a little harder, because something incidental to the conversation wasn't quite ringing true.

'Just think back, Nina. Was there anyone Billy called or mentioned or—'

'No. Now listen, I met Billy in January 2017. Here. In that chair. We made a night of it. A reckless night, okay, because I got pregnant. I told him a few months later because he had a right to know, only he wasn't interested. This is May 2017. I never saw him again. A year down the line – May 2018 – Billy is murdered, and that's when I found out he was a villain. Am I glad I met him? No. Am I relieved he's gone? Yes. Is my son losing out? No. Am I prepared to help Karmen Naylor? Yes. But I can't. Because—'

'You don't know anything.'

'At last you understand. Now can I get on? Or you'll never be a flapper.'

'With attitude.'

'Yeah, with attitude.'

Gradually the very image of a nineteen-twenties screen idol appeared in the mirror. The short hair on each cheek had been shaped into a neat curl; at the back, it was beautifully tapered to expose the neck. Then came the shock. Rapid chopping. A few Johnny Rotten spikes broke up the smooth layers, savaging any suggestion of orthodoxy or retro charm. Nina spoke of Obi, her son, who was now seventeen months old. He'd begun to walk . . . he'd learned a few words . . . he points at things . . . and she just hated leaving him at the nursery. Coming back to Billy, she said, the good thing was that his name didn't appear on Obi's birth certificate. It was as though he'd never existed. She didn't like lying, but her grandparents in Kontagora were going to hear about a guy who'd been run over by a bus. A businessman . . . no, a poet. A gentleman. The same story she'd one day tell Obi. No one would ever be the wiser. Nina held up a mirror so Tess could get an all-round view.

'You look fantastic.'

'I do.'

'A flapper with attitude,' added Nina, with a sing-song laugh.

* * *

52

As she drove along Lewisham High Street, a gobsmacking £95 lighter, Tess wished Benson had been with her. Because while Nina had finally cooperated, sort of, something had jarred. As Tess got further and further away from Snip-Snap, she became more and more sure she'd been played. She didn't know how, and she didn't know why. But it had happened. It was the sort of thing Benson would have latched on to and foiled. Taking a corner a bit too quickly, she wondered what he'd think of the super-short-punky-shingled bob.

10

Congreve's, the fishmonger's on Artillery Passage, Spitalfields, first opened its doors for business in February 1892. They closed, with a bang, in March 2009 after Archie, fighting supermarkets, discount stores and fish fingers, falsified some tax returns. Which had landed him in a cell with William Benson, in the final year of his incarceration for murder. When the legal establishment slammed door after door in Benson's face, the Congreves opened one of theirs, with Archie transformed from a trader into a barrister's clerk. A gold signet ring with his initials replaced the filleting knife. The public mockery had been widespread. When Tess heard, astonished to discover that Benson had made it to the Bar, she'd run to join the fight. They'd become Benson and de Vere, the most talked-about defence team in London. And then, without invitation, another fighter had come on board: Molly Robson, a wrestling referee who happened to be a legal secretary. When Tess pushed open the door of Congreve Chambers later that evening, she felt like she'd come home.

'Can I help you?' said Benson huskily.

'Look a little closer.'

Tess had walked straight into Benson's study, the Gutting Room, where the fish had once been cleaned. Files lay open, and photographs of blood spattering were strewn among pens and highlighters and Post-it notes, all on a naval captain's desk. Instantly her eyes snagged on the door that led to the delivery yard, where, two years back, she'd pinned Benson to the canvas and kissed him.

'There's something odd about Nina Osabede,' she said.

Tess recounted the conversation with Nina, mindful that for Archie and Molly the shock of her appearance had been quickly displaced by censure for having abandoned ship. She pressed on as if she'd never been away:

'What struck me most was the absence of emotional residue . . . that she'd been involved with an extremely dangerous man who'd done extremely bad stuff and that this man was the father of her child . . . someone who'd been slaughtered. There was no disgust. Or horror. There was no fear of the Naylors, even though she'd got up really close, no sense of a close shave. Nothing. Everything she said sounded rehearsed. She was in control. She delivered a speech. I just didn't know how to break it down.'

Tess reached for her hair, to give a shake, but it wasn't there. Instead, suddenly self-conscious, she touched her neck, and saw Benson's gaze fix on the exact spot.

'I was wrong, Will,' she said. 'Doorstepping Nina was a good idea. I'll do the same thing to her father. Maybe he knows what his daughter is hiding.'

Archie and Molly, usually vocal, said nothing. They were waiting for her to confess to something else she'd got wrong. But how could Tess go there? She'd couldn't share the reason. She couldn't share it with anyone.

'She's not the only one hiding something,' said Benson pointedly.

That produced a couple of nods, and Tess thought, it's time to leave, but then Benson added:

'The Kilgours are hiding something, too.'

'Like what?' said Archie, after a long moment.

Benson opened his mouth, breathed in and then shook his head:

'You'll find out at trial.'

'C'mon,' said Archie. 'Don't be coy.'

'No. It's just a hunch.'

'C'mon, spit it out.'

'Okay . . . there's more to the crime scene than I thought.'

'What the hell are you on about?'

'There's a path that runs behind HGT Ltd. It doesn't have a name. It doesn't appear on the prosecution's map of the *locus in quo*. And in the unused material there's a note of a phone call from a guy who was out for a walk on the night of the murder, and . . .'

'And?'

'He's called Cameron. I've looked him up.'

'Go on.'

'He's a professor of French literature. Retired. Specialised in the sixteenth century.'

'So what?'

'He's got a dog called Monty.'

'Ah yes, Montgomery. Think El Alamein, Molly.'

'No, Archie,' said Benson. 'The field marshal doesn't appear in the canon. And that's the literary term, not the gun. Think Michel Eyquem de Montaigne. That's my guess. An essayist much preoccupied with the subject of death.'

'Death?' said Archie.

'Death,' repeated Benson significantly. 'I've sent a message to the other side. I want the professor in court. I've some questions for him.'

'What's a man and his dog got to do with anything?'

'They might just be central to the case.'

'How?'

Molly, leaning forward to catch Benson's whisper, nearly slipped off her seat:

'It's another hunch. You'll find out at trial.'

Archie ground his teeth, smiling, while Molly, not wanting to, laughed, along with Tess, who did.

'This is the job, Team Congreve,' continued Benson. 'We could be representing Steven Bucklow tomorrow – remember him? The drug dealer pretending to be a van driver. The lowlife caught with three million quid stuffed into three suitcases, keeping shtum about a money-laundering operation – well, he's listed in the court next door to ours. Win or lose, it wouldn't matter. He's guilty. He knows it; we know it. For him, it's just a game of cat and mouse. Instead, we're acting for someone who's obviously innocent. The result counts. In different ways to different people. If I could pick my fights, this is the kind I'd choose. With you three at my side.'

'Do you think we can win, Rizla?' said Archie.

'We've got a shout.'

'I think you mean bark,' said Molly. 'Let's drink to Monty.'

And that was the beginning. Out came the hooch. Molly complimented Tess on the new hairstyle – she'd known a wrestler, a seventies sensation known as the Chopper, who'd sported a very similar cut – and Archie recounted his accidental meeting with Johnny Rotten, who'd been extraordinarily polite, and Benson, thinking of the twenties, said he'd have given his back teeth to wear spats and plus-fours and a straw boater. Tess listened, and she talked and she laughed, loving Benson for his genius and sensitivity.

Only her day wasn't over. She had another uncomfortable meeting to attend.

11

Rather than head home to Ennismore Gardens Mews in Knightsbridge, Tess went to Selby Street in Bethnal Green, and the consulting room of a clinical psychologist who'd once helped Benson. He'd told Tess she changed her hairstyle frequently, using colours and beads and silks. And that she wore bangles and bracelets and rings picked up from Cancer Research or the Red Cross, charity shops round the corner from where she lived. He'd said she was almost clairvoyant.

'I know you helped Will, and I'm wondering if you can help me.'

Abasiama never seemed to breathe or move. Benson had said that, too.

'I think Will helped himself.'

'I'm not capable of that.'

Abasiama's dark brown eyes were like magnets. Tess could feel them tugging at the fragments of her past.

'My specialism is the impact of war,' she said. 'Trauma. From witnessing atrocities. Or committing them. Then there's the living with lies. And anger. And fear. And guilt. And panic. And regret. I'm here for those who limp through life.'

Tess couldn't help but glance down. Abasiama's right leg was missing. Benson had said nothing about that. If she had a prosthesis, it was nowhere to be seen. There was no wheelchair either. Or crutches. Not even a walking stick. Suddenly Tess felt the push of tears. She'd long ago stopped limping. She crawled now, her fingers digging into the ground for leverage, while everyone smiled, thinking she looked just great.

'That's me,' said Tess. 'I live with fear, anger, lies and guilt . . . terribly consuming guilt. I want to be whole again.'

'Won't happen.'

'What do you mean?'

'You'll never be whole again.'

'Is there any point in me going on?'

'Only if you think going forward is better than staying where you are.'

Most counsellors have a box of tissues on a table, perhaps with some fresh flowers in a vase. Abasiama had a cactus.

'Okay. Let's try going forward. Until now, I've worked out a way of living as if everything is normal. I think I'm probably quite good at it. It's even been comfortable.'

'How long have you lived like this?'

'Since 2010.'

'What happened in 2010?'

'I can't tell you. Does that mean you can't help me?'

'Not at all. When did the comfort become discomfort?'

Tess wondered if she could identify a moment. And she could. 'After a kiss . . . after I kissed Benson.'

'Are you sure you don't need a relationship counsellor?'

'Benson has nothing to do with my problems. It was the closeness that made me realise I'd got used to hiding. And that I didn't want to hide any more. Not just from him. Everyone. I wanted to tell Benson everything about myself, and I couldn't. So I ran away. I just dropped him. But my work has brought us back together . . . and there's nowhere I can run. There never was.'

'Have you ever literally run away?'

'Yes.'

'Would that be in 2010?'

'Yes.'

'Where to?'

'France. Strasbourg. And then other places.'

'How did you explain to those around you what was happening?'

'I blamed a boyfriend who happened to be a bastard.'

'Did you break down?'

'Yes.'

'Were you prescribed medication?'

'Yes.'

'Did you take it?'

'No. I thought that was kind of cheating. I thought I ought to feel what I was feeling.'

Tess had never felt safer in her life than being here with Abasiama. She couldn't remember when she'd last breathed as easily. She took deep, refreshing breaths, and she let them out slowly. If she'd been in a pool, she'd have floated on her back, eyes closed to the sun.

'I found my feet eventually. In all, it took five years, and then I got a job in London. Pretended everything was fine. Looked up my best friend. By chance, this was when Benson opened his own chambers. He thinks I came to help him out of loyalty . . . because we'd clicked. But, deep down, I just wanted myself back. The self he'd known and remembered, when I was nineteen. The best of me.'

Tess stopped, expecting a question, but none came.

'But I found something else . . . a drive to prove his innocence. And from that moment – you might not believe this – I forgot my own secret. Maybe it was there, but it had lost its hold. All I cared about was uncovering the truth about Benson's past. And his emotional freedom. Because aside from his conviction, I could see he was still locked up, inside himself. That he wouldn't let anyone get near him.'

Again, Tess stopped, but Abasiama, absolutely immobile, just carried on watching.

'The investigation set me free. And not just from my own past. I was able to show him what I felt – real love. Because I knew he couldn't respond. But when he'd been vindicated, and I kissed him, he came out of the dark . . . and I was left standing there, wondering what to do next. How to take things forward when I wanted to go back.'

'Why not go back to France?'

'Because I'd learned it doesn't work.'

'Tell me about your father.'

'I beg your pardon?'

'I never repeat myself.'

'Why ask about my father?'

'I've no idea. I could have asked about your mother. But I didn't.'

'What do you want to know?'

'Anything. You choose.'

The light from that imagined sun had suddenly gone. Tess nearly got up and ran for the door. Her hands were on the armrests of her chair, ready for lift-off, her shoulders raised for the push. She held herself like this, tense and terrified.

'Do you want out or not?' said Abasiama. 'That's another choice.'

Without making any formal decision, and like someone watching someone they knew through binoculars, Tess rose and quietly left the room, not even pausing to say goodbye, being careful only not to brush against Abasiama's chair.

12

Benson took the path through the trees that led to Seymour Basin on the Albert Canal, and the only barge moored there, his home, *The Wooden Doll*. Suddenly, Traddles, Benson's cat, shot past him, and Benson laughed. He was the only cat he'd ever known who was frightened of his prey. He went after birds or mice, driven by instinct, but as soon as they turned around he fled. Opening the front cabin door, Benson flicked the light switch, but nothing happened.

'Do you play football, Rizla?'

Benson knew that kind of voice. It preceded the violence.

'Not really, no.'

'Take a seat. You know your way around.'

Benson could just about discern three or four large men, joined into a single mass of thick necks and bulging shoulders.

'I said sit.'

Benson felt his way to the small table facing the Aga. He slid onto the bench. The same voice continued.

'What about tennis?'

'No.'

'Snooker?'

'No.'

'Table tennis?'

'No.'

'Cricket?'

'No. Sorry.'

'Golf? You must play golf. Now that you're a celebrity.'

'I don't. Look, what's this about?'

'Tell you what. We'll try boxing. Do you box, Rizla?'

'No.'

'That's not what I've been told.'

'I've never boxed.'

'Split words with me again and I'll take your eyes out. I'm on about fighting. When you were inside.'

Benson's heart was banging out blood that wasn't even there, hurting the wall of his chest. He pushed himself back into the bench, avoiding the punches that hadn't yet been thrown.

'Yeah, you're impressive, Rizla. Took on bastards with a full-life tariff. People with nothing to lose . . . and you wouldn't back down.'

The growling and biting had been about survival. Marking out the territory he couldn't concede.

'We're impressed, aren't we, boys?'

None of the boys replied. But they were there, looming over the table.

'You see, this afternoon, we were wondering what made you tick, asking ourselves whether you were the sort of bloke we could have a sensible conversation with, you know what I mean? And my mates here, they said no chance. He won't listen. He'd rather spend months in hospital. Maybe die.'

'Listen to what?'

'Sense.'

'Look, what's on your mind? You can take whatever you want. I'm open to anything.'

'The boys don't agree. They reckon you're too . . . principled. That's the word, isn't it, boys?'

Again, that awful silence.

'Please tell me, what can I do?'

'Okay. Prove the boys wrong. Throw the trial.'

Benson looked into the heaving darkness. The voice came closer, with a quiet crunch and the whiff of a mint.

'Ever heard of Sonny Liston? The Big Bear?'

The speaker was inches away, two thick arms propped on the table.

'They say he threw the second fight against Clay. Liston went down from a blow that most people didn't even see. Did y'ever watch that, Rizla? The round-one knockout?'

'Yes.'

'Good. We understand one another. Thing is, the boys expect more from you. You don't lie on your back thinking of Tess de Vere's tits. Or even Molly's. For the avoidance of doubt – barristers say that kind of thing, don't they? For the avoidance of doubt, your honour, Little Winner gets life. You decide how and why. But you make sure the jury convicts her.'

The large shadows moved as one towards the door. And then, for the first time, Benson realised they'd not been alone. Footsteps were coming from the far end of the boat. Someone had been sitting there, listening, as if from the throne room. As this dark shape moved past Benson, there came the snap of aftershave and an ever so quiet double sniff, unintentional but given; and then, very casually, a trailing hand opened the fridge door. The inside light came on and then the voice came again, this time from the deck, through the open door:

'We've left you something to chew on.'

When they'd gone Benson again slid along the bench, his eyes on the illuminated interior of the fridge, hearing the low hum, feeling an imagined chill. He could see the yoghurts. A block of cheese. Milk. Worcestershire sauce. Half an onion. Two beers from Ettal. An open tin of baked beans. Another of corned beef. And a side plate . . . that hadn't been there in the morning . . . covered in cling film.

Benson lowered himself onto his knees, then tipped back with a cry. On the plate was a finger. And on the finger was a bloodied gold signet ring, engraved with an A and a C.

13

'I went out of the back door as usual, and they were waiting. I didn't have a chance.'

Having crawled into Bishopsgate, Archie had collapsed. A passing motorist, seeing the heap, had stopped and taken him to the Royal London Hospital on Whitechapel Road. When he'd come round, Archie, barely coherent, had called Benson, who'd then called Tess. Molly hadn't picked up, so he'd left a message. Benson, plunged into a living nightmare, brought the finger – still on the plate – to a waiting nurse, for transmission to the surgical team who'd attempt to reattach it.

'They knew your routine,' said Benson. 'They knew mine, too, and probably yours, Tess.'

Tess, ashen, nodded.

'They've been watching us for months. Ever since we took the case.'

A nurse came into the room with the calm haste that inspires confidence.

'You've a couple of minutes. Then we're taking Mr Congreve into theatre.'

She was gone before Benson could ask any questions. He turned to Archie. They'd given him a thrashing first. His eyes were pinched shut by blue swellings and his lips had been split.

'I'm sorry, Archie. You were right. Representing Karmen is dangerous.'

Archie seemed to drift off, so Benson turned to Tess:

'I've been inside with these people. They're not screwing around. If Karmen is acquitted—'

Archie's right hand yanked hard on Benson's sleeve.

'You were right too,' he said.

'About what, Arch?'

'Taxis.'

'Taxis?'

'The bloody cab-rank thing. We defend whoever turns up. Now do it.'

Archie's arm dropped, and the nurse, returning with a porter, tugged the bed and began wheeling it away down the corridor.

Benson lit up.

They'd found a couple of tree stumps on the pavement outside the hospital. An eerie calm had settled on Benson.

'We're on our own, Tess. We can't tell the court. We can't tell Karmen. And we can't go to the police.'

'We can get protection.'

'It makes no difference. They'll put someone you love in a wheelchair.'

'But the police can—'

'Tess. The police might be involved. Think it through. After Hudson's murder, they never investigated the people who were most obviously responsible. Instead, they charged someone who has no motive, accepting an obviously contrived crime scene at face value. The police are part of the plan. I'm not saying they sat down with the Ronsons in a pub and worked out who was doing what, but they arrived at a mutual under-standing, through Q. For whatever reason, the police would rather have the Ronsons in play than the Naylors – maybe the trick is to get the Ronsons later, letting dog eat dog first, I don't know – but this much is clear for now: Hudson gets taken out and Karmen takes the fall. Everyone's happy.'

Tess leaned forward into light thrown from the hospital, and all at once Benson glimpsed her on the day they'd first met. She'd been overwhelmed by the sheer weight of the Old Bailey – the stone and marble and stucco – all of it upstairs, threatening to crash through the ceiling. The threat had been imaginary. This one was real.

'We're part of the plan, too, Will. They were always going to come for the defence team. So far, everything's gone like clockwork.'

What bound them now went deeper than any affection or misunderstanding. They were looking into the same grave. What they did would determine whether or not they ended up buried, one beside the other. With Archie thrown on top. Which didn't bear thinking about.

'I think you just met Stuart Ronson,' said Tess.

'So do I.'

'And I think you met the team that killed Billy Hudson.'

'I'm sure I did.'

'Let's show them we won't look the other way, Will. Let's stop the clock, here and now. And whatever happens, happens.'

Benson looked towards the hospital, recalling the day Congreve's had reopened its doors for business. Archie had just been given a gold signet ring by his father. The man who'd shamed the family name had raised it to glory. He'd stretched out his hand, watching the play of light on his initials. Q, as much as anyone else, had brought about that amputation.

'And whatever happens, I'd like a quiet word with Q,' he said.

'I was just thinking of him,' said Tess. 'He's as vulnerable as we are. He's on his own. He can't go to the police. If he's exposed, he's dead. We can use that. We can help him choose to stay alive. We take him to another police force. And this time the game is over. For the Naylors. For the Ronsons. And for the police officers who hung Karmen out to dry. This could be the jackpot, Will . . . and if Nina Osabede's father knows anything, I'm going to find out what it is.'

Benson and Tess only decided to go home after Archie, out of theatre, told them he fancied a pork pie. With some Branston pickle. And a pint. And some cheese. And cashews. Salted. The essential man had surfaced unscathed from the depths. And anyway, Molly had arrived. With the remains of a cake.

Tess drove Benson to Seymour Basin, though he didn't invite her onto his barge. They sat in the car, near a pool of orange light thrown from a streetlamp, talking about Tony Naylor, broken but not beaten, and HGT Ltd, soon to be demolished, the Kilgours, left out to rot, and Nina who'd soon be gone . . . not forgetting Q, who'd gone nowhere. At the first pause, Benson opened the car door and they said goodnight.

Only that was wishful thinking.

The lingering smell of that silent man's aftershave and the sweat of his entourage remained in the air. And there were flashes of remembered horror. But none of these things kept Benson awake. It was gratitude. Because those animals had brought him closer to Tess than ever before. They'd been brought face to face with the true nature of their calling, a vision they'd first shared when they'd been little more than kids, a student and a defendant, two dreamers in a dismal holding cell below the Old Bailey.

PART TWO

The case for the prosecution

Friday 15th January 2010

The home of Mr and Mrs Lomax
Fulham, London

'What did you say your name was?'
  'De Vere. Tess.'
'You mean D-E, then V-E-R-E?'
'I do.'
'Two words?'
'Yes.'
'Your dad was French?'
'No. English.'
'Where from?'
'Warkworth. A village in Northumberland.'
'Near the coast . . . and there's a castle?'
'Yes. You've been there?'
'No. Just heard of it. A long time ago.'
Brian Lomax, a former sergeant in the British army, last-minute whistleblower and the overweight husband of Brenda, thought for a while, scratching his bare arms ferociously. He grimaced at the raw skin, blued by tattoos.

'It's the cancer,' said Brenda, on the edge of a stool by his armchair.

'De Vere?' he repeated.

'Yes.'

Mr Lomax turned to Peter.

'And you're Peter Farsely?'

'That's right.'

'F-A-R-S-E-L-Y?'

'Yes.'

'Well, that makes you a bit of an arse. Doesn't it?'

'I know a lot of people who'd agree with you.'

Mr Lomax thought some more, then he said:

'You're an item, you two.'

Tess quickly corrected him.

'We're work colleagues, Mr Lomax. And we're here to take a statement with respect to allegations you have made about a group of British soldiers who organised and carried out assassinations in Northern Ireland during the seventies with the tacit consent of the government. We'll video everything you say, and I'll write it up later for you to check and sign. Is that okay?'

'You're an item.'

'Stop it, Brian. She'll go red if you carry on.'

'It's in their eyes. And good luck to you both. We've had thirty-three years of fun and games, haven't we? It's been great. Best thing that ever happened to me. I love you, Brenda.'

Again, Mr Lomax grated his arms with his nails. Then his face darkened, and he stared out of anguished eyes towards the door.

'The archive's in the kitchen. I don't want it anywhere near me. It's all in there. There's nothing else to say.'

Brenda was eager and relieved.

'He's going to tell you everything, aren't you, love? You're going to get it all off your chest. You're going to tell them what where when and who, aren't you, love?'

Mr Lomax gave a shake of the head.

'Ah yes, the Who.'

'The who,' said Brenda with emphasis.

Mr Lomax thought for a moment.

'They were the best rock group that ever trashed a hotel toilet.'

'Who's that?' said Brenda, confused.

'The Who, who else?'

Mr Lomax addressed Tess.

'We saw them live in Kilburn. Do you know the name of their first single? It was – wait for it – "I Can't Explain".'

Then, both arms still tearing at his skin, he got up and left the room, coming back with a large carboard box. He dropped it by Peter's feet and fell back into his chair.

'They may as well listen. They deserve that much. Is the camera rolling?'

Peter, smiling uncertainly, pressed the record button.

'Action.'

14

Benson did in fact fall asleep. And he dreamt that Tess had found Q, that rogue police informant. He was a council employee who drove a bulldozer, a muscular entity with yellow teeth who kept rearranging his privates. Benson and Tess had cornered him with a couple of boathooks on the deck of *Little Winner*. They'd looked at each other in triumph. Because he'd agreed, in exchange for his freedom, to demolish a street of rotten houses. When Benson opened his eyes, he was sweating anger and reckless purpose. The resulting energy made him step on Traddles, cut himself shaving and drop his cuff-links. It fuelled his brisk walk to the Old Bailey, driving him into the robing room and onto the concourse outside Number 4 Court. And it pushed him towards Indira Shah

QC, who'd just emerged from a conference room with a CPS representative and DCI Anita Panjabi, the officer in charge of the case. The OIC who wanted to nail Karmen just because she was a Naylor.

'Good morning, Benson,' said Shah, with her rich purple voice, after Panjabi had moved away. 'Has Naylor seen sense?'

'Meaning?'

'Is she going to plead? I'm hoping she's been well advised.'

This was Benson's first case against Shah. There'd been three pre-trial hearings, and she'd attended none of them, owing to 'serious matters in the Court of Appeal'. A junior had been sent along in her place. All preliminary negotiations had been carried out by email. Delicately framed, in her mid-forties, with dark, liquid eyes, Shah had a reputation of making simple cases unpleasant for her opponent and complex cases unbearable.

'Why did the police leave so many leads unexplored? Why did they do nothing once they'd got their hands on Karmen?'

'Karmen? Keep some distance, Benson. You're a lawyer. Not a therapist.'

'You've spoken to the CPS. You've spoken to Panjabi. You know the wider picture. Why are they gunning for her when it's obvious she's been framed?'

'It isn't obvious to me. Or those who instruct me.'

'The Ronsons' fingerprints are all over the place.'

'Actually, Benson, they aren't. You might reflect on that.'

'I'm reflecting on the wider picture. Can you tell me why they're so sure she's—'

'There's a proper way to explore these questions, Benson. It's called a trial. If she's not going to plead, we must press on. Two matters. First, Professor Cameron. I understand you want him warned to attend?'

'I do.'

'He's in Lahel. With his wife. Marie-Edith.'

'Lahel? Where's that?'

'Senegal.'

'What?'

'Senegal. You should have asked earlier. Second, the Naylors and the Ronsons. Do you still want to address the jury on the matter?'

'Of course I do. That's why I insisted on a statement of police intelligence.'

'Just checking. The proper order is that you speak after me. I'll have the judge warned. Anything else?'

'No.' Benson paused, resigning himself to days of bruising conflict. 'It's a shame we couldn't discuss the background to this case as colleagues.'

'Shame?' Her voice had chilled. 'That's a word I'd avoid, if I were you. Along with colleagues. You're a convicted murderer, Benson, who claims to be innocent. And rather than appeal, you cherish the stain, to attract people like the Naylors, mocking the entire system of justice. They feed off your disgrace. I'd have you struck off for that alone.'

She hesitated, like an arsonist who'd set fire to a curtain, waiting for the uncontrolled lick of flame. But Benson gave no reaction and, realising none would be forthcoming, she spun on her heel and headed towards court.

As the door swung shut, Benson's eyes flicked right, to catch the CPS representative and DCI Panjabi. They were standing close together, whispering with their counterparts in *R-v-Bucklow* . . . and Benson was instantly flung into Number 1 Court, and the day of his own trial, twenty years ago. There'd been a lot of whispering then, too, and Benson had looked on, feeling sick, until Helen Camberley, his brief, had swept into court like an unleashed demon. The next thing Benson knew, he'd struck the court door with the flat of his hand and was striding towards Karmen. She looked up, diminished between two burly guards, her face white with anxiety.

'I believe you, Karmen,' he said. 'It doesn't matter what anyone else thinks. I'm here. And—'

'I'm innocent, Mr Benson. I swear to you.'

'—and I'm going to fight like I've never fought before.'

One of the guards – a stub of a man who looked like he foraged on steroids and broken glass – smirked, so Benson gave him a look: the kind you can only give after eleven years in prison for a crime you didn't commit; the loss of your mother while you were away; the breakdown of your father, who clung to your innocence; the rejection of your brother, who believed you were guilty; the spite of people who wouldn't give you a second chance; and the loss of that fragile part of you that gives and receives affection naturally and easily, but is now so damaged that all you can do is smoke, remembering who you once were, longing for who you might have been, banging your head against the peeling walls that will always surround you. It was the look of blueish death and it wiped the smile off his face.

'Try and relax, Karmen. Leave everything to me.'

Benson went to the area reserved for counsel, his eyes locked on the empty jury box. The twelve people who'd shortly be gathered there were the ones that counted. Not the witnesses, not the judge, and certainly not Shah. They were the keepers of the gate, and come hell or high water he'd persuade them to throw it open. In a trance of purposeful aggression, he watched Mr Justice Garway shamble onto the bench, the jurors take their seats and the clerk read out the indictment alleging that Karmen Naylor, on the evening of Friday the eighteenth of May 2018, murdered William 'Billy' Hudson. Then, still under Benson's determined gaze, the judge gave a polite nod and the trial began.

'Good morning, ladies and gentlemen. My name is Shah. I appear for the Crown. On my left is Mr Benson. He represents the defendant. You are about to embark on a disturbing journey. At the outset, I insist you put to one side the lurid headlines that this case has attracted, along with the hype and hysteria. Your task is to seek the truth. And you'll only find it if, as you examine the evidence, you remember two words of warning. I am sure my learned friend Mr Benson would echo them with absolute conviction: be careful.'

15

Finding Azuka Osabede was a straightforward exercise, because his address had been given in Nina's brief statement to the police. Tess went there, 'The Conifers', a sheltered housing project situated a half-mile or so from Nina's flat. Unable to spot a single tree, Tess did however find the warden, Mrs Chadwick, who explained that on Tuesdays a member of staff took Azuka to a church café on Clayton Road, where he worked as a volunteer. A great place for baked potatoes and coleslaw, if you liked that kind of thing. And so Tess found herself in a windowless vaulted room adjacent to a busy kitchen, facing Nina's father across a table as he peeled carrots.

'No one will listen to me,' he said. 'Not the police, not Nina, not Ekene. They think I'm blind. But I know I'm right.'

'Who's Ekene?'

'My son. Nina's elder brother. He's a good boy. A kind boy. But he thinks I'm from another planet.'

Tess was taken aback. First, because Azuka *was* blind, or had significant sight loss. Second, because Nina had made no mention of her brother when describing her family. And third, because Tess, in explaining who she was, had triggered an outburst that showed here was someone who had something new to say about Billy Hudson. And no one would listen to him. Tess immediately put aside the questions she'd planned.

'What are you right about, Mr Osabede?'

'Billy.'

'In what way?'

'He wasn't all bad. I told Nina to explain everything to the police, but she refused. She's the one who's blind, not me.'

'Explain what?'

'The attack. One of them had a knife. And then Billy turned up.'

Mr Osabede, lined and grizzled, lived again the shock and gratitude; it shone from his eyes. Nina had been walking on her own in Peckham Rye Park when she'd been surrounded by a bunch of youths. White boys. Racists. Five of them. They were—

'When was this?'

'A long time ago.'

'When, Mr Osabede, precisely?'

'Oh . . . August 2016. Nina was twenty-four. And Billy saved her life. I don't approve of violence, Miss de Vere, but sometimes, well, what can you do? And he gave those boys something to think about.'

Billy had taken Nina, crying and distraught, to the Be All and End All café, off Forest Hill Road, near the cemetery, and bought her a hot drink. A sweet drink. He'd calmed her down and then brought her home. Listening, her mind racing, Tess could see Azuka, arms outstretched, moving carefully around the flat, insisting that Billy stay to eat with them. He'd brought in all the neighbours. He'd called friends and cousins. They'd eaten a traditional Nigerian meal, and afterwards he'd taken Billy aside, into the kitchen.

'A man's life is written on his face, Miss de Vere. So I put my hands on him. I wanted to know who'd saved my daughter.'

Again, Tess, transfixed, watched in her mind as Azuka ran the tips of his old fingers over Hudson's brow – one of London's hardest hard men – around the eye sockets, down onto the cheekbones, the upper lip, the chin, feeling the lines in his skin, searching out the marks of his character made over a vicious lifetime. Ordinary creases, from smiling or frowning or squinting. And scars, where the stubble wouldn't grow.

'I lost my Oma, my wife, seventeen years ago. We'd looked at the world together, as one. And then, gradually, I lost most of my vision. There were no more clear lines, no sharpness, just a sea of colours and shapes and memories of how things used to be. Now I rely on these' – he dropped the peeler and raised his hands – 'and I feel things other people can't see, and I'm telling you . . . there was kindness in this boy.'

That, thought Tess with a sad smile, could have been deduced simply from his intervention to help Nina. It didn't change much. Hitler had been charming to his secretaries. He'd loved his dog. But Mr Osabede had spoken as if he'd discovered something altogether special. Something that shifted the balance of judgement. He reached into a brown paper bag and took out another carrot, and began drawing the peeler across the gnarled skin, revealing the bright orange flesh beneath. Firm cut after firm cut.

'He came to my home regularly. He ate at my table, with Nina. We laughed together.'

'Mr Osabede, were you aware what Billy did for a living?'

'Not at first, no. But my boy, Ekene, he found out. And he was not happy. You see, he was Nina's protector. When my wife died, Nina was only eight years old. She'd always been an angel at school, but after she lost her mother, she started getting into trouble with her teachers, and in her teens she went off the rails. And by then, I'd lost my sight. It was Ekene who held us together. It was Ekene who brought Nina back in line. He urged her to become a hairdresser. He paid for her training . . . he's a good boy, Ekene, with a good career on the railway. Since he left school. He's a guard. I'm proud of him, and Nina. I wish Oma had lived to see them grow . . . What was I saying?'

'Ekene found out what Billy did for a living.'

'Ah yes, and he was very worried. He told Nina to leave him, but she wouldn't. There was shouting and screaming, and Nina said she was old enough to live her own life and Ekene said she was putting the whole family at risk, and I . . . I couldn't see, and I was trying to bring peace between them, to talk things through calmly, but there was too much anger and upset.'

'And when you'd all calmed down?'

'Nina refused. She said Billy was special.'

Tess began to wonder if her own family situation had met its match. But she dropped the thought. Azuka was still sharing the agonies of being a parent. Six months after that first meeting with Billy, Nina had got pregnant, only she'd kept it secret. Imagine that. She'd said nothing. Not to her own father or brother. And not to Billy. She only spoke about it five months later, when she came home with a cut mouth. From Billy, who'd denied being the father. That was the end of their relationship. Even after Obi's birth in September, Billy never—

'Just pause there, Mr Osabede. You're saying Billy hit Nina?'

'Yes. He split her lip. I told her to go to the police, but she refused, and Ekene . . . he nearly lost his mind. Ekene, he is a strong man, a rash man, but thank God he controlled himself.'

With Azuka's permission, Tess took out a pen and pad and made a note of the dates, confirming what she'd just been told:

August	2016	Nina meets Hudson. H intervenes. Racist attack
January	2017	Nina pregnant
May	2017	Nina declares pregnancy Assault. End of relationship
September	2017	Birth of Obi

Tess did a calculation out loud:

'A year after that assault, Billy was murdered.'

'Yes. And he never met his son. Never asked to see him. Never accepted he was Obi's father. If he'd only seen him.'

Tess smiled another sad smile. This poor old man had failed to wonder if there was a connection between the assault and the murder. He just couldn't imagine that his children were anything but honourable people. He said:

'I was sad, for Billy. He died in such a horrible way. Ekene, he said Billy deserved it. So did Nina. They rejoiced over his death. They drank beer. When the Naylor girl was arrested, they clapped their hands. But no, I was sad.'

'Why, Mr Osabede?'

'I know he struck Nina; but he also saved her . . . and that is something I can't forget.' He put down the peeler and raised his hands as if they were scientific instruments of quite extraordinary precision. 'I know I felt something. He could have had a different future . . .'

Not expecting any helpful replies, Tess asked about the Kite, and Q, and whether Nina had ever mentioned these darker sides to Billy's life, but she hadn't.

'Hearing you ask such questions and looking back on the lives of Ekene and Nina, I wish I'd never left Nigeria. I knew there was crime. I knew there were bad people. I just didn't expect the endless distrust because of the colour of my skin. I never wanted that for my children. I don't want it for my grandson. If I could start again, somewhere else, I would do. You see, I've never got used to the . . . struggle.'

There was nothing Tess could say. Apologising for what the Osabedes had encountered and endured would have been trite. Vaguely ashamed, she thought it best to leave.

'It's been a real pleasure, Mr Osabede,' she said, rising. 'Thank you.'

But she couldn't pull away that easily. Mr Osabede continued with his work, and for a long moment Tess quietly stood there, watching him with immense pity. His hands had found what he wanted to see: a shred of decency in the man who'd saved his daughter's life. And she watched with admiration; he handled the vegetables slowly, piling the detritus to one side; this old gentleman who believed it was important for the world to know that something good could be said of an evil man.

16

'This is a most singular case, ladies and gentlemen,' said Indira Shah. 'On Friday the eighteenth of May 2018, late in the evening, Billy Hudson met this defendant, Karmen Naylor, at his place of work, Hither Green Tyres Ltd in south London. He was never seen again. In the days that followed, he made no phone calls and he sent no text messages. He wrote no letters. He withdrew no money from the bank. He didn't use his credit cards or debit cards or store cards. He wrote no cheques. He drove nowhere, flew nowhere, sailed nowhere. He didn't walk anywhere, and he didn't run. And that's because he was dead. When the police were summoned to the Hither Green premises on the Monday, two days after this meeting, they entered an abattoir. All that remained of Billy Hudson was his blood, some vomit and a few hairs. His body has never been found.'

With one reference to an abattoir, Shah had evoked the tabloid frenzy around the Hither Green Butcher. She'd brought into court the very sensationalism she'd urged the jury to ignore. Several jurors turned cautiously towards the dock, wondering what the Butcher looked like. Shah resumed only when they'd finished drinking in Karmen's features.

'A trail of forensic evidence led the police from that crime scene to a cottage on the Hoo Peninsula. A cottage owned by the defendant. And it led them to her boat. Which she took to sea the day after Billy Hudson went missing. I leave the rest, ladies and gentlemen, to your imagination. Unfortunately, I must also say the same about the defendant's motivation. Because as I stand before you today, I cannot tell you why the defendant killed him. I can't tell you whether she was angry, or resentful, or afraid, or threatened or vengeful. Only that she was merciless.' Shah appraised the defendant with the optimism of a newly appointed chaplain. 'It is my hope that in the days to come Karmen Naylor will take this final opportunity to explain what happened to Billy Hudson, and why. I'm hoping she'll allow some closure to those who've been left behind.'

Those left behind? Dear God, thought Benson. There was rejoicing and gladness when Hudson disappeared. There are people he battered out there, people now suffering permanent physical and mental harm, who – given the chance – would bathe in the blood the police had found on the floor. No funeral? There'd been untold numbers of carnivals. No grave? No one, save his mother, would have gone there, except to spit and laugh and show how violence dehuman-ises everyone it touches.

'Tony Naylor,' said Shah.

She let the name hang in the air.

'We may as well name the elephant in the room. Mr Benson will talk to you about him and his family in a few moments. That is his choice. For my part, I say this: we, the prosecution, look no further than this defendant for an understanding of what happened to Billy Hudson. We look no further than the evidence we have gathered for your consideration.'

That, thought Benson, was almost certainly untrue. Shah was about to exploit the blood link between Karmen and her father for all it was worth.

'The defendant is a clever and resourceful woman,' she was now saying. 'Whatever her father might have been doing, Karmen devoted herself to an upright, ordinary life. She did well at school. With top marks at A level, she secured a place at Newcastle University to study business finance and management, subsequently obtaining – in 2009 – a first-class degree. Rather than pursue the many career options that must have been open to her, the defendant found employment as a waitress in the hospitality sector. Two years in Newcastle. Three years in Leeds. Three years in Manchester. During those eight years, she only came home twice. Once after she'd finished her studies, and once to attend the funeral of her mother. In 2013. And it was only the near death of her father that brought her back permanently, after he suffered a debilitating stroke, in April 2017. She became his part-time carer, assisted by therapists and nurses of her choosing. She also became company secretary of HGT Ltd, where, as you now know, Billy Hudson worked. And it was at these prem-ises, on the evening of the eighteenth of May 2018, that, we say, a fatal confrontation took place. According to the defendant, when interviewed by the police, she'd arranged to meet Mr Hudson in the hope of persuading him to work elsewhere. They met in the reception area. Everything was convivial. He'd agreed to her request. We reject that expla-nation in its entirety, because of this we can be sure: Mr Hudson was murdered in his office that very night.'

Benson, noting everything down, was waiting for Shah to rehearse Karmen's incriminating association with the Naylor infrastructure, from her role as a director to her ownership of property – the first step towards painting her as a true Naylor, capable of Naylor conduct. But Shah was moving on to her next point . . .

'What can I say about Karmen Naylor's victim?' she said. 'As with respect to her father, I'm sure my learned friend Mr

Benson will be saying a great deal – so once more I leave the detail to him. I will confine myself to the following. Whatever a man has done in the past, whatever he might deserve as a consequence, and however disagreeable you might find viewing his life with surgical detachment – upon which I will insist – these courts protect everyone, good and bad alike, from the vagaries of the mob. Billy Hudson may not have been an innocent man. He may have deserved a cruel and nauseating end to his life. But this court will not sit by and allow him to be deprived of the justice he failed to show to others. It is the glory of our ancient legal system. And it falls to you to fulfil its sovereign mission.'

Shah sat down.

Benson well knew the merits of economy – it was the hallmark of forensic excellence – but Shah, he felt, had made the expert's mistake. She'd understated her case. And he understood how it had happened. Unable to identify a motive, she'd elected not to canvass one, out of fear that Benson might undermine her theory. But that decision had of necessity entailed another: not to marshal the incriminating evidence to support any theory at all. As a result, Shah had pared down her case to a bare adumbration of fact, leaving untouched Karmen's compromising links to her father and her relationship with Hudson. She'd said nothing about the murder of the Kite, and the shared modus operandi with Hudson's killing. All these key issues, and more, had been left unharnessed . . . and that gave Benson his opportunity.

'Mr Benson?'

Mr Justice Garway raised an eyebrow.

'I understand you, too, will address the jury.'

Benson rose to his feet. He was going to take control of the case.

'Yes, my lord. We're still in the presence of an elephant.'

17

Benson gave a nod to an usher and a copy of the police intelligence report obtained at his insistence was handed to each member of the jury. When the rustling of paper had stopped, Benson read out the text:

IN THE CENTRAL LONDON CRIMINAL COURT

R v KARMEN NAYLOR

**Metropolitan Police Intelligence Unit (Southern Division)
Subject: the NAYLOR ORGANISED CRIME GROUP
Valid until trial date: 15th January 2019**

1. When not a matter of public record, or otherwise stated, the information set out herein has been graded 'near certain' by Metropolitan Police analysts.

2. Anthony 'Tony' NAYLOR was the leader of the Naylor Organised Crime Group (the group). He has two children from a marriage to Susan MOIR (deceased): Ryan NAYLOR and Karmen NAYLOR.

3. It is understood Ryan now leads the group.

4. Operating south of the Thames, the group is involved in multiple criminal activities, including armed robbery, drug dealing, prostitution, extortion, fraud, skimming, money laundering, forgery and murder.

5. The group's principal rival is the north London crime family run by Stuart RONSON, against whom it has

been conducting a war of influence since approximately 2015.

6. William 'Billy' HUDSON was Tony NAYLOR's driver, bodyguard and enforcer.

7. At the time of the matter before the court, HUDSON based his activities at Hither Green Tyres Ltd (HGT Ltd), situated on Southbrook Road SE12.

8. On the 14th of August 2016 James 'the Kite' FITZGERALD, a RONSON operative and cousin to Stuart RONSON, was murdered by exsanguination at warehouse premises on Pancras Road N1, a property owned by Stuart RONSON. His body has never been found.

9. According to a covert human intelligence source, codename Q, the murder was carried out by Tony NAYLOR and FITZGERALD'S body was dumped at sea.

10. Tony NAYLOR was arrested and charged on the 7th of January 2017. However, he suffered a stroke three months later and the case against him was abandoned.

11. With respect to identity of Q, it was not HUDSON.

12. Karmen NAYLOR is a woman of good character.

With each change of paragraph, Benson had shifted his attention to a new juror. He was seeking a potential foreman and finally settled upon a middle-aged black woman wearing a chic blue leather jacket. She was the only person who'd stared at Benson, rather than the piece of paper that had been handed out. When Benson had finished, Mr Justice Garway said:

'So much for the elephant. Now for the spade. Or spades. Can we call things what they are, from the defendant's perspective?'

'Certainly, my lord.'

'You're telling the jury that people were lining up to kill Billy Hudson?'

'I am, my lord.'

'And at the front of that queue – no pun intended – was a member of the Ronsons?'

'Yes, my lord.'

'Who killed Mr Hudson in retaliation for the murder of Mr Fitzgerald?'

'Precisely, my lord.'

'Copying the manner of his death and the disposal of his body?'

'Exactly, my lord.'

'And, having done so, they framed your client, simply because she had the profound misfortune to be Tony Naylor's daughter?'

'Your lordship has summarised the defence argument in full. There's one final matter. HGT Ltd had a CCTV system that covered all entrances to the premises. Obviously, once it was turned off, anyone could approach the building without their presence being recorded. Similarly, as long as a visitor avoided CCTV cameras on the street, he or she could come and go, and, short of an eyewitness, there'd be no evidence they'd been at the premises at all.'

'Enabling Mr Hudson to have, shall we say, "professional" meetings?'

'Yes, my lord.'

'Have you got all that, ladies and gentlemen?'

The jurors nodded.

'Good. Now, don't allow yourselves to be distracted by the

gangland backdrop to this murder. This is a simple case. You've been given an outline of how to approach the evidence by each side. All you have to do is listen to it. But remember this: the defence doesn't have to prove anything. That burden falls entirely upon the prosecution. Are we ready to proceed?'

'Yes, my lord,' said Shah. 'I call Lisa Hudson.'

18

Benson listened with compassion. He'd read her statement long ago, imagining the woman, and her voice. He'd failed to anticipate her dignity; her quiet, devastating candour, as she went beyond the words on the page, volunteering more detail about her failure as a mother.

Lisa had been seventeen years old when Billy was born. She didn't know who the father might be, and, looking back, thought that was probably a good thing. At the time she'd been a resident in a council-run care home. After Billy's birth she'd been allocated a flat in Lewisham, with intensive support from social services. At first, things were fine. But then, with constantly changing social workers and frequently changing boyfriends, lots of drugs and no work, she began to make big mistakes. Going out and leaving Billy alone. Not having enough food in the house. Not doing the laundry. All the basics. As a result, Billy was often spending weekends with different foster families. By the age of eleven, he was working as a lookout and runner for the Naylors. Aged thirteen, he went into care. And that was the turning point for Lisa. When she'd consented to the care order, crying uncontrollably, the judge had said, 'I'm reserving this case to myself, Lisa. If you work hard and deal with your problems, Billy will be returned to you. I promise.'

Lisa did work hard. She went back to school. She saw a drugs counsellor every week. Four years later she'd obtained two A levels. She was looking for a job. And Billy, aged seventeen, came home. But by then it was too late. The state might have been responsible for Billy's welfare, with professional input and resources way beyond most parents' reach, but they hadn't done any better than Lisa. Billy had remained embedded in the Naylor group, working for Lewis Derby. A very frightening man.

'Things came to a head a year later, on Billy's eighteenth birthday,' Lisa said.

'The twenty-fourth of April 2006?'

'Yes. This Derby character turned up in the evening. To take Billy out for a drink.'

'What did you say?'

'Over my dead body.'

A very loud argument ensued between Lisa and Billy. But Lisa was powerless. Billy had grown away from her. He'd become part of a very different family. That was where he belonged now. As Billy, coat on, walked down the corridor, Lisa called out his name. Not aggressively. Not loudly. But like an anxious mother, seeing her son heading off to begin a long voyage.

'He turned. We looked at each other. And I heard myself say, "Don't come home until you've finished with the Naylors."'

'Those were your exact words?'

'I've never forgotten them.'

'Did you ever speak to Billy again?'

'No.'

Lisa stared at the floor as if it had opened up, and Benson looked in the same direction, seeing the year of hopeless struggle she'd endured with Billy before losing him again. Looking further, he glimpsed the boy who might have been a very different man. Shah broke the silence.

'Where were you on the night of Friday the eighteenth of May 2018? This is the night of your son's murder. Twelve years later.'

'I was in Rotterdam.'

By now, aged forty-six, Lisa had become a travel agent. She'd a steady partner, Neil Ashford, a theatre nurse at King's College Hospital. They'd decided to have a short break, from Thursday to Sunday, in Holland. A cheap deal. But Lisa had accidentally left her phone at work. When she came into the office on Monday morning – at Oyster Travel Associates in Camberwell – she found a string of texts and one voicemail.

'It was from Billy. He'd called me on Friday night . . . the night he was killed.'

Shah turned to an usher, who pressed a button on the court's sound system. Moments later there was a pause, and the sound of breathing. Then Billy Hudson spoke to his mother for the last time:

'Mum, it's me. It's Billy. Look . . . I'm just calling to say you were right. I was wrong. I should have listened. I love you. I've always loved you.'

The call ended. Shah waited, letting the eerie voice of a dead man linger. Then she said:

'I'm very sorry, Lisa. This is very difficult for you. But I must now ask you one more question. What did Billy say you were right about?'

Lisa was still staring into the opened floor.

'He was referring to our argument, I know it.'

'What had you said?'

'That if he ever let them down, they'd kill him.'

'Who are "they"?'

'The Naylors.'

'My lord, the chronology is as follows,' said Shah after a short break. Lisa had suddenly covered her mouth, and then her whole face. Visibly shaking, she'd sat down and been

91

given a glass of water. 'This much is agreed: Mr Hudson arrived at HGT Ltd on the night in question, at eight-fourteen p.m. He made this call to his mother five minutes later. CCTV cameras at a road junction twenty yards from the premises filmed the defendant's VW Golf arriving at eight fifty-eight. The prosecution argues as follows: allowing two minutes to reach Mr Hudson's office, the defendant and Mr Hudson were together for fifteen minutes. The Golf is filmed leaving the area at nine-seventeen p.m., moving at a high speed. The prosecution say it is during this fifteen-minute period the murder took place and the body was transferred to the boot of the defendant's vehicle.'

'And the defence argue that the defendant never went to Mr Hudson's office, and someone else could have had access to the premises after the defendant had left?'

'Yes, my lord,' said Benson, rising. 'Because the CCTV cameras at HGT Ltd had been turned off. They could have arrived immediately afterwards, or indeed at any time that evening. Either way, the premises remained accessible to covert intrusion and departure over the entire weekend.'

The sound of Billy Hudson's voice had brought his appearance to Benson's mind. He glanced at a photograph the police had obtained from an associate. For an enforcer, Hudson wasn't a large or imposing figure. If anything, he was short, for a man. But there was a tautness to his frame that suggested strength and speed. He had untamed black hair. His eyes had a glint of humour and intelligence. If you didn't know his background, you'd think he was a fun-loving rascal. Benson cleared his throat.

'May I call you Lisa?'

'Yes, of course.'

'Insofar as it was possible, did you keep an eye on Billy after he'd left home?'

'Yes.'

'How did you do that?'

'I followed him around sometimes, keeping my distance. I made friends with people on the fringe of his life. I'd ask them questions. They didn't tell me much. But it was something.'

'You mentioned Lewis Derby. He was Billy's line manager. Did you know that Billy put him in hospital?'

'Yes.'

'In 2008, two years after he'd left home.'

'I know.'

'Aged twenty, Billy shattered Mr Derby's jaw, two cervical vertebrae and his right shoulder blade. Using a hammer. The injuries were so severe Mr Derby has never worked since. Legally or otherwise. Did you know that?'

'Yes.'

'Do you know why Billy did this?'

'Because Mr Derby had disrespected the Naylor name.'

'Correct. And as a result, Tony Naylor made Billy his—'

'Driver and bodyguard. Yes, I know.'

'Did you know that between leaving you and meeting his death, Billy was arrested seventeen times for violence-related incidents?'

'Yes.'

'And none of the investigations came to anything, because all the witnesses refused to give evidence?'

'Yes.'

'Have you heard of the Ronsons?'

'Yes.'

'Did you hear about the murder of the Kite and the arrest of Tony Naylor?'

'Yes.'

'Did you know the Kite was an operative for the Ronsons?'

'Yes, I did.'

'And that in killing the Kite, the Naylors risked provoking an attack upon one of their own, someone high up, like Billy?'

'Mr Benson, I know nothing about the Ronsons. I'm a mother who lost her son. Don't expect me to tell you how and why.'

Benson glanced again at Billy's features, and he studied Lisa's. She was as delicate as he was strong; and yet, with the black hair and bright eyes, there was a striking similarity. She'd used her strength differently.

'I regret having to question you in this way, Lisa. I don't enjoy saying terrible things about your son. The fact is, he frightened a lot of people. And, as you say, he hurt them. Didn't that worry you? That one day one of these people might just come and get him?'

Lisa didn't reply, and Benson didn't press her.

'Weren't you also worried that, one day, the Ronsons might do to him what the Naylors had done to a Ronson?'

Again, Lisa didn't speak. She'd come to court determined to damn the family who'd stolen her boy from her; who'd exploited his vulnerability and ruined his life. She'd probably spent sleepless nights, these last few months, rehearsing her condemnation of the Naylors. This was her day. The only day she'd ever get. And she couldn't bring herself to acknowledge that anyone else might have been responsible for the murder of her son. Mr Justice Garway, being merciful, said she needn't answer the question. It was a matter for the jury. So Benson sat down.

19

Tess slid onto the bench behind Benson. Her mind was whirring with the lies of Nina Osabede and what they might mean, but all that would have to wait. Her eyes latched onto the man gripping the sides of the witness box. He was thin, pasty and terrified, with stress spots around a tight mouth.

Aged twenty-six, and the youngest of Jack Kilgour's sons, Greg had come to work at 7.30 a.m. on Monday the 21st of May 2018. He'd crossed the workshop and gone up the stairs to Billy Hudson's office. Why? Because he'd seen Hudson's car parked outside. Which was unusual, because he normally arrived, if he did at all, around 9 a.m. Standing at the doorway – marked D1 on the plan – Greg had seen pens and papers scattered over the floor, a broken cup and an upturned chair. As recorded by photo 35. But what had seized his attention was a large stain on the far side of the room, by an open door – marked D2 and shown in photo 37 – that led to the loading bay. He'd approached it slowly, his eyes following what looked like drag marks along the floor, reaching a manual roll-over shutter, which had been pulled down but not closed – marked D3 and shown in photo 38. Instinctively, he'd known the stain was congealed blood. He'd backed away, stumbled down the stairs and telephoned the police. It transpired that a heavy-duty 23mm extending wheel wrench was missing from a tool cabinet.

Greg had last seen Hudson at 8.45 a.m. on the previous Wednesday, the 16th of May. Hudson had explained he was off to Manchester, returning for a meeting with Karmen on Friday at 9 p.m. He'd told him to log the details into the online calendar used by the business.

'Was that standard practice?' asked Shah.

'Sometimes he did, sometimes he didn't.'

'Did Mr Hudson normally tell you where he was going?'

'No.'

'How would you describe his manner?'

'Tense. Stressed.'

But as he'd walked away Hudson had said, 'Take care,' something that had never happened before.

Shah sat down; and after a long pause, Benson came to his feet.

'Hudson goes to Manchester all stressed out, leaving HGT Ltd in the hands of your family and my client?'

'Yes.'

'How would you describe *her* manner?'

'Really cheerful.'

'And on Friday, the day of the murder?'

'The same. She was in a very good mood . . . and kind.'

'Wasn't she always kind?'

'Yes. Sorry, she was.'

'Do you mean that she gave you a cash bonus? You, your brother and your father. One hundred quid each. From her own pocket.'

'She did, yes.'

'Had *that* ever happened before?'

'No.'

'Miss Naylor went home, as usual, at six p.m. But you knew she was coming back later in the evening to meet Mr Hudson. Because Hudson himself had told you.'

'Yeah.'

'It was in the online calendar?'

'That's right.'

'Who could access that calendar?'

'Anyone in the Naylor family. Sometimes they put in real appointments. Others were . . .'

'Fake?'

'Yeah.'

'Creating a digital record to help support an alibi?'

'I don't know, Mr Benson.'

'Could anyone in your family access the calendar?'

'Yeah.'

Benson let the answers settle like snow on the ground. Then he broke the silence:

'Where's your brother?'

'Pete?'

'Yes, Pete. Where is he?'

'Scotland.'

'When did he go to Scotland?'

'A few days back.'

'Why?'

'He wanted a break.'

'What from? He's on the dole.'

'I don't know. Life in London, I suppose.'

'You didn't ask?'

'No.'

'Was he with you on Monday morning, when you discovered the crime scene?'

'No.'

'Was he ill?'

'He had to go to the dentist.'

'Why didn't you mention Pete in your evidence?'

'I wasn't asked.'

'Fair point, Greg. How old were you when you started working for your father?'

'Seventeen.'

'Your brother had already been there for two years?'

'Yeah.'

'What did you think when Tony Naylor rolled up – we're talking six months after you'd started work – and bought the business founded by your grandfather and built up by your father, and which you, and Pete who's in Scotland, were meant to inherit?'

Greg looked at Benson like a terminal patient pleading for a final injection of painkiller.

'I didn't mind.'

'Seeing your father hand over everything to Tony Naylor didn't bother you?'

'No.'

'Losing your future?'

'Not really, no.'

'Did your dad mind?'

'We never discussed it.'

'What about Pete? Did he mind?'

'No. Like me, he still had a job.'

'Where is he in Scotland?'

'I'm not sure.'

'Has he been there before?'

'No.'

'Who ran HGT Ltd? Your father?'

'No. Mr Hudson.'

'Did he often stay late at night?'

'On a Friday.'

'Why a Friday?'

'That's when he did the books for the Naylor family. Money was brought in during the week, and . . .'

'Were you well paid?'

'The money was all right.'

'You call less than minimum wage all right?'

'I never complained, Mr Benson.'

'I'm sure you didn't. Did Mr Hudson ever help out with the work?'

'No.'

'What kind of car have you got?'

'A Renault Twingo.'

'What year?'

'1993.'

'What kind of car did Mr Hudson have?'

'A Range Rover Sport.'

'2018?'

'Yes.'

'Did you like Mr Hudson?'

'Yes.'

'Because he said "Take care" once in eight years?'

'Yes. No . . . well, he was all right, sort of thing, with me.'

'Were you frightened of him?'

'No.'

'Greg, you've taken an oath to tell the truth. I'll try again. Billy Hudson was a gangland enforcer. Were you scared of him?'

'No, if you see what I mean.'

'I don't. Where were you on the night Mr Hudson was killed?'

'In a pub . . . the Blackstone Arms in Catford.'

'Where was Pete?'

'I don't know. He went home as usual.'

'Pete had access to the online calendar, didn't he?'

'Well, yeah, we all did.'

'I'm wondering if Pete – not as usual – went back to HGT Ltd later that evening, waiting for Billy to finish his meeting with Karmen?'

'No, no, no. He'd never do anything like that.'

'Like what?'

'Kill Mr Hudson.'

'Why not? Because he liked Mr Hudson, too?'

'No, Pete's not violent, is what I mean.'

'Are you?'

'No, no.'

'What about your father?'

'No. None of us are.'

'Greg, are you proud of the Kilgour name?'

'Yes. Absolutely.'

'What about your father and brother?'

'All of us, yes.'

'What kind of pride allows you to lie back and let people like Billy Hudson walk all over you?'

Greg's jaw stiffened. But he said nothing. Tension and fear had made his face deathly pale.

'Do you feel like a free man, Greg?'

'Yes.'

'Because Mr Hudson's dead?'

'No.'

'You preferred things when he was alive?'

'I never said that.'

'The tool cabinet. Was it usually locked at night?'

'Yes.'

'Who locked it on Friday evening?'

'Which Friday?'

'The night someone took a wrench and battered Mr Hudson with it. Who locked it? Was it you?'

'No, that was Pete's job.'

'Then why did the police find it open on Monday morning?'

'I don't know . . . you'd have to ask Pete.'

'But he's in Scotland. Have you got his phone number?'

'Erm, yes.'

'Give it to me, please.'

'What?'

'I want his number.'

'Now?'

'This instant.'

Benson took out his mobile phone, and before Shah could object – she was already on her feet – or the judge intervene (and he was scowling), it happened. Greg Kilgour, the youngest victim of a family trampled underfoot by the Naylors, cracked. He told the court what he'd failed to tell the police. About the guy who'd come looking for Hudson. The angry guy. Tess listened in astonishment. And when he'd finished, Mr Justice Garway checked his notes like a man displeased by bad grammar. Then, with a sigh, he turned to the jury: 'I knew I should have kept my big mouth shut, ladies and gentlemen. This case is no longer simple.'

20

They went to Grapeshots, just down from Congreve's. Tess ordered soda water. Benson pointed to a bottle of Spitfire Ale. And they looked at each other, still wondering what the hell had just happened. Tess felt the heat of a coming triumph. She couldn't say that, of course, and neither could Benson. But their shared elation made clear what each of them was thinking.

'I thought this case was all about a bent informer who can't be found,' said Tess.

'It still might be.'

'I thought we were dealing with the Ronsons.'

'We still might be.'

Benson had been freewheeling, recalling the resentment of Jack Kilgour. Pointing the finger at a would-be killer hiding in Scotland had forced Greg Kilgour to point a finger of his own. At a black man in his early thirties who'd come to HGT Ltd in May 2017. The month Hudson had dumped Nina Osabede. He'd driven right into the workshop on a black and chrome motorbike, jumped off and run up the steps to Billy Hudson's office. Standing in the doorway, with his helmet still on, he'd yelled, 'You can deny you're the father, but you can't hit my pregnant sister. You're dead.' Or words to that effect. With a few f—s. Hudson had looked stunned. But then, calmly, he'd taken a gun from a drawer and placed it against the head of the man who'd threatened him. Hudson had walked him backwards down the stairs and across the workshop. Reaching the motorbike, Hudson had said, 'If I ever see you again – and I mean ever: if I catch a train and you're on the platform, that's enough – Nina's dead. Along with her kid.' Pushed relentlessly by Benson on why the Kilgour family had kept silent about this encounter, despite every opportunity to tell the police, Greg had made a mumbled admission: they'd all been relieved to see Billy dead, and a Naylor in the dock at last. They hadn't cared which one. Or what for. The trembling wreck had then turned to Mr Justice Garway, pleading for immediate police protection for him and his family, and new identities and plastic surgery and somewhere to live and benefits. These are matters to be taken up with a solicitor, the judge had replied apologetically, like a ship's captain short of a lifejacket.

'Do we subpoena Azuka Osabede?' said Tess. 'Nina, too. And Ekene?'

'No.'

'Why not?'

'Lisa admits there were plenty of people wanting to kill her son, and the next witness gives us an example. That's a bullseye. It's all we need.'

'Nina lied, Will. She'd known Hudson for six months before she got pregnant; she'd always known he was a crook. He hit her, for Christ's sake, and then her brother threatened to kill him. All that shows they could have been involved.'

'Which is why she could have lied,' said Benson impatiently. 'This case isn't simply about having a motive and opportunity to kill Hudson. It's also about killing Hudson in a particular way, and framing Karmen. And I don't believe Nina and her brother would have come up with such a plan, still less carried it out. They'd no grudge against Karmen. Or the Naylors as a family. Shah knows this, and she's itching for me to call them. And that's not all. For all we know, they've both got cast-iron alibis, which would screw us. As things stand, we can exploit this threat from Ekene to our advantage, along with everything he said.'

It was a good point. The judge had sought clarification on the identities of those involved in the encounter. Shah had confirmed all the relevant details. The jury now knew about Nina, her child, the assault and the threat. Benson didn't need anything else. But he looked troubled.

'What are you thinking, Will? Tell me.'

Benson went over Lisa Hudson's evidence. She'd impressed Benson. With her dignity and forbearance. Her ability to face a jury, knowing that she was in part responsible for her son drifting into the world of the Naylors; and, by default, all he'd done thereafter. She'd hidden nothing. Her tragedy brought to life, graphically, what happens when you get involved with a criminal dynasty. Lisa was right: your days are on loan. Lose the favour of the king and you're finished.

'I've listened to that last phone call of Hudson to his mother countless times. But hearing it in the courtroom, with the jury, and Lisa standing there, motionless, still in that corridor . . . I got a sense of the two of them together. Hudson *was* referring to that last argument. He knew he was going to die, Tess. That night. And he realised he'd missed his chance to start again. That's why he rang his mother. It was goodbye.'

'And that, Mr Benson, is the prosecution case.'

'Yes, I know. And we've denied it. We've always thought Hudson's words could have meant anything. Because the person he was about to meet was a former waitress. The girl who wanted to rival Kwik Fit. He couldn't have thought, okay, this is it. My mother was right. Little Winner's about to brain me. Unless . . .'

'Unless what?'

'Unless Hudson's mind was on someone else. Someone he'd arranged to meet later that night, after Karmen had gone.'

Tess, like Benson, had never considered the possibility.

'Someone who knew everything about Billy and Karmen, and wanted to nail them both,' said Tess, returning to first principles. 'Someone who knew the CCTV cameras would be turned off; who knew how to come and go without being seen; who knew that Karmen would be there earlier in the evening. Someone who'd planned to mimic the Fitzgerald murder.'

'Exactly. And that points to someone very different to Ekene Osabede. Or Pete Kilgour. Or the youths who surrounded Nina. Or some mates of Lewis Derby. Or even one of the Ronsons, who Billy would never have agreed to meet. At least not on his own.'

'Who, then?'

'I don't know. And we might never know, because the police never carried out a proper investigation. Thankfully it's not our job either. All we have to do is make sure Karmen goes home. Which is why, for now, we're in a good place. We can point the finger at an angry man who threatened to kill Hudson at some point in the future.'

Benson examined the label on his beer as if it might contain a message. 'Which might be good news for Karmen,' he went on, 'but it's bad news for us. This is a trial I'm meant to be throwing.'

Benson finished his drink and stood up.

'Let's go and see Archie, and find out how much he's eaten.'

Tess wanted to say, 'Yes, great idea.' But when she opened her mouth, she said, 'Sorry, I can't. I've got other work to do. Pressing stuff.'

They walked down Artillery Passage, the energy of violent death between them, until they reached Tess's Mini. They said goodbye, with a touch to each other's arm, first from Benson and then from Tess. After he'd gone, head down, hands in his duffel coat pockets, Tess went to Selby Street, mindful that Abasiama was half-expecting her; that this was the kind of thing troubled people do. They storm off, and they come back when they've calmed down. Tess stared at the doorbell. She looked at the brass casing and the aged white button. And, thinking of the cactus, she turned around and went home.

21

With morning came Shah's last lay witness: Jennifer Reed, a barmaid at the Four Ravens, a pub less than a mile away from HGT Ltd, and Hudson's local. Reed was almost certainly the last person to see Hudson before he went to his meeting with Karmen. He'd arrived at roughly 7 p.m. and ordered a pint of Fuller's London Pride and a ham sandwich. He'd sat at the bar alone, eating and drinking. He was preoccupied, fidgeting with his mobile phone, sliding his thumb over the screen, spinning pages but reading nothing. He'd been wearing a crisp white shirt with red buttons and a light green cardigan. She'd thought he'd dressed up for a night on the town. As far as Reed was aware, Hudson had made no calls and received none. No one approached him. After about forty-five minutes he'd leaned over the bar and said, 'See you, Jenny,' which she'd found surprising, because he didn't normally say goodbye.

Another odd goodbye, noted Benson. The first had been to Greg Kilgour on Wednesday morning, prior to going to Manchester. He'd been tense then, too. And he'd been tense and worried when Karmen had met him an hour or so later that Friday night. But whatever was on his mind had nothing to do with her wanting him to move out so she could build up the business. Make it grow. Rival Kwik Fit. Something the jury would never know, because Karmen refused to give evidence.

'Mr Benson?'

'No questions, my lord.'

Shah began her reconstruction of the murder. Starting from the main entrance, she placed the jury in the shoes of the killer – understood to be the defendant – guided by the effervescent Dr Joy Sengupta, lead forensic scientist in the inquiry and a neurosurgeon specialising in trauma injuries to the brain. Since much of the evidence was agreed, she presented the findings of those colleagues Benson did not wish to question.

Abundant evidence demonstrated that the defendant had been in the reception area. Thereafter, it was reasonable surmise. Whoever the killer might have been, and no one but the defendant was known to have been in the premises, they'd selected a Radwerk 23mm extending wheel wrench from a tool cabinet. The wrench had never been found, but one of the same size and brand had been obtained for examination purposes. Its head section perfectly matched a deep indentation on the left jamb of door D1, the entrance to the victim's office. Hair, scalp tissue and blood had been founded embedded in the grain, all visible in photograph 36 of bundle A. DNA analysis confirmed these had all come from Hudson. Hence the most likely explanation was that the defendant had ascended the small staircase shown on the plan and struck Hudson a glancing blow on the head as he turned around. Given the disarray in the room – shown in photograph 35 – Hudson had stumbled forward, before collapsing by D2.

'Let's call that the end of stage one in the killing,' said Shah. 'I want to examine it more closely. The blow to the head. What can you deduce from the crime scene?'

'Given the depth of the indentation in the wood, and the

dislodging of hair and flesh, I believe Mr Hudson sustained a significant cranial fracture, potentially with bone depressed into the brain.'

'What symptoms would you expect to see?'

'Unconsciousness or drowsiness . . . loss of balance . . . breathing difficulties . . . impaired vision . . . loss of speech or slurring . . . vomiting . . . limited or no muscle control . . . the list is long.'

'What would happen to Mr Hudson's heart rate?'

'It could slow down or continue as normal. The blood pattern analysis suggests that latter.'

'Assume Mr Hudson was conscious and able to see clearly and process his surroundings without difficulty—'

'That is unlikely.'

'Assume it. Would Mr Hudson have been able to resist a second attack?'

'Absolutely not. A considerable amount of vomit was found on the floor, by D2. This had not been projected from a standing or even crouched position. It was a low-level ejection, with limited force, like coughing, and that persuades me Mr Hudson had collapsed. He might have retained sufficient vision and mental acuity to comprehend what was happening to him, but he would have been quite powerless. All he could have done was watch.'

'Thank you, Doctor.'

Benson established his main point immediately:

'The forensic trail stops at the door to the workshop?'

'It does, yes. But that does not mean she didn't enter the workshop or, indeed, the room where the murder took place. Forensically, her assertion that she remained in the reception area can't be proved.'

'Any more than you can prove she struck him on the head, cut his throat and opened the shutter to the loading bay?'

'Accepted, Mr Benson. I can't prove any of that. Because the body was removed.'

'Ah yes, the removal of the body.'

'It's the most distinctive feature of the case.'

'I agree.'

'With a murder of this kind, involving direct contact between the assailant and the victim, the chances of finding some transfer evidence is high. Which is why I believe the removal of the body is tantamount to the part-cleaning of the crime scene.'

'Or the re-enactment of an identical murder, like that of Mr Fitzgerald?'

'Or both. Either way, a vast amount of evidence has been lost. That's why professionals do it.'

Benson wondered if it would be fitting to cross the courtroom and embrace Dr Sengupta. The reference to cleaning had been one slip-up; the aside about professionalism had been another. Taken together, they were a gleaming gift.

'Is it your suggestion that Karmen Naylor, a career waitress, had secretly acquired the skills and knowledge of an experienced killer?'

'That's not for me to say.'

'It is.'

'I'm sorry, I can only look at the evidence. My point is that removing a body is a sensible precaution. It's one thing to clean surfaces and objects, if they've been touched or marked; it's another to try and remove incriminating material from a body. That's a far harder task. It can even be impossible.'

'But nobody cleaned the tool cabinet, the door frames or the floor. No one cleaned anything. Which is why my client's fingerprints and DNA were found in all the places you'd expect to find them. So removing the body had nothing to do with part-cleaning anything, did it?'

'Perhaps not.'

'Which means the killer or killers were indeed professional.'

'What do you mean?'

'They left no trace that they'd even come and gone. Have you seen that before, Dr Sengupta?'

'Yes, Mr Benson. I have.'

22

Stage two of the killing, announced Shah. Exsanguination. In lay terms, bleeding to death.

To deal with this element of the case, Shah called Dr Josephine Merrin, a blood-pattern expert from Glasgow with extensive experience in torture, gangland murders and the interpretation of crime scenes where no corpse has been found. She'd visited HGT Ltd on the afternoon of Monday the 21st of May, the day the police had been summoned by Greg Kilgour.

Since the floor to Hudson's office had an absorbent surface, Dr Merrin had been unable to carry out volume calculations to determine how much blood had escaped from Hudson's body. Was this an impediment to determining whether death had occurred, and how? Absolutely not. Let's take the movement of blood to the head, she explained. Blood moves under high pressure, propelled by the beating of the heart, through the carotid arteries. It drains, at a slower rate, through the jugular veins. Cut the former, and we're talking pump-action gushing. About 75 millilitres of blood with each heartbeat. It is therefore remarkably easy to establish if a catastrophic injury had been sustained simply by analysing the blood spray pattern – if there was one. And in this case, a textbook example had been found towards the bottom of D2. Since the vertical spurting columns were low down (16.4 centimetres from the base at its highest), Dr Merrin concluded that Hudson had been attacked while he lay on his back, with his head close to the door, a hypothesis confirmed by the distribution pattern of the vomit. The two taken together – blood spray on the door, proximate to vomit – convinced her that a carotid artery had been severed. Mr Hudson's cardiac output was unknown, but assuming 4900 millilitres per minute, with 10 per cent going to each carotid – there are two of them – Mr Hudson would have bled out in five minutes or less.

'Let's assume my client is the killer,' said Benson, rising to his feet.

'Okay.'

'Let's further assume that she parked her car by the loading bay of the premises with the boot open, ready to receive Mr Hudson's body.'

'Okay.'

'She's prepared and she's determined.'

'Okay.'

'My client was with Mr Hudson for fifteen minutes. The prosecution case is that she clubbed him, cut his throat, let him bleed out, dragged his body eight yards to the loading bay shutter, opened it, rolled the body into the boot, pulled the shutter down, shut the boot and drove off. That's a lot to get done in a compressed time frame.'

'It is. But it can be done.'

'If you know what you're doing?'

'Yes.'

'And you remain calm and focused?'

'Yes, that would help.'

'The carotid is about an inch and half below the skin?'

'It is.'

'To the side of the neck?'

'Yes.'

'To cut it deliberately – if you are acting swiftly – requires a basic knowledge of anatomy?'

'That would help, too.'

'Let's now assume my client is not the killer.'

'Okay.'

'And that she didn't park her car by the loading bay with the boot open, and she didn't know where the carotid artery was located, or at what depth, and by temperament was not likely to be calm and focused during and after a violent incident. In those circumstances, what are the chances of her carrying out this attack, moving the body, and escaping from the crime scene, all in fifteen minutes?'

'Not very high, I admit.'

'Close to nil?'

'Perhaps.'

'Thank you, Dr Merrin.'

Since Shah had no re-examination of the witness, Mr Justice Garway thought that was a good place to stop for lunch. So did Shah, who, upon the judge's departure, quickly left court as if to confirm a reservation. Benson found her absolutely inscrutable. Her case was falling apart, but she showed no sign of panic. There was just this commitment to the continuum: the unfolding of evidence, seemingly indifferent to its impact on the jury. Benson had never seen anything like it in his life.

23

After an early-morning conference and a committal hearing at Camberwell Green Magistrates' Court, Tess intended to join Benson at the Old Bailey, but she found herself heading down the road towards Peckham Rye, and the Be All and

End All. The relationship between Nina Osabede and Billy Hudson – this meeting of charm and violence – intrigued her. More to the point, she wanted to chase down the lies. An impulse that turned into a hunter's fixation when, on turning a corner, she saw a black and chrome motorbike parked near the café entrance.

The room was divided into cosy booths by wooden partitions. As far as Tess could make out, they were all empty, save the one in which Nina was seated, facing a young man wearing a black padded jacket. Watching them intently was a tall man at the counter, slowly drying dishes. The only noise came from the radio. A phone-in on LBC. Someone had called to talk about immigration. What it was to be English. Tess lowered her head. She moved quietly, but not too quickly. She positioned herself in a booth adjacent to the Osabedes, who were so engrossed in conversation that they hadn't noticed her approach.

Tess listened.

'Things aren't going to plan,' said Nina. 'They know about you. Not good.'

'I did what I did. Any brother would have done the same.'

'You should have done nothing.'

'You shouldn't have told me he'd smacked you in the mouth.'

'If you'd minded your own business everything would have worked out fine. I had it sorted.'

'You needed me, Nina.'

They didn't speak for a while. Tess heard the tinkling of a spoon on ceramic.

'Look on the bright side: whatever happens, we're made,' said Ekene.

'Not if we end up dead.'

Tess stood up and leaned on the partition.

'What plan?'

Nina swivelled to one side. She stared at Tess and Tess stared back, alternating between sister and brother.

'"What plan?" I said.'

Nina's eyes flashed with anger.

'Life, Miss de Vere. Life isn't going to plan. My brother once threatened to kill Billy Hudson. And now it's been mentioned in court. Given that Billy was murdered, there's a lot of room for misunderstanding. There's a lot of nasty people out there. And that's not all, my name is—'

'Nina, you lied to me. I know Billy saved your life. I know he denied being Obi's father. I know he hit you. I know you rejoiced when he was killed. I know you—'

'You just don't get it, do you? My name is out there now. Along with Obi's. I didn't want him to know anything about his father. Who he was or what he'd done. He'll find out now, one day. I tried to keep things hidden, okay? That's why I never spoke to the police. It's why I never spoke to the media, and it's why I didn't want to speak to you.'

While speaking, Nina had stood up. She now walked off, leaving her brother still seated at the table.

'You're Naylor's solicitor?' said Ekene, reaching for his helmet, and rising. He came close to Tess, close enough to make her uneasy. 'I swear on Nina's life, Obi's life and my father's life, we had nothing to do with Hudson's murder. Okay?'

'Are you threatening me?'

'No. Just educating you. After I left Hudson, I couldn't walk the length of a train without thinking a passenger was going to kill me. I came home wondering if someone had taken my dad out for a walk. I wondered if Nina had made it back from work. After Hudson's death, we felt safe. The threat had gone. But now I'm being blamed for the killing and that puts us at risk again. Because of you. If anything happens, to any of us, it will be your fault.'

He moved quickly away; through the window, Tess watched him straddle his motorbike. Nina leaped on the back, just as the engine roared into life. They both leaned forward, like TT racers on the Isle of Man, and then—

'You're a solicitor, are you, involved in the Hither Green Butcher trial?'

Tess hadn't heard him come near, any more than Nina and Ekene had heard Tess. The man she'd seen at the counter, still holding a tea towel, had crossed the room, and was sniffing and looking over his bony shoulder. He was one of those forty-odd-year-olds whose patchy three-day stubble looked as if he'd last shaved with a pair of blunt scissors.

'Yes. I represent Karmen Naylor.'

'Right, well' – he glanced round again – 'you can't trust people like that. You know what I mean?'

'I can't say I do.'

'Blacks. They're not like you and me. That's why they lied to you. I've seen it all my life. They'd be better off back where they came from, if you catch my drift. Better for them, better for us. Better for the country. I let them in here because, well, they're all on benefits and I might as well get my money back—'

'I'm not interested in your racist—'

'I think you might be, Miss Solicitor.' He leaned closer. 'I was going to tell you for free, but since you've hurt my feelings you'll have to pay.'

Tess could only look at his tight, bloodless lips, recoiling from the sewage that sloshed around behind his teeth.

'They came here for months,' he said. 'The two of them, always together on that bike. With a woman. That's three. But they called themselves the Four Ravens. Do you want to know the rest? If you do, dig deep into your pocket.'

24

'My lord, I will now move to stage three of the killing,' said Shah.

By which she meant the disposal of Hudson's body.

The role of guide was entrusted to an expert in fibre transfer evidence, Dr Jonathon Tupton, who broke the trail to disappearance into four parts: the loading bay at HGT Ltd, the defendant's VW Golf, the jetty at Allhallows, and the boat, *Little Winner*. The connecting thread, he quipped – to the judge's displeasure – came from Hudson's shirt.

The evidence was uncontested in its entirety.

Dealing with the loading bay, intermittent blood smears consistent with a body having been dragged across the wooden floor stretched from the place of death to the shutter area. White threads from a Poliny Barns dress shirt along with green fibres from a Baz Howks woollen cardigan had caught on slivers of planking along the same route. The same for a red mother-of-pearl button, which been found in the horizontal base rail of the shutter system. The attached cotton thread indicated it had been torn off, presumably when it became trapped in the rail as the body was rolled into the vehicle on the other side. These precise fibres and threads had also been found on the jetty, with more evidence of dragging, along with traces of blood and another red button aboard *Little Winner*. Such, then, was the road taken, from HGT Ltd to the sea.

'Using a VW Golf. And I have to say the boot is *remarkably* large . . . especially when the rear seats are down.'

Twirling his half-moon glasses, Dr Tupton enthused with the wonder of a salesman about the 52.7 cubic feet of space.

'That's four suitcases. Making it perfect for . . .'

Benson drifted off. Or rather he focused on the photograph of Billy Hudson. Whoever killed him had hit him bloody hard. The indentation in the doorframe had split the wood, suggesting pent-up hatred or its best replacement, the indifference of a contract killer getting on with his job. Benson angled the photo, looking at the amused expression. There'd been no smile on that Friday night. He'd known what was going to happen. And knowing there was no escape, he'd made one valiant decision: to die looking good.

'I don't know if the boat and car had been washed,' said Dr Tupton, repositioning his glasses. 'Both had been exposed to the elements for months. As a result, only the faintest traces of blood remained. But we found 'em. In tiny cracks. Thanks to Ben, Jim-Jam and Mimi. Springer spaniels. Astonishing creatures. They—'

'Thank you, Dr Tupton. Wait there, please.'

'Forensic scientists, CID, uniformed police and three extraordinary dogs. That's quite a team.'

'You missed out the army. We got the army in, too. With helicopters. And divers. Looking for the body.'

'And all you found was a trail of Smarties from where Billy Hudson was murdered to where my client owned property?'

'Do you really think dropped Smarties is an appropriate image?'

'I do, yes. Because these clues were planted for children to pick up.'

'That'll do, Mr Benson,' said the judge.

'I'm sorry, my lord. Dr Tupton, I fail to understand why you never considered the possibility that my client has been framed.'

'Why should I?'

'Because no evidence of the body was found in the boot

of the VW. Because no evidence of the assault was found on my client's clothing or in her car or in her house or in her cottage. Ben, Jim-Jam and Mimi sniffed themselves dizzy and they still found nothing. Except outside. Places to which everyone and his dog had access.'

'She could have destroyed her clothing. She could have used a plastic sheet. She could have worn gloves. She could have—'

'That's a lot of "could haves", Doctor.'

'That's what a crime is, Mr Benson. Could haves that actually happened.'

'I'll remember that one, thank you. Do you think the evidence found on the Golf, the jetty and the boat could have been planted?'

'It's possible. But anything's possible.'

That one throwaway remark was all Benson needed. He quickly moved on.

'One last matter: my client weighs sixty-one kilos. Mr Hudson weighed in at sixty-four. In order to get his body into the rear of her waiting car, she had to drag, manoeuvre, roll and shove – and probably jump to the ground, to heave and pull – before she could shut the boot. Allowing five minutes for the bleed-out, that gives her ten minutes to reach the CCTV camera on Southbrook Road. All on her own. Let's move from "could have" to "must have". She *must have* needed help to move the body. Do you agree?'

Dr Tupton thought for a while, and then hit back.

'I'd say "probably".'

Which was more than Benson wanted anyway.

'Thank you, Doctor.'

Benson had a host of other questions. He dropped them all. He'd made his case: someone, for good reason, had killed Billy Hudson. They'd wanted to make it look as though Karmen was the killer, who'd then bungled an attempt to incriminate the Ronsons. It was obvious. To everyone except the prosecution's expert witnesses. And Shah, who was checking her phone.

'I think we'll call it a day, ladies and gentlemen,' said Mr Justice Garway.

25

'Mr Benson, you're a genius,' said Karmen.

Tess agreed. But then she'd always agreed. She'd made it to court for the majority of Benson's cross-examination, and had now joined him in a conference room near the cells.

'I know I shouldn't say this,' said Karmen quietly, 'but I don't think the jury is impressed.'

'Neither do I,' replied Benson, also quietly. 'More importantly, neither is the judge. Depending on how things end up tomorrow, I'll make an application to have the case thrown out.'

'And if you succeed, what happens?'

'Let's leave tomorrow until tomorrow.'

Karmen's face contorted with feeling. She was so near the exit to the courtroom. To freedom. The door handle was almost within reach.

'I could have chosen anyone to defend me, Mr Benson. Do you know why I picked you?'

'I don't need to know, Karmen. But don't forget, I'm nothing without Miss de Vere.'

'I'm sorry, I didn't mean to leave you out, it's just . . . watching Mr Benson in court, I—'

'Don't worry, I know what you mean,' said Tess.

Karmen turned to Benson, her face shining.

'You're brilliant. With every question someone shrinks and something falls down.'

'We aren't out of the woods yet,' said Benson. 'Try not to think beyond this moment. Read poetry. That's how I survived.'

'"We're the three ravens. We remove the fourth,"' said Tess. 'That's what he heard the woman say. And he can't have made that up.'

'Ravens?'

'Yep. And that little gem cost me five hundred quid. I had to go to a cashpoint.'

They were huddling in a low-lit corner of the Ausonian Muse, an Italian wine bar in an alley off Ludgate Hill, minutes from the Old Bailey.

'The woman . . . did you get a description?'

'No. He never saw her face. She always wore a hat or scarf and sunglasses. And never the same hat or scarf. She knew what she was doing.'

But she'd also made a slip-up when she'd allowed herself one grandiose moment, just when a caller on LBC got lost for words. The woman, sliding brown envelopes across the table to each of them, had said, 'We're the three ravens. We remove the fourth.'

'A payment?'

'What else? Tickets to the opera? They're involved in the murder.'

'Wind back, Tess. Give me Nina's chronology again.'

Hudson and Nina had first come to the Be All and End All in August 2016. Nina had been in tears, presumably in shock, because of the racist attack, not to mention seeing Hudson kick the shit out of five people. He'd bought her a large cup of tea, asking for loads of sugar. Buster, the owner, had never seen either of them before. But from that day on, Hudson and Nina had come to the café regularly. At least once a week. Sometimes more. It became their spot. Same booth, away from the windows. Hudson always with his back to the wall and facing the door. They were an item. Holding hands. Whispering. Up to no good, probably. Buster had no idea who Hudson was. He'd just wondered why a good-looking white guy hadn't found himself a busty blonde. You know, a more natural pairing. Then, in May 2017, they stopped coming.

'After Nina told Hudson she was pregnant,' said Benson.

'The same month he hit her and Ekene threatened to kill him.'

'How's he sure of the month?'

'His wife left him at much the same time.'

Buster never saw Hudson again. But he did see Nina. A month or so later. So we are now in June. A motorbike pulls up. She's the passenger, her arms wrapped around the rider. Buster thinks she's got a more appropriate boyfriend, because he's black.

'It's obviously Ekene. A few minutes later, this woman turns up, sunglasses and so on. They meet about four times over the next few weeks. Always in the same booth. And it's on the last occasion that she hands over the money.'

'"We're the three ravens. We remove the fourth,"' quoted Benson. 'They named themselves after Hudson's local. They were planning to get rid of him. But who is this woman?'

'I think it's Q. The CHIS is a woman, Will. Not a man. And she's close enough to the Naylor business to have heard about Hudson pulling a gun on a guy crazy enough to have threatened him. Which gave Q her opportunity.'

'For what?'

'To recruit him, and then his sister. If you think it through, they're ideal for the job. Nina was no angel. The wayward kid stayed wayward. She went out with a gangster when she knew he was a gangster, and she had a child with him. She'd seen Billy in action and she hadn't run away. Quite the opposite. It brought them together. And as for Ekene, he hated Hudson from the moment he met him.'

'Did Buster say anything else?'

'Yes. He only found out who Hudson was when he saw his face on the news. After the murder. He didn't want to get involved, so he said nothing to the police, and they, of course, left him alone, because they never knew Hudson and Nina had been regulars.'

'And so the police were never told about these ravens either.'

'That's how it goes. Important leads. All left unexplored.'

Buster, said Tess, had nearly crapped himself when, just before the trial, Nina and her brother had come back to his café. Why? The girl had been an associate of Hudson. He didn't know about the break-up and assumed she was well in with the Naylors. Tess told him he had nothing to worry about.

'And what about Q? Did she turn up, too?'

'No. He never saw her again. Which makes sense. Q organised things. She paid up and then she dropped out of the picture. Whereas these two . . . until they got named in court, they were enjoying themselves. They'd come back to the place where they'd done the planning. Now they're scared. With good reason.'

Benson gently swirled the wine around his glass.

'You're right, Tess. It seems they were involved after all. But it still doesn't make *complete* sense.'

'How so?'

'I've said it before: kill Hudson, fine, but why agree to do it in a way that shafts Karmen? They've got no problem with her. They don't know her. Haven't even met her.'

'I forgot about that.'

'And remember, Hudson sensed he was going to be killed that night. But he couldn't have known what the Osabedes were up to.'

'I forgot about that, too. We're lucky, Will. Or maybe I

should say Karmen's lucky. This stuff is all relevant, and it could help her, but it's out of reach. Thanks to you, though, she doesn't need it. And I have to say, when it comes to Hudson I don't care if whoever killed him gets away with it. He was a nasty piece of work. He died the way people like him always die. The justice system never got its hands on him. Someone else did. So what?'

Benson twirled his glass again, watching the wine swing up to the lip and down again.

'Because the justice system got its hands on Karmen.'

26

Another impression struck Tess the next morning, when she got to the Old Bailey. She thought of the thousands of man and woman hours. The dog hours. The tins of Pedigree Chum. The cost of experts, lawyers and court time. The downright bloody hard work. All made necessary because someone had put down Billy Hudson. What prevented the endeavour becoming a charade – as Benson observed – was the fact that innocent people got chewed up by the machinery. While getting them out gave meaning to a defence lawyer's existence, it was the duty of the police to make sure it didn't happen in the first place. In this case, the obligation had fallen upon DCI Anita Panjabi. Her evidence-in-chief took most of the morning. The investigation, she said, had led ineluctably to the defendant, though the defendant had admitted nothing when interviewed, save to accept she was the one who'd organised the meeting with Hudson for the Friday evening when the murder had taken place. The point, stressed repeatedly, sounded anodyne.

* * *

'Do you have any doubt that Jim "the Kite" Fitzgerald was murdered by Tony Naylor?' said Benson after lunch.

'None.'

'Do you doubt that he died by exsanguination and his body was dumped at sea?'

'No.'

'Because the informant Q told you so?'

'Yes.'

'And because you are confident Q can be relied upon?'

'That's right.'

'DCI Panjabi, you've been in the Serious and Organised Crime Unit for six years. During that time have you ever known the murder of a gang member by a rival organisation to pass without retaliation?'

Panjabi drew a long breath, aware that Benson already knew the answer to his question, that she couldn't prevaricate.

'Never.'

'There's usually a hierarchy to such killings, isn't there? Kill a pawn, you lose a pawn. Kill a bishop, you lose a bishop?'

Another slow breath.

'Yes, that's generally the case.'

'The Kite was close to the king. So was Billy Hudson. They carried the same weight on the board?'

'You might say that.'

'Might I ask who died on the Naylor side, in payment for taking out the Kite?'

Panjabi stared straight ahead, avoiding eye contact with Benson.

'No one,' she said.

'But someone must have gone down. It's a jungle out there. The Naylors had hit Stuart Ronson's cousin. They could hardly sit back and do nothing.'

'I'm sorry, I can't give you a name.'

'I've got one. According to the Metropolitan Police Intelligence

Unit (Southern Division), only one senior Naylor player has died since the Kite was bled to death and dumped at sea. His name is Billy Hudson. Who, according to you, was bled to death and dumped at sea. Did it even occur to you that the two killings might be connected, that Billy Hudson might have been killed by the Ronsons?'

'Theoretically, yes. But all the evidence pointed towards Karmen Naylor.'

'Let's stick with the theory. Did you interview any member of the Ronson family?'

'No.'

'Determine their whereabouts on the night Mr Hudson was killed?'

'No.'

'Did you interview anyone who worked for them?'

'No.'

'Anyone who knew them?'

'No. But I should say, Mr Benson, to make the best use of resources, investigations have to be targeted. We are satisfied we found the person responsible for the crime.'

Benson looked at the juror wearing the blue leather jacket; the black woman with whom he'd established a subtle form of discourse. She, like the other members of the jury, wasn't impressed. Addressing them as much as Panjabi, Benson followed a similar pattern of questioning, dealing first with the oppressed Kilgours and then the Osabedes. The one-word reply came again and again; Tess counted seventeen of them: 'No.' Interviews had not been carried out. Movements had not been traced. And so on. Until, finally, no, DCI Panjabi had no idea why Karmen Naylor might have killed one of her father's most feared and loyal captains.

'We now know the Kilgours hated the Naylors and Mr Hudson.'

'They did.'

'We now know that Pete Kilgour went into hiding in Scotland when this trial opened.'

'Yes, we do.'

'Pete, who left the tool cabinet unlocked.'

'So I understand.'

'I don't suppose you know if there was any form of contact between Pete Kilgour and the Osabedes, Nina or Ekene or both?'

'No, I don't.'

'That's a pity. Let's stick to what we know, then. We know that Mr Hudson abandoned Nina Osabede, his girlfriend. We know that he denied being the father of her child. We know he hit her when she told him she was pregnant. We know her brother, enraged by that attack, told him he was a dead man.'

'We do, yes.'

'And we know that someone killed Mr Hudson.'

'We do.'

'DCI Panjabi, are you any good at maths?'

'Well, I've got an A level.'

'Didn't you think to add up the evidence?'

'Much of what you said has only emerged in this trial, so I couldn't have added up anything.'

'And whose fault is that?'

'Mine, I suppose. But even if I had done the maths, as you say, I remain convinced we found the person who murdered William Hudson. It was Karmen Naylor. No one else.'

'Found? With respect, you spent more time looking for the body than you did for the killer.'

That was a comment, not a question, and when Benson sat down it was as though Panjabi had been left hanging out to dry, to drip her endless denials.

'I have no re-examination, my lord,' said Shah.

'Does that conclude the case for the Crown?'

Shah was about to reply when the court door swung open, and a thickset man with heavy black glasses entered the room. He signalled to the CPS representative sitting behind Shah.

'One moment, my lord.'

A hushed discussion followed between the three of them. When they'd finished, Shah's shoulders slumped. Tess couldn't work out if it was relief or exhaustion. Whatever the explanation, Shah nodded. She then addressed the court.

'Having taken instructions, my lord, the Crown seeks an adjournment in order to reconsider the future conduct of this case.'

'That seems a sensible move to me, Miss Shah.'

'My lord, given the gravity of the matter, I need a conference with a number of Crown officials, some of whom are not available until tomorrow afternoon. Might I suggest the court reconvenes on Monday?'

'Any objection, Mr Benson?'

'None, my lord. But I would make an application for bail.'

'And that,' said Shah firmly, 'would be resisted. I have not yet closed my case.'

Mr Justice Garway sighed his weary sigh. The issue could be argued at length, but in real terms his hands were tied. Karmen still faced a murder charge. And that was a key-turner.

'Monday morning it is. Ten thirty. Bail denied.'

Tess and Benson nudged their way through a crowd of journalists thrusting microphones and cameras into their faces. The questions came like popped corks amongst the clicking and flashing. Glancing at one another – these moments are best shared – they made no comment. Eventually, free of the bustle and the pushing and cajoling, they turned into Newgate, heading back towards Congreve Chambers.

'Shah is genuinely malicious,' said Benson, relaxing. 'She's about to throw her hand in, but she wants Karmen locked up for as long as possible. Just to make her suffer.'

'It's no justification, Will, but you've humiliated Shah. Her case is in shreds.'

Back down in the cells, Benson had explained to Karmen that senior figures in the CPS had already begun to express their disquiet, and Shah would almost certainly abandon the prosecution on Monday morning. If she didn't, Benson would make – as promised – the application of no case to answer. Given the judge's attitude, and his remarks in open court, that application would succeed. They'd left Karmen trembling with disbelief.

'Reputations have suffered, too,' continued Tess. 'Panjabi and the CPS have messed this one up, and Shah did nothing to repair the damage. The prosecution should never have been brought. Now they're all tarnished.'

They were walking side by side, discussing Panjabi's reckless smile of defeat, thrown as they'd left court; and, working backwards, the parade of floundering witnesses . . . not bothering to mention the implications of this farce for themselves: the torture and death that almost certainly lay around the corner. Karmen was about to be released – when, according to Stuart Ronson, she was meant to be going down. The trial had not been thrown. In silence they turned into Artillery Passage. With the swing of arms, their knuckles brushed against each other. Twice. Three times. A fourth. The touching was no longer an accident. Tess sensed Benson was angling his hand to catch hers. She opened her own, feeling the cool of sudden perspiration, and then—

'You won't believe it.'

Tess and Benson stopped in astonishment. Standing outside chambers was a black-eyed Archie, one hand clutching the *Evening Standard*, the other – in a plaster cast and bandaged – raised in the air, as if to explain himself by semaphore.

'You've got visitors. It's Tony Naylor. And his son.'

27

Tony Naylor sat at Benson's desk in the Gutting Room. Standing to one side, arms folded, was Ryan. The father wore a tracksuit. The son wore a suit and tie. The father hadn't shaved. The son's aftershave spiced the air. The father was lean. The son was bulked up. The father bristled with lost power. Ryan was . . . Benson wasn't sure where the contrast lay. But it was there. He had the smarmy confidence of a usurper. The son of the king, dressed in Hugo Boss and anointed with Calvin Klein, had taken the throne, leaving his brain-damaged master to think he still called the shots. Something like that.

Tony tapped his index finger on Benson's desk, as if to press a button. Ryan sniffed and spoke:

'My father says you've got balls.'

Interpreting that as a compliment rather than an observation, Benson gave a nod of recognition, keeping things ambiguous.

'You slagged off the Ronsons. And you've slagged off the Naylors. Respect.'

Tony pushed out his lower jaw; Benson began to sweat. Tony tapped his middle finger. Ryan spoke again:

'My father says you are the only brief out there who'd believe Karmen's story. He says you're the only brief who knows what being banged up does to your mind. He says you're the only brief who'd risk his balls for a punter.'

Benson edged towards one of the client armchairs, glancing at Archie, who was staring at him from the other side of the room. Their eyes locked in mutual understanding. Benson slowly lowered himself down as Tony tapped his ring finger.

'It's why my father picked you,' said Ryan. 'Now he wants to thank you.'

'The case isn't over, Mr Naylor. It's never over until the judge says so.'

Tony put his elbows on the ship captain's desk, blinking erratically. He opened his mouth, pointing into his throat with a finger.

'I can't . . .' he said. 'I can't . . . you know?'

Benson said he understood. Tony narrowed his dulled watery eyes, pushing out his lower jaw again, pointing now at his head. He began stabbing his temple, hard enough to make a noise. He meant, okay, I can't speak, but I can think. I know what's going on. And if I click my fingers, whoever I want gets stiffed. Of course he couldn't see Ryan, whose sneer had pulled his lips apart.

'I said my father wants to thank you,' said Ryan. 'He's sent a message to the Ronsons. If they touch you, your family, anyone here, their family, anyone you care about, then they'll pay. You've got our protection. For life.'

Tony flicked his head and Ryan reached for a walking stick that was leaning against the wall. He gave it to his father and Tony led the way out, dragging one foot across the floor, grimacing, swaying from side to side. Behind him, arms out ready to catch him if he fell, came Ryan, his amused protector.

After they'd gone, Benson turned to Archie. He was sitting on the old iron radiator by the window, his injured hand in the air. Neither of them spoke.

'He discharged himself,' said Molly, coming in with a box of Mr Kipling Bramley Apple Pies. 'Everything's gone well with his paw, it seems. He's been told to keep his hand above his heart. He's been given tons of paracetamol. He's been told to keep an eye on this and that, and I've told him he's a big lump and should have—'

'What's wrong, Will?' said Tess, her eyes shifting between Benson and Archie. 'This is seriously good news. It's unorthodox, sure. But we've got the sort of protection the police can't provide. I want to drink to that . . . because I quite fancied staying alive.'

Engrossed in his thoughts, Benson went to a cupboard and took out a jerrycan of hooch made by Archie and Molly to a recipe from HMP Lindley. He reached for some plastic cups, and began pouring.

'The Ronsons were never our problem, Tess,' he said.

'What do you mean?'

'We don't need protection. Not from them, anyway.'

'Archie, what's going on? Am I missing something?'

'No, Tess, I am. Or I was. It's been sewn back on with a needle and thread.'

'Pack it in. Explain what's happened.'

Benson handed out the cups of hooch, then leaned on the front of his desk, legs crossed at the ankles.

'Tess, the man who came on board my boat and sat in the darkness while his mouthpiece told me to throw a trial was not Stuart Ronson.'

'And the person who stood in a shadow while his crew cut off my finger wasn't Stuart Ronson either.'

Benson looked towards the open door of the Gutting Room.

'I've smelled that aftershave once before. And I've heard that sniff once before. On one and the same occasion.'

'Same for me, Tess.'

'What the hell are you two saying?'

'It was Ryan Naylor,' said Molly, wondering how best to explain the threat and the violence. 'I don't think he likes his sister very much.'

28

'Have you seen the headlines, Mr Benson?'

Karmen soared into the interview room at HMP Denton Fields clutching a copy of the *Daily Mail*. The deathly pallor of the previous months had vanished overnight. Her cheeks were flushed. She was smiling. Freedom beckoned.

'They're saying you blew them out of the water. That the Director of Public Prosecutions should pay for the costs of the trial himself. They're calling it the Hither Green Bluster. Even the Attorney General has said—'

Benson stepped into her path, as if to block access to the taxi that might take her home. His authority was irresistible: Karmen stopped moving. Reaching out, he took the paper from her hands and laid it on the table.

'Take a seat, Karmen.'

'What is it? What's wrong?'

'We need to talk.'

Karmen slowly lowered herself onto a battered plastic chair. 'What's happened?'

Benson waited until she was quite still.

'In relation to the case against you, nothing. All is well. Don't worry. I expect to hear from the prosecution over the weekend.'

'Then everything's fine, isn't it? I'm going home, aren't I, soon?'

'I hope so, yes.'

Karmen turned to Tess.

'Is there a problem?'

'Yes, Karmen, there is. The night before the trial a group of men came to visit Mr Benson. They were already on his boat when he got home. They told him he had to throw the trial.'

'I don't understand. Mr Benson . . . what did they mean?'

'They told me I had to ensure that you were convicted. To demonstrate this wasn't a polite request, they'd used a pair of bolt cutters to remove one of my clerk's fingers. They'd put it in my fridge.'

Karmen didn't react at first. Then, ever so slightly, her breathing quickened as her chest began to close in.

'Oh God. I'm—'

'Until last night, we were convinced that these were Stuart Ronson's boys. And that Stuart Ronson was there. We now think differently.'

'What happened last night?'

'Your father paid me a visit. To thank me for winning the trial that hasn't yet been won.'

Karmen placed a hand on her throat as if to loosen a collar.

'You can't think he had anything to do with the attack on your clerk . . . or wanting you to throw the trial. That's impossible.'

'I agree. But your father didn't come alone. He came with Ryan. And it was Ryan who came onto my boat. It's Ryan who wants you framed for murder, Karmen. Not the Ronsons.'

Again, and amazingly, Karmen barely reacted. Eyes narrowed, she looked into the distance, perhaps conjuring her childhood and the years that had unfolded thereafter, years of separation and rejection. She frowned, reconsidering so many moments – arguments or slights, things said or done, Tess didn't know – and then Karmen's hand slowly clenched. She whispered:

'You're sure of this?'

Benson explained in greater detail what had happened: on his boat, and during the conference in chambers. And for the first time – relying on a sniff and a smell – the argument for the identification of her brother in the dark sounded rather weak. But Karmen needed no further persuasion. White-knuckled and pale, she said:

'You're also saying Ryan betrayed my father?'

'Karmen, none of this concerns you. You have to think of yourself.'

Tess spoke quietly:

'As soon as this trial is over, you should get out of London. Don't hang around. Don't even go back to Manchester. Go somewhere new. Start again.'

Benson was nodding.

'You can't get involved in working out what Ryan is doing and why. Miss de Vere is right: you simply have to vanish. If you do, I think you'll be fine. Because you were fine before. Start asking Ryan questions, or speak to your father, and you'll end up dead. And not just you. I've seen how these things work out: once the killing starts it spins out of control.'

Karmen lowered her arm from her throat to her lap.

'He always hid it so well.'

'Hid what?' asked Benson.

'His resentment. From the moment I was born. My father has absolutely no idea. Never did. Never will.'

She stood up, no longer quite present. She didn't seem to notice that Tess and Benson were watching her with concern, or that they'd come to their feet. She walked past them towards the interview-room door, signalling through the window to the guard that the meeting was over. The door opened and she slowly walked out, turning suddenly, as if she'd forgotten to tip a diligent waiter.

'As ever, Mr Benson, thank you. Thank you for everything.'

29

They stood on the pavement in the shadow of the high prison walls. It brought to Benson's mind his reunion with Tess only a few days earlier, when they'd come to meet Karmen for the last conference prior to the trial. They were no longer strangers. They'd inched back to where they'd been, their hands brushing against each other. And yet, with the case as good as over, he sensed another parting. It was in her manner. The way she stood back. The way she'd folded her arms and kept glancing sideways.

'You've done it again, Will,' Tess said, hugging herself. 'What a case.'

'Yes, what a case.'

'I'm not sure we could have done much more.'

The note of finality was there, in her voice. She was wrapping things up before moving on.

'I feel so sorry for her,' said Benson, drawing things out. 'She's done everything possible to escape her background . . . but her background keeps chasing after her.'

'It's worse,' said Tess. 'She'd have been better off never even trying. Then she'd have got the protection of her family. Now she's more exposed than the Kite. At least he could rely on his uncle. Karmen has no one.'

They fell silent. Tess twisted the toe of her shoe on the pavement, as if extinguishing a cigarette, while Benson thrust his hands in his duffel coat pockets.

'You know, I've never done a case where I didn't have a good idea about what really happened . . . do you know what I mean?'

'Yes.'

Another twist of the foot.

'There's the innocent and the guilty,' Benson went on, 'and sometimes they all lie. But the facts add up to something, regardless of the writhing around, and we can glimpse it . . . but not this time. I can't make complete sense of anything.'

'Neither can I.'

Ordinarily, after a big trial, there was a gathering in chambers to celebrate or commiserate. The tension would ebb away, dissolved by the camaraderie of those who had fought – winning or losing – for someone else. Those present would talk about the case. It wasn't simply natural, it was necessary. Rather like words spoken at a wedding, or a funeral. This time, Benson was sure, there'd be no get-together. Tess would be too busy. Here would have to do. An uneven pavement outside a prison.

'We couldn't have made this stuff up,' he said. 'We've got the Osabedes working with Q to get rid of Hudson. Q is a police informant with a long-standing grudge against the Naylors. The Osabedes seem to have pulled off the killing, mimicking the murder of the Kite, framing someone they'd never met and who'd never done them any harm. At the same time, we've got Hudson resigned to his fate and saying goodbye to the world and to his mother. Then we've got Ryan trying to put down his own sister, even as his father hopes to save her . . . when both of them must think the Ronsons, their arch-enemies, are responsible for the whole bloody mess. I swear to God, Tess, I've never done a case like it.'

'Neither have I.'

She untangled an arm and glanced at her watch.

'Look, Will, I'm sorry, I've got to go. I've a mountain of work. Do you want a lift?'

The question contained all the confusion of the past few days. The hint of intimacy, and the reluctance. The drawing near and the drawing back. She wanted him and she didn't want him. Benson knew this terrain. He'd spent years behaving just like Tess.

'No, I could do with a walk,' he said.

She took out her keys and looked away.

'I may not be free on Monday, so I might send Georgina in my place. Is that okay?'

'Of course. Whatever's best for you.'

Suddenly, after hesitating – like someone on the edge of a cliff, resisting the wind – Tess stepped forward and kissed Benson on the cheek. It was a friend's kiss. It was a final kiss. It wasn't half enough, and they both knew it. For Benson, it was an agony. Her hair had brushed against his skin. He'd caught the scent of perfume from behind her ear. He'd seen the light of loneliness in her eyes.

'Goodbye, Will,' she said, backing away. 'You really were brilliant.'

Benson watched her go. He watched her cherry red Mini swing around the corner out of sight. She'd accelerated too hard and braked even harder for the turn, tilting the car on its axles. There'd been a burst of fumes and a show of weak red lights. And yet, though she was gone, she lingered. She'd left something behind, and not just the scent, but a cry for help, suppressed but insistent; unheard, yet heard. At least by Benson.

'You're not getting away that easily,' he said.

PART THREE

distressed (adj) **1** (of prison furnishings) simulated marks of age to create a vintage appearance. **2** an emotional state to be completely suppressed in order to survive incarceration.

Monday 18th January 2010

Hollingtons Solicitors
Covent Garden, London

'Okay,' said Julia. 'Roll it. Play the video.'

Tess and Peter were back in Julia's sixth-floor office. Former Sergeant Brian Lomax peered out of the television, scratching his cancerous skin. And he told of a group of soldiers who'd been so frustrated by the rules of engagement they'd decided to take the war into their own hands. Three intelligence officers and three Special Forces soldiers. All based at Lisburn Garrison.

'Everyone involved was frustrated. Officers to other ranks. We knew who the key players were. We knew who'd killed British Armed Forces personnel. Our friends. Lads with wives and kids. And there was nothing we could do. Officially.'

'Officially?' came Peter's voice off camera.

'Well, that's a stupid question, Mr Arsely. Why else are we here?'

'The name is Farsely. Tell us about your unit.'

Mr Lomax had been a member of the Information Management Detachment. The IMD. A paper-pushing outfit within the British Army Intelligence Corps. Their function was basically clerical. Intel obtained by units on the ground ended up in their Portakabin. They joined any dots and circulated the results to interested parties. The information was then filed away.

'One night three of us got talking with some of the Special Forces lads who patrolled the countries in unmarked cars. They were out looking to make arrests, using information they'd got from us. Needless to say, they were armed . . . and bound by the rules of engagement.'

'And one of you wondered how much easier it would be if those rules didn't apply?'

'You're quick, Mr Arsely. I'll give you that.'

The wondering became a decision. An uneasy decision for Sergeant Lomax, but a decision nonetheless. They decided to 'neutralise' a well-known PIRA shooter. It would be a one-off operation. For once, they'd be fighting on a level playing field. So the IMD lads handed over some paperwork about the fella's movements – where he lived, where he could be found, and so on – and the lads in the car basically found him one night and shot him.

'They just wound down the window and took him out.'

'In the aftermath, how did the lads in the car account for the use of ammunition?'

'There was nothing to account for. They'd used bullets from a captured PIRA arms dump. Put to one side for this outing.'

'But someone in command must have wondered if there was a link between the shooting of a PIRA operative and the movement of the patrol.'

'They didn't.'

'They let it go?'

'They didn't let anything go. Because they never asked any questions.'

And that, said Mr Lomax, was the beginning. Sensing questions wouldn't be asked, the one-off operation became the first in a series of unofficial executions. In effect, three *members of the IMD teamed up with three Special Forces soldiers.*

'We called them the Blood Brothers. And they called us the Blind Eyes. Because that's what we did. We looked the other way. Like everyone else. From our CO, all the way to London.'

There was a pause. Then Peter spoke again.

'Let's talk names.'

'Well, we used code-names. Pointless, really. But it introduced some . . . distance. Between who we were and what we were doing. You know what I mean? It helped me, anyway.'

They'd each chosen their own alias. Mr Lomax had gone for Bluebell. There'd been a corporal . . . he'd gone for Flywheel. And there'd been one commissioned officer. A young lieutenant. Ruffcut.

'He'd just turned twenty-two . . . didn't even need to shave. Poor kid. He should never have joined the army.'

'Why?' came Tess's voice off camera.

'Because he was an idealist. He'd joined up to do something good. Make things better. He'd ended up doing something bad. Made things worse.'

'Names aren't code-names, Mr Lomax,' said Peter.

'That's all you're getting. Along with the files. It's the files that give you the names of the ten people we killed.' There was a long pause, and then Mr Lomax grimaced. 'We thought we were fighting fire with fire. But in the end, it wasn't as simple as that.'

'Because?'

'We set up innocent people. By accident. People who had nothing to do with the PIRA.'

'How many?'

'Four. Four men who should be looking after their grandchildren this afternoon, and instead are buried in Milltown Cemetery. That's why we stopped. We couldn't rely on the intelligence, and we couldn't rely on the Blood Brothers. End of story.'

Only that wasn't quite the end. The uneasy Sergeant Lomax had kept a copy of the paperwork used for each killing. He might have turned a blind eye, but his conscience had insisted on preserving the evidence. A private archive of ten files.

'You can have 'em,' said Mr Lomax, tearing at the skin on his arms. 'It's up to you what you do with 'em.'

Peter turned off the television. They were quiet, listening to the muffled sound of street entertainment in Covent Garden. Someone was doing a show. Magic tricks. Or dancing. Maybe both. Then Julia said:

'He told me there were eleven files. Not ten.'

'Makes no difference,' said Peter. 'We've been through them. They contain nothing incriminating. All they show is that certain individuals were the subject of intense surveillance. There's no link between that information and their subsequent deaths. There's no evidence anything was sanctioned by anyone. There'll be no cases in London, The Hague or Strasbourg.'

Julia shook her head.

'He said he could join the dots from targeting to execution. With names.'

'Julia, he didn't even tell us about himself. Except that he was Bluebell.'

They were quiet again. The show went on.

'He didn't name names,' said Peter; then, after a wicked pause: 'He didn't point the finger.'

30

'I don't understand myself,' said Tess. 'We were walking down the street. My hand brushed against his. I wanted to take it, and if we hadn't met someone I'd have done so. Why would

I do that? Why would I put myself in the position I want to avoid? I can't allow myself to get close to him, otherwise I'd have to tell him about my past.'

Abasiama had opted for an exclusively yellow hair arrangement, comprising yellow beads and yellow threads woven into the black strands, with streaks here and there of yellow dye. Tess had the impression she was getting too close to the sun. Her scalp tingled with sweat.

'I was wondering why I expose myself to risk.'

Abasiama seemed to be waiting. As if they hadn't left off from last time, and she'd nothing to say until her last question had been answered. Then Tess remembered that Abasiama never repeated herself.

'You asked me about my father,' she said finally.

'Yes, I did.'

'You asked me to tell you something about him. Anything. You said I could choose.'

'Yes, I did.'

While Tess had been emotionally winded by the question, she'd been unable to forget the words. They'd tugged at her, rousing her from a kind of sleep. She'd found herself seized by an altogether peculiar energy. Something reckless. She'd redirected it into the trial. But now it was all but over, this rashness-on-the-move had brought her back to this room.

'Anything at all?' she said.

'Anything.'

Tess let her mind go blank. Then, in the darkness of her imagination, she saw her father.

'He loved Barna Woods,' said Tess. 'We went there often when I was a child, to listen to the redwings.'

She was staring at the figure in her memory: he was absolutely still, straining forward, one hand held in the air as if to silence the rest of nature by command. Tess was there, too.

They were waiting, waiting, waiting; and then it came. The song from high in the trees.

'I don't think you chose that recollection,' said Abasiama.

'You're right, I didn't. It's how I always think of him . . . if I don't try. He just appears, by my side, in the woods.'

'How old are you?'

'About ten or eleven.'

'Is this a special moment?'

'Yes.'

'What makes it special?'

'The silence we shared. We didn't need to speak. It was in the waiting and listening . . . we understood each other. It was a kind of communion.'

'When did you last see your father?'

'A few days ago.'

'Where?'

'Hammersmith.'

'Is there a difference, for you, between the man in Barna Woods and the man in Hammersmith?'

Throughout this exchange, the energy that had brought Tess back to see Abasiama had begun to drain away. Exhaustion came like a drug through a drip.

'Yes. Because he broke my trust. I came to learn the silence we shared was based on a lie. Perhaps it couldn't have been otherwise. Perhaps deceit is the only way to handle certain truths. Point is, I found out what he was hiding. And he changed in my eyes. The silence we shared changed. The waiting changed.'

'When did he break your trust? Before or after Barna Woods?'

'Before I was even born.'

Abasiama allowed the peculiarity, perhaps the incoherence, of the reply to sound in Tess's mind.

'You mentioned waiting,' said Abasiama.

'Yes . . . it's present whenever we're together. Quiet or talking, it's there.'

'What are you waiting for?'

'A confession, I suppose.'

'Would that make a difference?'

Tess wasn't quite sure, save she knew she wanted to hear the truth from his own mouth.

'Maybe, because it would bring the lying to an end. For both of us. Then we'd be in an honest place, rather than a false one . . . which is where we are now.'

'You want to be in a place of failure with someone who isn't who you thought they were?'

'I want to reconcile myself to who he is, and if he told me who he was, and what he'd done, then maybe I could cope better . . . with what has happened. With what I've done.'

'Did you ever think of putting him out of his misery?'

'You mean tell him? Tell him what I know?'

'Yes. Why wait?'

'Because . . . because it's up to him?'

'Is it? You're the one who's changed. As far as he's concerned, the man who went to Barna Woods is the man who went to Hammersmith. And he's right. They're no different.'

A bead of sweat ran into one of Tess's eyes.

'I couldn't . . . I just couldn't.'

'Because certain truths can only be handled by deceit?'

'No, no, it's not that. It's . . . complicated.'

Tess squinted with the sting of salt. Abasiama said:

'Tell me something about your mother. Anything at all. You choose.'

Tess instantly visualised Orla as she'd last seen her: adrift in the rented flat, a sort of shimmering fallen angel, her eyes brimming with sorrow and guilt.

'She has no idea who she married,' said Tess quietly.

'None whatsoever. She's no idea who I am either, who I've become . . . You see, it's not just my father who lives a lie. It's me. And my lie is tied to his lie. We've both lost ourselves. And yet . . . and yet for some reason my mother blames herself.'

'For what?'

'I'm not sure. The distance. The silence. The waiting. I can't imagine anything else.'

Tess dropped her gaze, waiting for Abasiama to continue with this disembowelment without anaesthetic, cutting question after cutting question, until her guts were on the carpet. She heard her breathe in. There was a clink of beads. And then she said:

'It's only fair I tell you I think your lying has reached this room. You've lied to me. In quite a sophisticated way, actually. You've used the truth to create a totally false impression.'

Tess didn't move a muscle.

'I don't believe you dropped Benson simply because you feared telling him about your past. I don't believe you came to see me simply because you didn't want to live with guilt any more. I don't believe you've simply been damaged and that you've done damaging things. While all these disclosures are true, they are not the truth.'

'What, then, is the truth?' said Tess in a whisper.

'I think your past caught up with you,' replied Abasiama. 'I think your hand has been forced. In my experience, this happens not because guilt has become too heavy a burden to carry. It happens because of someone. Someone from the past walks into the present. And the present – what's been cobbled together after the damage and the trauma – is at risk of falling apart. Am I right?'

Tess didn't reply. She just walked out of the room. And again, ridiculously, with the carefulness of hardened superstition, she avoided touching Abasiama's chair.

31

Benson went to his local corner shop, seeking a carton of milk and a newspaper. The *Daily Mail*'s Hither Green Bluster approach had kicked off a trend, if not a competition. There were multiple variants. He liked the Hither Green Combustor, since it referred to himself. However, the version that appealed most was the Hither Green Fluster, because Shah's face appeared beneath the headline. She'd been snapped in a flap, leaving the Old Bailey. Benson bought that one and went to his bench on the deck of *The Wooden Doll*, intent on devoted reading, as a monk might savour scripture. After mocking Shah, the writer went on to discuss *R-v-Bucklow*, the case of the drug dealer would-be van driver caught with three million quid in three suitcases. It, too, had been adjourned. No reason was given. But it seemed that a plea would likely be offered, given the weight of evidence against the accused. Which didn't surprise Benson, because—

'Oi.'

Benson looked up at the shout. The first things he noticed were the black beret and the long black coat. Then he placed the voice.

'I might have told you to keep away from me, but that doesn't mean I have to keep away from you. I imagine that's the kind of point you like to make, isn't it, Mr Benson?'

'It is.'

He watched the woman cross the landing deck and step elegantly on board.

'I've been complicit in a kind of cover-up,' she said. 'Friends don't do that. They uncover what ought to be uncovered. I don't propose to explain myself any further. What do you say to that?'

'I've no Earl Grey,' replied Benson. 'How about moderately unpleasant instant coffee?'

* * *

147

Sally Martindale said Benson had been right. After Tess had left Hollingtons in 2010, Strasbourg or no Strasbourg, she'd gone off-grid. Despite years of friendship, she'd dropped Sally, just as she'd later dropped Benson. There'd been no communication. No calls or letters. Just the odd postcard, until 2015, when Tess returned to London.

'It was quite bizarre,' said Sally, beside Benson among the pots of herbs, a light breeze coming off the water. 'She rang up and said let's go out for cocktails. Simple as that. No explanation. No apology. No embarrassment.'

They'd gone out, got hideously drunk and talked. They'd covered the years as if these things happen, prompted by career changes and – that most human of shortcomings – forgetfulness. Tess had spoken of the exaggerated bureaucracy of European institutions, the internecine politics and the overwork – oh it was all so boring – and somehow, feeling hazy, Sally had been won over. And what did it matter? Tess was back.

'What reason had she given for leaving?' asked Benson.

'Some nonsense about an Irish caprice. She made her mind up overnight. But I'd always thought it was because she'd fallen out with Peter Farsely. She's never denied it. She just wouldn't tell me what happened. And she still won't. I tried last week.'

'Well, Tess's departure from Hollingtons had nothing to do with Peter Farsely. Not as such.'

'How do you know?'

'Because I met a friend of his. Another solicitor. A year or so ago. At a hypnotist's – I was trying to stop smoking and so was this guy, and we got talking, because he'd heard of me and knew that I'd worked with Tess. He gave me Farsely's take on why they'd broken up. He'd said things were going great, but then she dumped him over his attitude to a case.'

'A case?'

'Yes. Apparently, he was all for letting it die, for the greater good, while she wanted to keep it alive, on grounds of principle. And rather than thrash it out, she'd sent him packing . . . after he'd paid for a monumental takeaway.'

'What's a takeaway got to do with anything?'

'No idea. Anyway, I asked about the case. Lawyers take different views all the time. But there's no collision between pragmatism and principle. You're instructed. You assess the evidence, you get on with it. You don't take a private decision to let things die because you think it's better for everyone. That's an extraordinary rationale. Only governments can make that kind of judgement.'

'So Tess was right.'

'Absolutely. So I can imagine her wanting to step back from Farsely.'

'But not give up her job and leave the country.'

'Exactly. That's why I decided to take a closer look at that case, if I could trace it.'

Benson had done a trawl of the work handled by Hollingtons in 2010. He'd pored over newspaper columns, legal articles, court papers, reported decisions – anything and everything – seeking a reference to Tess and Farsely. And he'd found a short article dated Tuesday the 9th of February in the *Belfast Telegraph*. The result of a leak from an unidentified source. A meeting had taken place the previous day between two lawyers from Hollingtons – Tess de Vere and Peter Farsely – and the investigation arm of the Historical Enquiries Team of the Police Service of Northern Ireland. While there'd been no official statement or press conference, it was understood the lawyers had handed over various documents, until now privately held, that might assist in the resolution of certain unsolved murders.

'Tess mentioned this,' said Sally; she'd been nodding as Benson spoke. 'An old soldier had contacted Hollingtons wanting to clear his conscience, to confess what he'd done during the Troubles. Tess and Peter went to interview him, here in London. I wanted to know what happened – I'm from an army family: Household Cavalry – but she just brushed it off. Said key papers were missing. It had been dead in the water.'

'And yet she dumps Farsely because he wants to let the thing die, when it was already dead?'

'It doesn't make sense.'

In July of that year, Tess spoke of her Irish caprice. She'd landed a job with an international this, that and the other, and she left Hollingtons in August.

'Only you're saying she didn't last a week?'

'At the end of September the post was advertised again. She'd rented a flat overlooking the Rhine. She walked out of that, too. The landlord only found out when he'd secured a judgment for non-payment of rent. These things leave a trail, but that's where it ends. Where she went and what she did afterwards, before returning to the UK, I've no idea. That's why I came to you.'

'I'm sorry I sent you away.'

'Don't be.'

Sally sighed.

'She must have had some kind of breakdown. It didn't even cross my mind. I got those postcards, and just put them on the mantelpiece.'

'Where were they from?'

'The South of France. Montpellier. Marseille. Aix-en-Provence. One-liners: "A sunny break from boredom in Strasbourg" kind of thing. No real information. No invitation to join her. I never saw them as a signal. Maybe they were cries for help.'

'If they were cries, she didn't want you to act on them. There's nothing you could have done. Fact is, in 2015 – five years later – she's feeling better. She lands a job at Coker and Dale and comes back to the UK. She's strong enough to call you and pretend nothing happened. And she came to me.'

They didn't speak for a moment. Then Sally gave a *humph*.

'I might as well tell you: she always felt for you. As for any others . . . *les autres*, to quote Gainsbourg, *on s'en fout*. From the moment she saw you go down part of her went with you. And when she came back to London and found out you'd made it to the Bar, she went to join you. But at the same time, she threw herself into proving your innocence. Because – oh God, this sounds like Rodgers and Hammerstein – she still felt for you. Only she needed to know you hadn't lied to her. But here's the thing. 2017. Just when we find out you'd told her the truth, she drops you. And, in a way, she dropped me, too. I've seen very little of her.'

That Tess had been 'interested' in him, as the phrase went, came as no surprise to Benson. That it went back to his trial certainly did. He'd felt the same. They'd both been so young. So different. If he'd never been charged with murder he'd never have met her. Because he'd been convicted of murder they'd been parted. And so it had begun. And now a new crisis, her crisis, was underway. Would they ever catch each other up?

'There's been a coincidence,' he said. 'Something happened in 2017, after I'd been proved innocent. It's unrelated. And all she could do was step back, because she doesn't want to talk about it. She's trapped in a bigger story, so she's trying to protect us from its implications . . . That's my guess.'

'So what do we do now?'

'We go back to where the trail went cold. 2010. But first—'

'I know. You're busy.'

Sally reached into her pocket and took out a newspaper cutting.

'We'll wait until the Hither Green Trussed-her is over.'

She'd saved a cartoon from the *Guardian*. It showed Benson roasting Shah over a fire made from the prosecution's witness statements. They laughed together, nervously aware of a new familiarity, and then Benson went below deck to make that coffee.

32

Tess hadn't anticipated Abasiama's merciless exploration of her life. She'd expected her to flush out some emotional contradictions and make recommendations on how to handle the inner conflict. What she hadn't foreseen was this horrible commitment to facts. Events. She reminded Tess more of a police officer than a therapist. She wouldn't be going back. There was no way back. Not without—

'Tell me what you're thinking.'

Tess felt her mother's soft hand on hers. They were sitting on a bench in Ravenscourt Park, a short walk from the rented flat by the Thames, and not that far from Sally's. Sally, whom Tess had failed to contact. Sally had sent a couple of WhatsApp messages, suggesting they meet up at the weekend. The blue ticks – Tess hated them – showed Sally they'd been seen. But for some misty reason Tess had hesitated to reply. And then she'd forgotten. And now, late on a Sunday afternoon, Monday beckoned.

'Nothing, Mum. I'm just glad this case with Karmen Naylor is over. It's one of those great moments in the job – when you get the result you're fighting for, and you know it's right.'

'I told you not to worry, didn't I?'

'You did.'

Her mother's hand was still on hers, lightly, as if she might not have permission.

'Tess, I wanted to meet you alone, because I have something to tell you.'

They'd gone out after another awkward lunch at the flat, her father remaining behind. As they'd walked out of the door, Tess sensed this had been organised. A decision between parents had been made. Tess's father had avoided eye contact.

'I think you've noticed the strain.'

'I have.'

'Well, put simply, it's my fault.'

Orla took her hand away; Tess immediately seized it, bringing it back towards her.

'I had an affair, Tess. Years ago. Many years ago. When you were small. I've kept the secret all my life. As I've got older, it's gradually squeezed the life out of me. I had to tell your father. I couldn't live with the dishonesty. I told him a few months ago. We came to London to get away from where it had happened. And to give us time to put things right. I'm sorry. Sorry for breaking something that you thought was good and simple.'

'What are you talking about?'

'Your childhood.'

Tess couldn't quite register what she'd been told. She couldn't see her past clearly, or grasp what she felt. The good and simple had been shattered long ago. And not by her mother. What did she think and feel about there having been someone else in her mother's life? Her mind was a blur. She felt nothing. She chose to lie – not to deceive, but to share a gift.

'Mum, it was good and simple; it remains good and simple.'

The affair had lasted a month or so. A visiting lecturer from Australia had come and gone, and he'd gone with a small piece of Orla's life. How did it happen? Orla made no excuses; she just gave the facts. Tess's father had become very insular after her birth, as if a bond had been broken between him and Orla. Which, in a way, it had. He was no longer the centre of her universe. And he had been. To an extent, what had happened was rooted in the early years of their relationship. Orla, a graduate student from Ireland at the Royal College of Music, short of money, had pinned her name to various noticeboards, offering lessons in Gaelic. She'd only secured one pupil: an introverted, secretive doctoral student in Irish history. A walking anomaly, he'd been the very archetype of the posh-speaking sons of Albion who'd brought fire and famine to Ireland. But what had attracted Orla hadn't been his diligence so much as his profound diffidence. It was only gradually that he'd opened up about himself, and the friendless years he'd spent at sea, his spare time buried in books and music. She'd invited him to hear her play the cello. And that had been the beginning. The confirmed solitary had allowed someone into his life. He'd opened up, and out . . . becoming, in time, more Irish than the Irish: someone Orla hadn't met, someone different; wonderful and new and devoted. They'd left London for Galway.

'But with your birth, something snapped. He became self-absorbed again. Not for weeks or months, but years. It was as though he'd become that withdrawn student once more, only this time he was out of reach. I tried and tried and tried . . . and then I met . . . I don't want to use his name. Do you mind? He means nothing to me. He was just there when I felt . . .'

'Abandoned?' supplied Tess.

Orla didn't adopt the word. Because to do so would be to diminish her responsibility. She'd half-nodded, then stopped herself.

'I wish it had never happened. Obviously. I don't recognise myself in what took place. I can't even remember much. But it's been there, in my past. It was there whenever we were together as a family.'

Her regret and remorse had been unbearable. All the more so because as Tess had grown, her father had sort of grown, too. He'd come out of himself. He'd discovered an extra-ordinary joy, simply watching Tess; playing with Tess; just being with Tess.

'Your father returned to who he'd been before you were born. The distance between us had gone. But by then there was this knot inside me. A tight, strangling knot, and in the end, I just couldn't ignore it any longer. I hoped against hope that your father would understand. That he'd have room in his heart to forgive me . . . after all the years we've been together; after all we've shared. I'd hoped he'd think it didn't really matter.'

Was it an affair, thought Tess. Was it even a fling? Whatever it was happened almost forty years ago. Sure, it had been a mistake. And the mistake had lasted longer than a night, or ten minutes in the hay. There'd been a few weeks of insanity. But the greater sanity was everything that had been lived afterwards; everything they'd built as parents: the memories for Tess; memories of absolute mutual devotion.

'Forgive me, Tess. If I could go back and—'

Tess tugged at her mother, drawing her close enough to smother the phrase. She held her tightly, eyes clenched shut, unable to speak. She felt the fragility of her mother's body, the loose assembly of bone and wasting muscle. She was getting old. Tess didn't want regret to define her wonderful life. She pushed her mother away, a hand gripping each shoulder, as if to give her a good telling-off, but Orla said:

'Don't say anything, Tess. Please. All I ask is that you understand your father. Understand his disappointment and anger.'

Tess felt her throat contracting. The knot that had nearly strangled her mother was around her own neck.

'I've a plan,' said Orla with false brightness, blinking in the winter sunlight. 'I've organised a party for your father. It's his seventieth birthday next week. I've been sending messages all over the place, to people who've been part of his life. From the beginning, after he left the merchant navy, as a student, right through to the end of his academic career. It's going to be a surprise. I'm hoping he'll see his life afresh, with pride . . . and maybe me. What do you think?'

Tess gripped her mother's shoulders even tighter, out of affection, but also to keep her own balance. She stared deep into her watery, defenceless eyes, and she said, choking,

'I love you more than you'll ever know, Mum. More now than I ever could have imagined.'

Orla's eyes shone with grief and gratitude.

'But there's one thing,' managed Tess. 'I hope you've invited the Australian.'

33

Benson's mobile went ping.

He'd been flicking through *Benson's Guide to the Underworld*, thinking of his one-time editorial assistant. At the age of twenty-two Doyle had done something crazy. He'd started a fire in a block of flats, trying to frighten his ex-girlfriend. Thankfully, the new boyfriend had put it out. For that act of madness, Doyle had received an IPP. An imprisonment for public protection sentence. The tariff had been set at nine months, which meant that once the nine months had expired, Doyle's fate had been put in the hands of the Parole Board. And they'd never let him out. The thing is, the man he'd become, aged thirty-six, had nothing in common with the kid who'd struck the match, but he was still inside, serving time.

Ping.

Benson glanced at the illuminated screen. It was an email

from Shah. Why was she contacting him late on a Sunday evening? The message was characteristically succinct:

Benson,
Please find attached a Notice of Additional Evidence, a witness statement, and the relevant application seeking leave to do all that is necessary to advance the true case against your client.

The evidence is relevant to motive. It also discloses a number of other grave offences. I propose to continue with the present trial and leave these other allegations for future proceedings. However, if you seek an adjournment, it will not be opposed. Should you do so, however, I propose to amend the indictment and deal with all outstanding matters at the same time when we return to court. It's your choice.
Indira Shah QC

Benson opened the witness statement on his laptop. He scanned the contents, gradually understanding Shah's opening speech. He understood the police as well, and why they'd left the Ronsons alone. In retrospect, it was all so bloody obvious. And Benson hadn't seen it coming.

His phone rang. It was Tess. Her voice was unnaturally calm:
'Have you read what I've just read?'
'I have.'
They were both silent. Tess broke the tension:
'I don't know what to think.'
'Neither do I.'
'None of this material is even hinted at in the police intelligence report. They must have had suspicions, but they said nothing.'

Benson closed his laptop, as if to wind back time and light another Sobranie, when a victory, a righteous victory, was almost at hand. They'd been in a good place. Leaving aside the mystery of the Three Ravens, which was not before the court, Benson had shown that Hudson had more than one enemy who was prepared to kill him; that the premises had not been secure from the moment the CCTV cameras had been turned off, permitting access to anyone who knew Hudson was there; that a threat had been made by a man enraged at Hudson's treatment of his sister; and that the time frame for Karmen to have carried out the killing was so compressed that she couldn't have done it without extra-ordinary composure or removed the body without assistance. Given there was no evidence of anyone being at the premises besides Karmen, and given that she had no motive to carry out the attack, it had seemed far more likely that the perpetrator had been a professional. That the manner of killing aped a previous murder strongly suggested that a revenge killing had been ordered by the Ronsons, with evidence being planted on Karmen afterwards.

Such was the case before the jury. And the judge – who'd probably made enquiries about the next trial on his list – was almost certainly planning to set Karmen free tomorrow morning. But now everything had changed.

'Our good points remain good points,' said Tess.

'Not all of them. Unfortunately, it doesn't really matter. What's alleged against Karmen is so serious, so off the scale of expectation, that if the jury accept it they'll think she's capable of anything, including the murder of Hudson, even if they can't imagine how she did it. Shah now has her motive, Tess. She's got a second bite of the cherry.'

Benson pictured Tess sitting alone in the dark. He listened to her breathing and watched the movement of her lips . . . she was chewing the side of her mouth. He was fairly sure she'd been crying. And not because of Shah's email.

'We could ask for an adjournment,' she said finally.

'Is that the best move? We'd lose what we've gained. And next time round, there'll be five defendants in the dock – or five star witnesses, if they decided to cooperate – and the murder charge will be just one in a list as long as your arm.'

'I can't think clearly,' she said.

Benson knocked out another cigarette, listening to Tess's breathing. He imagined her looking out of a window onto the night lights of London. Someone in the dark facing the dark. He lit up and pulled smoke deep into his lungs. After a moment of suspense, his head began to reel and the wave of sickness came, softening the impact of confusion.

'What are you going to do, Will?'

'I'm going to bury my head in the sand until tomorrow morning.'

'And then what?'

'Hopefully, when I pull it out, things will be clearer. I'm not sure we can save her. Maybe she can't be saved. Maybe she shouldn't be saved. Maybe—'

'Will?'

'Yes?'

'Don't blame yourself. It's not our job to see past our client. If Karmen's lied, then, incredible as it may seem, Karmen's lied. She's been caught out. The fact we believed her shows the job hasn't destroyed our faith in humanity. We've kept hold of something important.'

'Thanks, Tess. Goodnight.'

Benson smoked cigarette after cigarette, recalling all his conversations with Karmen. He'd seen the anxiety in her eyes. He'd listened to the light shake in her voice. He'd felt his guts turn with compassion for the innocent facing annihilation. She'd stared to one side, speaking of the family she'd tried to escape, whose terrible acts had cast a shadow over every step she'd ever taken. She'd caught Benson's eye, once or twice, fearful, it seemed, that he might have joined the queue of people who didn't believe a word she said; who thought she was just another Naylor.

Had all that been a performance?

Could she have fooled everyone for so long? From her late teens onwards? Those friends she'd met during freshers' week? Her tutors? The owners of those restaurants? The clients who'd ordered the set menu? Could they all have had no idea what Karmen was really doing? And could Karmen have lived a pauper's life for years until, with her father falling ill, she was forced into the open?

Or had she been set up?

There are times, thought Benson, when you have to follow your gut. When you have to go with all those natural responses that make up the anatomy of trust; those moments of recognition that bind your experience to someone else's. Otherwise you're lost. Even to yourself. You could never trust a single instinctive reaction. And Benson, scanning the statement once more, made a choice. He'd trusted Karmen on first meeting; he'd trust her now.

PART FOUR

A second bite of the cherry

Monday 8th February 2010

Offices of the Historical Enquiries Team
Police Service of Northern Ireland
Belfast

The files in the box had been labelled the Lomax Archive. A rather grand name for nothing of evidential value. A jigsaw where all the important pieces were missing. Julia – sensibly – thought the best thing to do was hand everything over to the Historical Enquiries Team. Who knows, she said, they might have other documents. They might have sources who could take this very sad tale forward. And so Tess and Peter went to Belfast. There, a DCI called Flynn flicked through each of the pages, in each of the ten files, and looked up, wondering why Hollingtons had bothered to contact them at all.

'There's nothing new here. It's just surveillance material.'

'There's a videotape, too,' said Tess. 'Lomax speaks of a group of rogue intelligence officers who teamed up with some Special Forces personnel to organise and carry out assassinations.'

So Flynn watched the video. And then he looked at Tess and Peter again, with the same expression.

'This is useless. The evidential chain is incomplete.'

'An official body has to keep the little that there is,' said Peter. 'We think the HET is the obvious candidate.'

With that, DCI Flynn was in agreement. His disappointment – and it was bitter – arose because he'd hoped that finally, with a list of specific killings, he'd get sufficient evidence to institute investigations and prosecutions. He slumped back in his chair.

'There's nothing I can do. Not without names. This Blind Eye is still looking the other way. He's got to face up to what he's done. I need names.'

On the way back to London, Tess couldn't erase the black-and-white images from her mind: the hazy photographs of those who'd been targeted. And while they were all legally innocent, it was the four who'd had nothing to do with the fighting that had unsettled her. Those who'd been morally blameless. Gunned down on a street corner or coming out of a shop. Just living their lives as best they could, keeping out of the conflict. The PIRA usually claimed its own, and after each of these four killings a statement had been issued denying that the deceased had ever been a volunteer. As DCI Flynn said, the records kept by Lomax only showed that the victims had been under surveillance. Nothing more.

'And that,' said Peter, ordering another gin and tonic on the plane, 'is the end of that. Thank God.'

'What about the four?'

'Collateral damage, Tess. It's called war. Name me a peace that ended with justice for everyone.'

He had already said something similar. She'd pushed his swashbuckling to one side. But this time his words punctured something inside Tess. And even though he reached for her hand, and she held his, and even though they'd probably carry on as usual, and make love and eat Chinese – or maybe the other way round – she knew their relationship had been

*damaged. Possibly irreparably. She didn't know. She didn't
want to think about it. All she could hear was a soft, inner
hiss of escaping air.*

*'I'll have two of them,' she said to the steward, pointing
at the Gordon's. 'Go easy on the tonic.'*

34

'It's all lies, Mr Benson,' said Karmen, pushing the witness
statement across the table. 'Not only have I never met him,
I've never heard of him. You don't actually believe any of
this, do you? You can't . . . you simply can't.'

Benson put the statement back in his file.

'These are extraordinary allegations, extraordinarily detailed
and extraordinary serious. I needed to know your response.'

'Well, it's extraordinary clear. I'm Karmen Naylor. People
will believe anything about me. Even you.'

'No, Karmen. That's not true. But I have to scrutinise every
shred of evidence.'

'There's nothing to scrutinise. He's made it all up. Can't
you object?'

'Yes, I can. But the evidence won't be excluded. The court
will simply grant us an adjournment to consider the allegations
made against you. Miss Shah will draft a new indictment,
listing all the offences implied in the narrative, along with
the existing murder charge. And when we come back, this
man won't be alone. There'll be a slew of other defendants
and supporting witnesses.'

Karmen stared into space.

'If we press on today, as Miss Shah wants, then I just face
the murder charge?'

'Yes.'

'But whatever happens, I'm going to be charged with these other offences . . . and there'll be another trial?'

'Yes. That's right. A much bigger affair.'

'When?'

'A few months' time.'

The muffled sounds of the Old Bailey at work reached them. Doors banging. Lawyers talking. Guards jangling their keys. The room seemed to contract. They were all pulling on the same limited amount of air.

'My own brother wants me put away for life,' said Karmen, more to herself than Benson or Tess. 'Why? Because he's angry and bitter and jealous. Because my father loved me more than him. Because I didn't need the family to survive. I come home and I end up being accused of murder . . . and just when I'm about to be released, someone comes forward and says everything possible to make sure I'm convicted.' She looked up. 'This has to be Ryan's work. He's out to get me, at any price.'

This reading of events had occurred to Benson. It was the most obvious interpretation, assuming Karmen was innocent. But it was an argument the court would never hear. Because he couldn't prove that it was Ryan who'd told him to throw the case, which, in turn, would prove his desire to harm his sister. And even if he could, at that point he'd have to withdraw from the case. He couldn't give evidence and represent Karmen at the same time. Benson was about to explain the dilemma when Karmen said:

'Miss Shah wants to press on because if I'm convicted it will make it easier to prove the case against me in the next trial?'

'Exactly.'

'I'll be presented to the jury as the woman who killed Billy Hudson because of a failed money-laundering operation?'

'Yes. She's also covering herself, in case any future witnesses retract their evidence. That often happens when gangs are involved. This way, if she wins, she's guaranteed at least one conviction.'

'But if you win, Mr Benson . . . I come back to court as a person of good character?'

'Yes.'

'There'd be no murder charge on the indictment, and you could argue forcefully that the previous jury must have concluded that I'd had nothing to do with the events surrounding the murder.'

'That would be a given.'

Benson was impressed. Karmen had seen to the heart of her situation instantly; much faster than he'd done. She'd seen the nuance, too, which was legal, and quite beyond her experience in the restaurant trade. To reach the same place, Benson had needed burn after burn and a bad night spent sifting possible outcomes. An obscure doubt flashed across his mind, moving so quickly it left no trace of its passing. He looked at Karmen, who in turn looked towards the door, as if noticing the noises on the other side for the first time. The air in the room had grown warm and thin.

'I don't want an adjournment, Mr Benson. I want the name of Billy Hudson out of my life.'

On entering court, Benson strode directly over to Shah. She was at her place, browsing her notes with the air of someone pleased with the scope and contents of a menu.

'You were waiting for this to happen, weren't you?'

'Yes.'

'You knew our case was possibly connected to another?'

'Yes.'

'You knew the police intelligence summary was inaccurate?'

'Read it again. It's accurate only until the date of disclosure.'

'I asked you about the wider picture.'

'You did.'

'And you said nothing.'

'Because I owed you nothing. You were entitled to what is disclosed through the proper channels. Now, in the proper way, you've been told the rest of your client's grubby story. I assume she's now going to plead?'

'No.'

'Good lord. Then you'll want an adjournment?'

'No. And I won't be opposing your application for leave to admit the new evidence either.'

'That, Benson, shows foresight. Because you'd lose.'

Benson appraised Shah with reluctant awe. Her emotional control was astonishing. She'd fought the case, losing ground each day, keeping faith in a wider strategy. She'd framed her case tightly, leaving gaps to be filled in later, if and when Bucklow cracked. And, for whatever reason, he had done. That was quite a story.

He decided not to tell Shah about the *Guardian* cartoon he'd pinned to his toilet door. He might have to take it down.

'You deliberately said nothing in your opening speech about context and motive because you didn't want to commit yourself to an account you'd have to withdraw?'

'Correct.'

'And now you're going to address the jury as if you're letting them know the truth behind the confusion . . . and I'm left looking as if I might have been hiding something.'

'It's called skill, Benson. It also happens to be true. On both counts. Which is why I don't trust you.'

There was a loud knock, and the judge shuffled onto the bench. He spoke before he'd even sat down.

'Miss Shah, I presume I'll be sending everyone home. Am I right?'

'You're quite wrong, my lord. Thanks to the generous cooperation of my learned friend, not to mention insight, we can proceed. He's taken instructions. He does not seek an adjournment. My application stands uncontested.'

'Really?'

'Yes, my lord,' said Benson. 'I've spoken at length to my client and she insists there's nothing to be gained from any delay.'

'Very well.'

The application to admit additional evidence was granted, the jury was brought back into court, and the judge explained what had happened over the weekend. A supergrass – not a term he liked, but it was common parlance – had come forward with grave evidence against the defendant. In due course he'd give them directions on the matter, but for now he required them to remember that the evidence they were about to hear was relevant only to the existing charge of murder. The defendant was not on trial for anything else. Particular care was needed to ensure . . .

Benson's thoughts were on a squat individual with bad breath about to enter the witness box. He'd once insisted on Benson representing him. He'd changed his mind pretty damn quick. Once he'd learned that Benson had already been booked by a Naylor.

35

'Give the court your name, please,' said Shah.

'Steven Bucklow.'

His mouth worked as if he was chewing gum, but in fact he was moving his tongue around – which, if Tony Naylor could get a grip on it, would be torn out of his mouth. For months Bucklow had said nothing. He'd come to a courtroom, just down from Benson's, and he'd listened to the case being spelled out against him, knowing Karmen was doing the same thing next door. And then, over the weekend, that tongue had started to wag. Bucklow had decided to become a cooperating witness. Which is to say, someone who gives evidence against his associates in return for what might be called favours. In due course, Benson would enumerate them.

'Are you a professional criminal?'

'Well, it's what I do.'

'Do you have numerous convictions for dishonesty and violence?'

'Loads.'

Shah read out the list, not to be straight with the jury, but because if she didn't Benson would. This way, Shah could mould the answers to her advantage.

'Why should this jury trust you?' she said.

'Because I'm going to tell you what no one in their right mind would tell anyone, right? I'm going to put my life on the line.'

He was shorter and wider than Benson remembered. But the same feral glare, bright with self-interest, lit his narrowed eyes.

'Tell the jury about the nature of your work.'

Bucklow had been dealing in drugs since he was eleven. And he was now thirty-two. He'd started out delivering wraps in Denton for his father. He'd ended up running his own show in south Manchester. He'd become a player, holding his own.

'The game changed in 2014. That's when I shifted league. If you like, I was headhunted.'

'Who by?'

'Karmen Naylor.'

She'd arrived in Manchester, ostensibly working at the low end of the restaurant trade, whereas she'd actually been on the third stage of a secret project expanding the influence and reach of the Naylor family. Using her business savvy, her name and the promise of wealth, she'd taken on promising drug dealers, backed them with product and hired muscle, and moved them up the rankings.

'How do you know this?'

'She told me herself. During the first meeting. She said she'd started off in Newcastle, then gone to Leeds, and now she was moving into Manchester. In each city there was a captain. I was to be that captain. The idea was to build a national network of cooperating players.'

'What was in it for you?'

'Promotion. From League Two to the Premier League.'

'For those who don't follow football, do you mean from small fry to big shot?'

'Yeah. Though no one ever called me small. Or a fry.'

The captains met every few months. To discuss marketing, distribution and revenue. A common system was being put in place to monitor growth and efficiency. To ingrain mutual support, intelligence and protection. Their names: Jed Farmer in Newcastle; Tim Vernay in Leeds; Bucklow in Manchester. Each captain had their own team.

'My lord, those who worked with Mr Bucklow were arrested this morning, as were Farmer and Vernay. Should they cooperate, other arrests will follow. They will all be the subject of separate proceedings. Mr Bucklow, what was in it for the Naylors?'

'Sixty per cent.'

'Their role?'

'They were the FA. The governing body.'

Which wasn't entirely accurate, because they took responsibility for supply. Either through direct importation or intermediaries. The captains knew nothing of that. They just received the product. Always free. Always on time. Always in the quantities required.

'Did you always deal with Karmen Naylor?'

'Nah. Once things were underway, she was planning on moving to Nottingham, so she sent the top guy from London. Billy Hudson. He was her eyes, ears and voice. That's what she'd told us. But we remained answerable to Karmen.'

'What about Tony, her father?'

'Never mentioned.'

'Ryan, her brother?'

'Never mentioned.'

'Tell us about the nature of the scheme itself. You were based in cities. But—'

'We'd gone country.'

'Explain the term, please.'

'Well, you know, it's going OT. "Out there". The police call it "county lines".'

'The "lines" being the phone lines dedicated to this kind of activity?'

'Yeah. We've got the product. We use runners to get it OT. We give the runners mobile phones. We call them, day or night, and tell them where to go. It's easy. I just carried on watching the footy.'

Benson examined the photograph of Billy Hudson, the fun-loving rascal, wondering why he hadn't ended up running Kwik Fit, or some other company. He'd had the required talent and dedication. How had he ever got involved, willingly, with 'going OT'? The practice of supplying drugs in rural communities and small towns, using vulnerable children as the dealers. How had he sat with those captains, discussing the grooming of kids from pupil referral units or care homes? Or forcing them to work through debt bondage? How had he agreed to sending them on trains and taxis – under the nose of the British Transport Police, or, using private hire, under the nose of no authority at all – to make deliveries to adult gang members waiting in a short-term let or a hotel? How had he slept at night? How had he gone to Manchester on Wednesday the 16th of May 2018 to supervise the first stage of a money-laundering operation, the fruits of this God-awful exploitation? According to Greg Kilgour, he'd been stressed, presumably by the scale of responsibility, rather than any moral self-disgust . . . while Karmen, oblivious to what was happening – assuming she was telling the truth – had been dishing out bonuses. Her mind on a weekend at Allhallows.

'The money arising from this business. How was it handled?'

'We took our forty per cent and cleaned it ourselves. The sixty due to Karmen was counted and collected by Tim Kershaw. He runs Kershaw Construction Ltd.'

Kershaw had also been arrested earlier that morning. And, again, if he opened up, other arrests were anticipated. Benson had to marvel. Bucklow had pulled down everything the Naylors had built in secret. Years of work. An industry producing millions per year. Wiped out in a matter of days, while Benson had been reading testimonials to his own perspicacity.

'Kershaw brought the money in used cement sacks,' said Bucklow. 'He'd bring them to one of his building sites. Billy would come up from London, confirm the count and put the lot into suitcases. My job was to take 'em to Heathrow.'

Where Kenny Lynam, in baggage handling, would arrange for their transmission to Dubai.

Benson waited, and sure enough it came. Lynam had been arrested that morning; and further arrests were to be expected, here and in the United Arab Emirates. And, consequent upon those arrests, others would no doubt be incriminated and apprehended.

'How many times have you done this?'

'Once a year for three years. Prior to that I don't know how Karmen handled her share. She brought in Kershaw to centralise things. And I became the driver to get a bonus.'

'How much?'

'Twenty-five grand.'

'How many suitcases did you normally transport?'

'It varied.'

'Can you tell the jury how much money you must have transported over that three-year period?'

'In all, I'd say nine to ten million quid.'

'At the request of whom?'

'Karmen Naylor.'

'On each occasion?'

'Yes.'

'Okay. Let's focus now on the day of your arrest. Thursday the seventeenth of May 2018. My lord, to place things in context, this is the day before Mr Hudson was murdered.'

'Thank you, Miss Shah.'

'Where did you meet Billy?'

'South of Manchester. A house renovation. Kershaw had come and gone, so I didn't see him this time. Anyways, I turned up, and Billy put the cases in the van, and then he called Karmen on speakerphone. He said, "All done, Karmen," and she said, "Good work. See you Friday night," and then Billy cut the call.'

'He called her Karmen?'

'That's what I said.'

'Did you recognise the voice?'

'I've spoken to Karmen on a burner for years. It was her. No question.'

'Tell the jury what happened next, please.'

'Billy gave me the news from London.'

'Which was?'

'With Tony out of action, the Naylors were falling apart.'

'Use Hudson's words, please.'

'Those are his words. He said the brother and sister were at war. Always had been, ever since Karmen had gone to that private school. He hated her and she hated him. And Ryan hated Billy, too, because Tony had always preferred him to Ryan, his own son . . . which is sad, if you think about it. Your dad is meant to—'

'Was that the end of his remarks?'

'Nah. He said if you—'

'His precise words, please.'

'He said, "If I were you, I'd cut and run. Because if anything goes wrong, today or tomorrow, we're both dead. Me first, and then you. Same for the lads in Newcastle and Leeds." So I said why don't you cut and run, then, and he said, "It's too late for me. I'm in too deep."'

Bucklow had then headed south: M56, M6 and the M1. The van had been intercepted and ultimately stopped, just south of Northampton. From the moment he'd seen the flashing lights, he'd thought of Billy's words. He'd never forgotten them. After Billy's death, he'd been rehearsing them on a daily basis.

'Last Friday I made my decision. I cut and run. And here I am.'

36

Mr Justice Garway adjourned the court for an early lunch, so that Benson's cross-examination could begin first thing in the afternoon. Tess, Benson and a still-bandaged Archie left the Bailey and went to a table in the upper room of the Crown and Thistle, by a window onto Paternoster Lane. The staff, knowing their regulars, knew what to bring. A plate of sandwiches, a bottle of water and a pint of Fuller's London Pride for Mr Congreve, who gave his verdict as soon as they sat down:

'Bucklow might be lowlife, but he's convincing.'

Tess nodded. Bucklow heard live was very different from Bucklow on the page. His fear was palpable. He was on the run, trying to hold onto his life.

'It all hangs together,' said Archie. 'The money is intercepted on the Thursday and Hudson is killed on the Friday. The two events are linked. Why would he lie?'

'The question is whether Karmen killed Hudson, Archie,' said Benson. 'That's all we're asked to think about.'

'But that question is linked to whether Karmen organised the northern development. He says she did. Again, why would he make that up?'

'Ryan's people will have told him to cooperate. He's been told what to say.'

'But why would Bucklow fall into line?'

'Because he knows that God himself can't protect you once the Naylors have decided to take you out. This way, Bucklow gets a new birth certificate and an assurance from Ryan that no efforts are going to be made to find out the name. It's a good outcome for him.'

'These arrests in Newcastle and Leeds,' said Archie. 'It shows Bucklow's telling the truth. I mean, who else could have set up this league of dealers, if it wasn't Karmen? She's the one who did the moving around.'

'Ryan used her as cover. Planning for a day like today.'

'So what's going to happen when Farmer and Vernay and the others are brought to trial?'

'They're all going to say exactly what Ryan's people tell them to say. Because he's the brains behind the northern development, not Karmen. He's the one who took over from his father, not Karmen. He's the one Hudson rang up once the suitcases were in the van, not Karmen. He's the one who had a motive to kill Hudson on the Friday night, not Karmen . . . when he knew Hudson had planned to meet her. By the way, he's the one who told us to throw the trial and had your finger lopped off.'

'But why would Ryan have Bucklow reveal all that crap about childhood hatred?'

'Because it's what Hudson said. It's realistic detail. All Ryan wants is his name swapped for Karmen's. The rest stands . . . which is why it sounds so bloody convincing.'

The sandwiches arrived and Tess began eating, slowly, pondering Benson's argument.

'What about the Ravens?' she said. 'If Ryan is involved in Hudson's killing, and so are the Ravens, then they must have been working together. But that's bizarre. All he had to do was use his boys. They're the experts. They're the people who know how to mimic the murder of the Kite, if only because they were there, with Tony, when he did it.'

'But what about—'

'Stop,' said Archie. 'There's no point in moving pieces around the board. We need more information.'

He was right. Bucklow's evidence had changed everything. Prior to his disclosures, the jury only knew about Shah's weak case. They knew that Ekene Osabede had threatened to kill Hudson. They knew Hudson had hit Ekene's pregnant sister. But they hadn't heard what Buster had heard shortly afterwards. They knew nothing about the woman who'd met the Osabedes in his café. They knew nothing about the two envelopes he'd seen being slid across the table.

'There's nothing we can do, Archie,' said Tess. 'The Osabedes would never admit anything. And neither would Buster.'

This time it was Benson who ate slowly, brooding on the argument. Then he said:

'There is.'

'Who?'

Archie laughed. Tess smiled, and then frowned, realising Benson had a plan. And that carrying out the plan would fall to her.

'There is someone we can pressure into talking. Someone no one would dream of approaching. Someone who might lead us to Q.'

He glanced at Tess; Tess glanced at Archie, who said:

'Don't worry, Tess. All I need is one good arm. I'm coming with you.'

37

How am I going to do this, thought Benson.

Shah's preference to continue with the trial, rather than seek an adjournment, was a gamble. Sure, she was trying to bag at least one conviction, but it also meant she was relying on one witness to make the case against Karmen. It was a high-wire act. Which meant that if Benson could nudge Bucklow off balance, it wouldn't only be the Manchester captain who'd tumble through the air. So would Shah's strategy – if a strategy could tumble.

But with nothing new to say, without evidence to demonstrate dishonesty, how could he show Bucklow was a liar? Benson had nothing to hand except what Bucklow had already said, and Mr Justice Garway was looking at him expectantly, eyebrows raised. Unsure of what to do, Benson rose, like a bird leaving its nest for the first time, knowing it must fly or else fall.

'You're putting your life on the line?' said Benson.

'Yeah.'

'Let's look at this decision a little more closely.'

'If you want.'

'For now, I won't contradict what you've told the jury. I'll pretend it's all true.'

'It is.'

'So let's get this right. You're a sort of midfield player in a county lines game run by the Naylors.'

'I'd say centre-forward.'

'You're also involved in the laundering of the income generated.'

'Yeah.'

'Until last week you'd refused to cooperate with the police. You'd said nothing to anyone about anything.'

'Nothing.'

'No one knew the fixtures were organised by Karmen Naylor?'

'No.'

'No one knew about Farmer and Vernay and Kershaw and Lynam?'

'Nah.'

'All the police had was a van driver from Denton in Manchester with three million quid in three suitcases.'

'Yeah.'

'You were facing a red card. Which is to say prison. You know the rules: all you had to do was keep quiet. And when you came back on the field, you'd get promoted.'

'Billy told me to cut and run. And I did. Because I didn't want to end up like him.'

It was as though Benson heard a whisper in his ear.

'That, Mr Bucklow, is a lie. It's the central lie that shows everything else you've said about my client to be complete and utter invention. If the terrifying Karmen Naylor wanted you dead, you would have been relegated the same night as Billy Hudson. "Me first, then you." Remember? No one could have saved you. Instead, you've been breathing fresh air for over a year. Which means you were on the team. It means you still are.'

'Yer what? You think I'm still with the Naylors? It's because of me, right, that everyone knows they've been operating outside of London. For years. It's because of me that everyone knows about the county lines. And the money laundering. I'm the one who's brought the league to an end.'

'Only the northern game, Mr Bucklow. London is still in play. Tell me, in the criminal world, speaking to the police, like you've done . . . doesn't that make you a non-league amateur?'

'My learned friend might like to ask a proper question,' snapped Shah.

'Sure. What did you get in return, Mr Bucklow?'

Bucklow shifted in the witness box, his mouth loosening into something like a grin.

'What's the package, Mr Bucklow?'

'For what?'

'Giving evidence today, and all the other days to come?'

'I'll get a reduced sentence.'

'What else?'

'Protection while I'm inside.'

'And when you come out?'

'A new identity.'

'What else?'

'A house.'

'What else?'

'Money.'

'What else?'

'That's it.'

'Don't you have a dedicated officer to help you resettle and handle any problems?'

'Yeah, if you like.'

'Don't you have someone you can call if ever you get into trouble, or something goes wrong?'

'Yeah, if you like.'

Benson waited, as if considering a pile of goodies on the oak table in the centre of the courtroom.

'You've done pretty well out of this, haven't you?'

'I'm getting what I deserve.'

Benson stared again at the table. He stared at it for so long he could feel the eyes of the jury, Shah and the judge upon him. When the silence became dense, he said, as if observing the wood rather than the rewards:

'To get where you are now, there's only one person you haven't named.'

'And who's that?'

'Everyone else has been sent off. Farmer, Vernay, Kershaw, Lynam – they're all facing serious amounts of time . . . Everyone except for one man. He's still in play. And, funnily enough, you want us to believe he never approved of what you were up to.'

Benson didn't need to name him. Bucklow knew who Benson was referring to.

'He wasn't involved,' said Bucklow. 'I've only told you what Billy told me.'

'He's the one who's been trusting you, isn't he? He's the one who told you to blame my client for this sickening game you've been playing. He's the one who gave you your life in return, so you could sell it on to the police.'

'I never spoke to him. I've never met him. You've got it wrong.'

'I think you might be right, Mr Bucklow. I have got something wrong. You're not quite the amateur I thought you were.'

'What am I then?'

Benson raised his eyes; everything depended on the impact of his answer to the question. A question he wasn't obliged to answer because, in court, he was the interrogator, not the witness. But he'd lured Bucklow into asking it. Looking towards the jury, Benson formulated his reply. Either they'd agree with him or they wouldn't. He seemed to soar over his own fugitive doubt.

'I'd say you were Ryan's man.'

* * *

As Benson sat down he realised what he'd just done. Until a few moments ago, Benson – along with Tess, Archie, their families and anyone they cared about – had enjoyed the unqualified protection of the Naylors, should the Ronsons decide to bring on the dogs. That promise now lay in shreds on the floor. He'd torn it up in the most public and provocative way. Every detail of his cross-examination was already online, reported live from the courtroom itself. Ryan was probably reading it at this very moment, sniffing at strangely unnerving intervals. Maybe he was reading it out loud to his father. Maybe his father couldn't quite grasp what Benson was implying, and Ryan was having to spell it out, watching the milky clouds gather in his father's eyes. Benson ought to have foreseen this outcome but, strange as it seems, he'd given it no thought. He turned aside, and saw that Shah was regarding him intently. For the first time he identified in her fixed expression something as foreign as it was sincere. Respect.

38

Tess parked in a side street off the Old Kent Road, roughly in between the South Eastern gas works and the New Cross waste processing centre. Between a fart and a crap, said Archie as they pushed open the grubby door to Ruth Mowbray and Co., solicitors to the Naylor family. The word company had a purely legal meaning. Mowbray had no associates or assistants. She didn't even have a secretary. Dressed in a white, closely tailored trouser suit, she was frowning over a folded copy of the *Daily Telegraph*, struggling with the last clue to the crossword.

'Just hang on, will you,' she said, tapping a biro between perfect teeth.

Her office was devoid of anything remotely personal. Even the scratched desk and worn chairs seemed not to belong. Neither did the red plastic Ikea desk lamp. There were no pictures or legal books, no calendar on the wall, no telephone or notepad, just a laptop, which was open, and two large grey filing cabinets with all the drawers pulled out an inch or so. There was an air of winding up after the removal van had gone. The room, curiously, was spotlessly clean. And Tess knew, at once, that it was always so; and that these tired furnishings had always been there.

'Done,' Mowbray said, smiling, and threw the biro into the wastepaper basket. She then stood up, unfolding the newspaper, and laid it carefully over the high headrest on the back of her chair, as if to protect her coiffure from any foreign matter. 'I don't know who you are, porky,' she sighed, nodding at Archie and resuming her seat, 'but you're de Vere. What do you want?'

Tess was nonplussed. She looked at the large open wings of the newspaper. It was covered with biro marks – jumbled capital letters, scratched-out words, dashes, scribbles, doodles and, of course, the filled-in crossword grid. She'd planned to put Mowbray under pressure, insinuating – obedient to Benson – that Mowbray was part of the conspiracy to frame Karmen. Why? Because she was the one who'd pushed the papers across the table for Karmen to sign in June 2017; the papers that put her at the heart of HGT Ltd, telling her she was only replacing her father.

'If there was a conspiracy to nail Karmen, that's when it began,' Benson had said. 'All of her life, with her father's blessing, Karmen has nothing to do with the Naylor business. When she came out of that room she was the most important person in the company, even if she didn't know it. She had power. Even if she couldn't use it. It made her a target, if only for the Ronsons. Mowbray must know all this. And she has said nothing. I should have seen this from the outset: if anyone is our link to Q, it's her.'

'What do want me to do?'

'Threaten her. Say you'll speak to Tony.'

'If you're right, Ryan's got her back. She'll laugh in my face.'

Which is exactly what happened when Tess finished a punchy speech prepared with Archie earlier that morning.

'I am Q, you fool,' she said, touching a curl of sculpted blonde hair. 'That's how Tony kept tabs on what the police did and didn't know. It's how we fed them information and disinformation – and they paid for it, too, through the nose. It's how we got rid of local opposition. It's how we made them think Tony came from another era. It's how we hid the northern gig. It's how we told the Ronsons Tony had done the Kite himself.' All at once Mowbray's eyes sparkled with mischief. 'The plan was to wait until the day before Tony's trial, and then I'd have got cold feet, backed out and told them I was better in place as a CHIS than blown . . . and Tony would have walked and my handler would have calmed me down, given me a bonus, told me that I was *important* . . . that I could still do something *good* with my life. All I had to do was keep the information flowing. Of course, Tony had his stroke, so that rather spoiled the fun.' The shimmer of amusement suddenly vanished. 'We were in real trouble. Billy wanted out. I wanted out. But once the new management was in place I thought the future was more than secure – we were in the ablest of hands. But now Bucklow's gone and blown it. The stupid northern prat.'

Tess, while listening, had been reading some of the scribbles on the newspaper. Amongst the workings-out, Mowbray had written in large capital letters:

WHAT DO I DO NOW??????
OOPS!!!!

AGHGHGHG!!

'Unfortunately, the good times are over,' she said, sliding open a drawer in her desk. 'When you came in, I thought it was the pigs. Which would have been very quick, actually. I mean, Bucklow's only just finished singing, and to get me they're going to need people coughing in Dubai: about the money, the offshores, the trusts, the dividends, the ghost companies . . . That was all me, you know. And I was good at it. Really good. Creative to the point of art.' She sighed more nostalgia. 'I don't suppose my Arab friends have squealed yet. But they will. It's only a matter of time.'

'Get ahead of the curve, Ruth.'

'Ruth? Try Mowbray.'

'Sorry. Ms Mowbray.'

'I prefer Miss. I'm single and old-fashioned.'

'Okay, get ahead of the curve, Miss Mowbray.'

'Which curve?'

'The judicial one. You can speak out before the police even get here. You can give evidence in Karmen's defence.'

Mowbray reached inside the drawer and removed a small pink bag. Little finger extended, she slowly drew back the zip and took out a round compact. Flicking open the lid, she checked her lips in the mirror, pursing and releasing them, pouting and smiling. Still looking at herself, she said:

'It's been a hell of ride, and it ends as it should, with a bang. And some surprises. You think you know people, but you don't. I never knew Billy had been banging that tart from Peckham. Never knew he might have had a sprog. Billy as a dad? Dear God. I'd have called social services myself if it was true.' Mowbray flapped her eyelashes, and stubbed a stray speck of black liner off her right orbital bone. 'Another shock is the size of Bucklow's knackers. They're real swingers. I never would have expected him to bite the hand that fed him. Or steal from us. But that's what happens when you wash your dirty linen in public. Billy should have kept quiet about that.'

Tess and Archie glanced at each other.

'What do you mean, steal?' said Tess.

'There were four suitcases in that van when it left Manchester. There were three when the pigs stopped it. Where did the other case go? I'll tell you what I think. After leaving Billy, Big Balls made a detour. To some hovel and a hag. He gave her a million quid and then went back on the road. They were planning to vanish after the drop off, only Bucklow got lifted first, because someone was speaking to the pigs . . . a little runt, who's probably still at it. I must say, that came as a surprise to me. The lightning-bolt kind. Sure, all families have their—'

'I said you can take control of what's happening, Miss Mowbray.'

'Yes, I heard you. I'm tempted to laugh some more. You really have no idea, do you?'

Tess glanced at more scrawl on the *Daily Telegraph*:

OH SHIT. HOW COULD YOU BE SO BLIND????

'Truth be told, Tony had been losing his touch for a while,' said Mowbray, powdering her cheeks with a pink pad. 'Standards had been slipping . . . in London at least. So after he had that stroke, it was a chance to bring everyone back into line. There was a reshuffle. And it pains me to say this, because I've worked for Tony all my life, and I love him, but things were better. Turnover was rising. People knew where they stood. Fear had been put back into the organisation. Real fear.'

'Miss Mowbray, now is your chance,' said Tess, raising her voice slightly. 'You can blow the northern prat out of the water. You can save Karmen – she needn't be dragged into all this. You can give Tony some peace of mind.'

'I can, can I?'

'Yes. Make a sworn statement now. And when the prosecution case is over, step into the witness box. Like Bucklow.'

'Yes, I suppose I could. You know, the irony of it all is that stupid, northern Bucklow has cut a reasonably good deal. Benson is right about that. I must say, Benson's good at what he does. Very good indeed. He's even opened my eyes to what I should have seen – tell him that from me, will you? I hadn't realised what the runt was capable of. Anyway, he was right about Bucklow. He gets out of the game with quite a package, paid for by the state, and a million quid that no one but the Naylors know about. Of course, Benson doesn't appreciate that last bit, but—'

'You can get out, too, Miss Mowbray. I'll help you. I'll make sure that—'

'De Vere, are you religious at all?'

'What do you mean?'

Mowbray snapped shut the compact, dropped it into the small pink bag and slowly closed the zip, her little finger floating once again.

'Do you know your Bible stories?'

'A few.'

'How about the Prodigal Son. Do you know that one? He ends up snuggling up to some pigs.'

'Yes, I know it.'

'Well, let me tell you a different version. One with a twist. Are you ready?'

Tess glanced at Archie. His eyes were fixed on the newspaper covered in desperate graffiti.

I'M NOT READY.

'Sure,' said Tess. 'Fire away.'

Mowbray's mischievous smile returned like sunlight on gaudy wallpaper.

'That, Miss de Vere, is precisely what I intend to do. Hear me out first, will you?'

Benson stared at the court door, willing it to open; for Tess to come through it, flanked by Archie, and for them both to take their seats behind him. The feeling of being exposed to Ryan's very particular displeasure refused to abate, and he wanted company. But the door only opened to reveal a tall, angular man who strode purposefully towards the witness box. Once in place, he looked at Shah expectantly.

'Give the court your name, please,' said Shah.

'Deputy Assistant Commissioner Desmond Oakhurst.'

'Outline your responsibilities.'

Benson knew about him already. Oakhurst was one of those urbane senior police officers who frequently appear on television, either to discuss trends in crime and the response of law enforcement agencies, or to comment on a crackdown or the successful outcome of a major campaign. The greater part of his career had been spent fighting organised crime. He was the National Police Chiefs' Council lead for county lines. And as such, he was not usually in charge of operations on the ground. The current case was an exception. And it had come about after a member of the public had contacted Crimestoppers, insisting he had intelligence for DAC Oakhurst's particular attention. After receiving an assurance the call would not be recorded or traced by the Met, the man was put through.

'When was this?' asked Shah.

'The fifth of June 2017.'

Benson wrote down the date in large numbers, circling it twice.

'What did the man say?'

'That he could deliver me, on a plate, the northern business of the Naylor family.'

'What was your response?'

'Considerable disappointment and irritation.'

'Why?'

'There couldn't be any northern business. Like everyone else involved in my line of work, I thought the Naylors were an old-fashioned gang strictly limiting their activity to south London.'

'Old-fashioned?'

'I mean a gang that operated in the age-old ways of hands-on pressure and violence. Suspicious of the internet and technology. Local in their outlook. Resisting expansion. They'd long been seen as something of a throwback to the time of the Krays and the Richardsons. In the underworld they had, let's say, a vintage cachet.'

But the caller had gripped Oakhurst's attention by revealing the name of the Metropolitan Police's only high-level informant in the Naylor set-up. Q. And then he'd grabbed him – so to speak – by the throat.

'He said he'd leave Q in place. But if I didn't play ball, Q would be blown. And Q would end up bleeding to death. And dumped at sea.'

'What did you conclude about the identity of this caller?'

'Most importantly, he was for real. He could deliver what he was offering. Second, he had to be part of the Naylor set-up, someone disaffected by the direction things had taken in the north. Someone committed to its old-school character and was prepared to go to extreme lengths to restore it . . . someone, therefore, with a vested interest in the politics of the family business. Someone who was playing a calculated game, because while he knew Q was a CHIS – a covert human intelligence source – he'd done nothing about it. He'd left Q unharmed precisely so he could make this move, to secure my confidence and cooperation. These conclusions – about the man's standing – were confirmed by the direction of our conversation.'

'Please elaborate.'

'He knew all there was to know about Naylor strategic thinking. And practice. He told me they'd been playing the police for a decade, in order to hide what they were really doing.'

'Which was?'

'Putting themselves in the vanguard of contemporary drug-dealing; which meant developing county lines networks throughout England, beginning in Newcastle, Leeds and Manchester. In due course, they intended to target other cities, as well as establishing schemes in Wales and Scotland. In tandem, they'd already begun to forge links with criminal organisations in Europe and beyond. Only someone intimately involved with the Naylor family could know such things.'

'Such, then, was the strategy. You mentioned practice.'

'In order to implement this strategy, the Naylors had decided to build these networks in secret. By so doing, they'd get a solid national structure in place without having attracted the attention of . . . people like myself. You see, it's relatively easy to pick a single weed. But a field, where all the roots are connected – that's another matter. This is where the old-fashioned image came into play. And this is where Q was used to great effect in misleading police intelligence officers.'

'How?'

'It's very simple. The Naylors used Q to keep the police thinking retro Tony would never look further than the south bank of the Thames. As I've indicated, to my shame, the ploy worked.'

'Why shame?'

'It is my job to anticipate this sort of trick. But no one had ever questioned the reliability of Q's material. It had always been accurate and of high value – vital to securing the arrests of numerous criminals outside the Naylor set-up. Multiple criminal operations had been foiled.'

'This man, then, had your full and undivided attention.'

'He did.'

'How did he propose to deliver on his offer?'

'By giving me the weakest link in the chain, he said. I asked for the name, and he said I'd have to wait. I asked for how long, and he said about a year. I'd be given seven days' notice. And when I was called, I'd be told all I needed to know. Between times, I was to make no note of the call or speak to anyone about what I'd been told. If I did, Q would pay the price, and slowly. Then the line went dead.'

'What did you think?'

'I didn't know what to think. Calling a year in advance of a tip-off was bizarre to say the least. I still don't know why I was given so much time. There was nothing I could do. Nothing I could plan for. And, as a consequence, I did absolutely nothing. I even began to wonder if I'd been played myself . . . but then the call came, as promised, about a year later.'

'When, precisely?'

'Wednesday the ninth of May 2018.'

Oakhurst was told to prepare to seize a vehicle on Thursday the 17th of May. He was given the driver's name, the make and registration number, the route to be taken and the time to intercept.

'He explained that funds were being transported to Heathrow as part of a money-laundering operation. As to how the money had been acquired, he recounted, in effect, everything Mr Bucklow has told the court. I replied that I needed hard, reliable evidence, because what I was being told on the phone would be of no use in a court of law.'

'What was the man's response?'

'He told me not to worry. That, once arrested, Mr Bucklow would tell me absolutely everything.'

'Can you recall his words?'

'He said, "Bucklow will hold out, but in the end he's the sort who cracks." And he was right.'

Subsequent to this second call, on the 9th of May, Oakhurst had brought together representatives of the National Crime Agency, the National Economic Crime Centre, the National County Lines Coordination Centre and the Metropolitan Police Serious and Organised Crime Unit. Together, led by Oakhurst, they'd planned Operation Sparrowhawk. A few days later a tactical team had swooped on that otherwise innocuous van heading down the M1. The caller's confidence turned out to be well-founded. Bucklow, the driver, had held out. But he'd cracked eventually.

'Please wait there. I imagine Mr Benson has some questions for you.'

'Were you surprised when Mr Bucklow told you that Karmen Naylor, a waitress, was the architect of an immense criminal enterprise, rooted in three cities, involving numerous personnel, all answerable to her?'

'I was stunned.'

'Like you were stunned to learn that retro Tony wasn't, in fact, so retro. That he'd been leading you on?'

'Yes, that's fair.'

'There's a parallel?'

'Yes.'

'Let's see how far that parallel goes. You never once questioned the veracity of intelligence emanating from Q?'

'No, I didn't. None of us did. The misleading information . . . the one big lie . . . had been buried in a heap of reliable material. Q was misled and so we were misled.'

'Have you questioned the veracity of what Mr Bucklow told you?'

'The scale of arrests confirms the reliability of what he told us. Think of Mr Bucklow what you will, as a man, but he has delivered up the entire northern business of the Naylor Family Crime Group.'

'You see, this is what bothers me, DAC Oakhurst. I accept you've been given a great deal of reliable material. And everyone in this court can only be glad that a wicked criminal business has been wiped out. I'm just wondering if you're making the same mistake all over again.'

'Meaning?'

'You've swallowed everything Mr Bucklow said, just like you swallowed everything said by Q. And once again, amongst all the good stuff you've been fed one big lie. And once again, you haven't spotted it, because you've failed to consider the possibility.'

'What possibility?'

'That someone has set out to frame Karmen Naylor. Someone has made it look as if she had a motive to kill Billy Hudson. Someone has told Mr Bucklow to put her name at the centre of this northern scheme. And so he turns up in court, swapping one name for another. That's quite easy to do without tripping yourself up, isn't it?'

'Those are all matters for the jury to decide. They now know as much as I do.'

'You know that little bit more.'

'And what is that?'

'The sound of the voice of the man who gave you Mr Bucklow. Tell me, did you give any thought to who it might be, this man who left Q in place? This man who was part of the Naylor set-up and knew Naylor strategic thinking in detail?'

'At the time?'

'Yes, even as he was speaking to you.'

'I did, yes. But it was nothing but surmise . . . just a hunch. It has no value. None whatsoever.'

'That's for the jury to decide. Give us the name that came to you when you put the phone down.'

'I can't see what I thought then has anything to do with what subsequently transpired.'

'The name, please. Let's see if your hunch matches mine. And the jury's.'

DAC Oakhurst looked over to Shah, expecting help. But none came. He pulled a face, to minimise in advance what he was about to say.

'Ryan . . . Ryan Naylor,' he said. 'But I really wouldn't attach much weight to a guess. At the time it was just a straw in the wind.'

'Did you clutch at any others?'

'No . . . no . . . I didn't.'

'Thank you, DAC Oakhurst. No further questions.'

40

'Okay, you know the boring version,' said Mowbray. 'A selfish shite heads off to a distant land and blows his inheritance. When it's all gone, he ends up in a pigsty, where he finally sees the light. So he goes back home, says sorry and his dad says no problem, son, and he – that's the dad – throws a party, gets the caterers in, buys his son a new suit and celebrates the return of a generally decent bloke who'd left his shite with the pigs. Now, the big brother, who's always been a decent bloke, gets annoyed, because he's done the good thing, day in, day out, and got bugger all in return, and the dad says, look, son, we're cool you and me, always have been, always will be, but your brother's no longer a shite. And that's worth a bob or two.'

Tess felt deeply ill at ease. There was a kind of madness in Mowbray's expression. A strange light in her eyes. Her heart rate had increased, reddening her face and straining her lungs.

She was like a diva, all made up, ready to walk on stage for the last time.

'Now, another version,' she said, baring polished teeth. 'No sentimental crap. A girl heads off to a distant land with nothing but her name. She blows nothing, because there's nothing to blow. Instead, using her name as collateral, and her student loan she *sells* blow . . . and other stuff. She doesn't *spend*. She *earns*. And most important of all, she keeps away from the pigs. When she's made a pile – and I mean a pile – she comes back and says, Dad, you never took me seriously: look at this. And she chucks the money in the air and the dad says, bloody hell, that's more than your inheritance. But there's no party. The girl doesn't want one. Instead, she heads off to another distant land, and it's the same story. And then another. She just keeps raking it in. But then, you know life's a bitch: the dad blows a blood vessel in his brain. He's left hobbling around. He can think, sort of, but he can't speak. That's when the girl finally comes home. And the dad finally throws a party. He gets the caterers in, and a band, and they celebrate the return of someone who made something out of nothing. Now, the big brother, who's always done his best, and has never had a party, gets annoyed, because he's been shown up for what he is. A plodder. And the dad says, through his trusted lawyer, relax, we're cool you and me, you'll always have pocket money, but get used to this: she's the future, not you. And do you know what the big brother did? He cried. Then he got drunk at the party and was sick in the toilet. And two days later he went and snuggled up to the pigs.'

Mowbray leaned back in her chair, keeping her head forward so it didn't touch the newspaper. Tess looked into those wild eyes, wondering how to handle the rising hysteria.

'You're saying Karmen took over from Tony?'

'I'm beginning to know what Jesus felt like. Must I explain everything, oh you of little—'

'Karmen set up the northern business? All on her own?'

'You're surprised? When her mother found out, she topped herself. Poor Susan. She still thought Karmen was the Virgin Mary . . . she'd loved that nativity play, Susan . . . but she never quite left the front row. Silly cow.'

'Karmen runs the Naylors?'

'Who else? Ryan? He couldn't update his own computer. He couldn't even clean up the toilet – that was left to me.'

'When was this party?'

'Oh God, are you still trying to work everything out? Third of June. That's when Tony crowned Karmen. Fifth of June: it's official, Karmen became company secretary . . . here in this room. Come the afternoon, Ryan called Crimestoppers.'

'You know this for sure? Ryan making the call?'

'Well, I didn't listen in. We didn't tap his phone – I wanted to, but Tony just couldn't track his own boy – but who the hell else would want to bring down everything Karmen had worked for? Everything she'd built through sacrifice and shame – and Karmen had swallowed her fair share, playing at being a waitress, year in, year out. Who else would want to see her banged up for life? Who else stood to gain the crown once she and Billy were gone? The answers are Ryan, Ryan, and Ryan. God, you're slow.'

'You're saying Ryan killed Billy . . . or arranged his killing?'

'Well, it certainly wasn't Karmen. She trusted Billy. She trusted him almost as much as Ryan hated him. And boy, did Ryan hate Billy.'

'Why?'

'Why? Are you just plain stupid? Billy was the son that Tony never had. While Billy shadowed Tony, Ryan was left to check the slot machines. It was only after Karmen took over that Ryan finally woke up, and he realised if anything happened to Karmen, Billy was next in line, not him . . . that he'd never run the Naylors . . . that his blood meant nothing. Now, speaking of Ryan, it's time you went. I think he might well be on his way over here. You see, in effect, Ryan is in charge now, and, well, we haven't been on the best of terms. Not after I laughed when he cried. More to the point, I'm Q, remember. I've served my purpose. And unfortunately, I've served my purpose as trusted lawyer, too. All in all, I'd say my time's up.'

Mowbray peered into the drawer. Gingerly, she put her hand into the gap, reaching for the back. When she drew it out, she was holding a pistol. Gripped in her small, manicured fingers, it seemed enormous and too heavy to hold. A bright red nail slid over the trigger.

'Do you know who gave me this?' she said cheerily. 'It was Billy. He popped by on his way up to Manchester. He knew something was going down, he could feel it. Something wasn't quite right. And he says use it. If anything goes wrong, don't let him catch you. He was on to Ryan. He knew the runt had gone over.'

Tess didn't move, in part because the gun was pointing directly at her. Archie rose slowly, hands outstretched, and placed himself between Tess and the threat.

'Err, Ruth, Mrs, Miss . . . put the gun down, shall we?'

'Clear off, fatty. You too, de Vere. Unless you're not squeamish.'

Tess leaned to one side, to see past Archie's bulging frame – a move as instinctive as it was unwise – and her eyes met Mowbray's. She'd positioned the muzzle beneath her powdered chin. A crushing silence filled the room, as might follow an explosion. It pressed against Tess's eardrums, causing a ringing pain. And then Mowbray winked.

'Please yourself,' she said, and pulled the trigger.

41

It was early evening. The crack from the pistol still rang in Tess's mind. She could still see the bouquet of blue and red on the *Daily Telegraph*. She could still see Mowbray's head, thrown back in a kind of savage ecstasy, her arms limp in sweet surrender. Worst of all was the blonde hairdo. Viewed from where Tess was sitting, it had kept its curves and loops, as if nothing had happened.

'How are you feeling?' said Benson.

'Fine and dandy.'

Tess and Archie, stunned and sickened, had gone through the motions. With their backs to Mowbray splayed in her chair like a fallen angel, they'd called the police and an ambulance. They'd given brief statements, careful to disclose nothing that would prejudice their current role as members of Karmen's defence team. Who'd have thought legal professional privilege would cover a confession prior to a suicide? But it did. They'd finally met up with Benson when the court rose at the end of the day. And they'd come back to the low lights and warmth of Ennismore Gardens Mews and opened a bottle of whisky. Molly had turned up, and she'd cooked. Fish fingers and peas. They'd eaten together. They'd watched a documentary on sea turtles. And they'd barely spoken until Archie, still shaken, had decided to go home, and even then he only said goodbye. He'd reached out and taken Tess's hand, as if to acknowledge they were bound together for life. Molly had followed him out of the door, coming back seconds later to embrace Tess, before turning to run after Archie.

'Mowbray's told her story, Will,' murmured Tess in the new quiet between them. 'We know Karmen's a crime boss. We know Bucklow told the truth. Can we withdraw from the case?'

'Sorry, no.'

'Why the hell not?'

'Because we *don't know* if Bucklow told the truth, and that's because we don't know if *Mowbray* told the truth. More to the point, even if she did, we're only concerned with the murder of Hudson. And Mowbray said Karmen wouldn't have done it. The fight goes on.'

'Are you sure?'

'Yes. I checked with the Ethics Committee of the Bar Council. Unfortunately, they also think I have to "accommodate" the allegations, just in case they are in fact true.'

'And what does that mean?'

'I can't push the idea that Ryan was behind the northern operation, or the money-laundering scheme.'

'But that leaves Shah an open door to say it was Karmen.'

'It does. We can still deny it, because Karmen denies it, but yes, our hands are now tied. I can no longer suggest that Ryan was Bucklow's . . . team manager.'

'But that's crazy. When it comes to the speeches, Shah can now say Karmen killed Hudson because he'd lost millions, and we can't contradict her?'

'Not quite. I can still blame Ryan for the murder. But I need another motive.'

'Like what?'

'I'm working on that. Look on the bright side: we're not going to represent Karmen in the next trial.'

'Why not?'

'We'll be dead. Because everything Mowbray said is true.'

Tess laughed.

It was a tale of childhood resentment. Of sibling ill-feeling that had eventually turned murderous. Tess forced her mind to consider the helpless Susan, trapped in a relationship with gangland Tony, mother to a delinquent son, desperately wanting to believe her daughter was different. But she'd turned out worse. She'd been brilliant, sparkling with initiative, and she'd used it to devastating effect. She'd deceived the world, as she'd deceived her mother. And with those skills of mock innocence, vulnerability and indignation at being misunderstood and judged and rejected, she'd deceived Tess and Benson. And maybe the jury.

'How are you feeling?' said Benson.

'Like I said, fine and dandy. Do you realise, Ryan started planning to frame her when he still had a hangover, immediately after that party? By the time Karmen took over, he'd worked it all out. How he was going to get rid of his rival and his sister, and everything she stood for. The only question was when. And to think, it all comes back to Karmen going to a private school and Ryan being sent to the local comp. Do you think things might have turned out better if he'd gone to Eton? Or was it that nativity play . . . because he'd never been Joseph?'

'Tess, I'm not listening. You need to relax.'

'We got it wrong, Will,' she said, and gulped down the whisky. 'Again and again we got it wrong. But who cares? We've done our job. I reckon Karmen's going to walk.'

'Tess, you're tired. You've had a bad day. It's time to have a good night. Have you got a spare room?'

'Why?'

'Because I'm not leaving you. So if I can't have the spare room, I'll have the sofa. And if I can't have the sofa, I'll kip outside the front door. But you're not staying alone tonight.'

'I'm fine. Honestly.'

'Sure you are. Bed, sofa or street? Which is it?'

Together they made up the bed. Tess cast the sheet, with a flick of her wrists, and together they tucked in the corners, making sure it was tight. Then they struggled with the duvet cover, trying to match the buttons with the holes, only to discover one was missing. They each plumped up a pillow.

And Tess got a towel. And a toothbrush. And some pyjamas, left behind years back by her father. They talked, carelessly, though Tess couldn't properly engage. She was just aware of Benson – his body, his movements, his sounds – as he warded off Mowbray's bloodied ghost.

'Goodnight, Tess,' he said, leaving the door ajar.

Tess lay in the dark, feeling the growing ache of hunger in her body.

The trial was all but over. It had ended – to quote Mowbray – with something of a bang. There was nothing else to be done. Come the morning, Shah would close her case and, since Benson had no intention of calling Karmen to give evidence, speeches would follow. Benson would weave his magic and . . . She gazed into the darkness, straining to hear any sound coming from the spare room; of bare feet touching the carpet, coming closer. But she caught nothing. Not even a sudden, sleepy tug of air, or the whisper of brushed cotton when someone rolls over.

The hunger, painful now, arose from something much deeper than desire, or longing or loneliness, though they were all involved. It came from the abiding fretfulness that had somehow entered through a back door into her life, like a stray cat seeking comfort, and the wretched thing kept sidling around, emerging out of the dark when she least expected it, bright-eyed and trembling. Driven to follow its lead, she swung her legs out of bed. Quietly, she left her room and went towards the door left partly open, her eyes on the thin, dark column beside the jamb, her breathing short and erratic. Reaching it, she stopped. And she stayed there, not daring to move any further, hearing the tick of the grandfather clock yet totally unconscious of the passing of time.

I can't just go in, she thought, with the coolness of sweat inching down her back. If I go in, I stay in. I won't ever come out. I'll have to tell him everything, tonight, now, before I even touch his hand, but will he understand? Will he forgive me? How could he, when I don't understand or forgive myself? How could he be any different?

Without daring to speak for Benson, without summoning whatever he might say, for comfort or condemnation, Tess turned around and retraced her steps, her toes curling into the thick pile of the carpet.

42

That Ryan could be implicated in the murder of Hudson had not been considered by Shah. Or, inevitably, the jury. And not the press, who now focused their commentary on the brother whose potential significance had been left unexplored until Benson had cross-examined Bucklow. None of them – advocate, juror or journalist – knew about the attack on Archie. None of them knew that Benson had been told to throw the trial. But these hidden details had opened Benson's eyes to the possibility of Ryan's involvement, allowing him to exploit anomalies in the evidence. Now Ryan's name was all over the front pages. His name was on the radio. His photograph, blown up and doctored to communicate danger and gangland aggression, peered from newspaper stands and magazine racks. To quote the crime correspondent of *The Times*, it was a paradox. If there was an elephant in the room, it had been Ryan Naylor, only no one had noticed him until Benson had pointed him out.

'I owe you an apology,' said Shah, throwing her copy of the paper on a conference room table. 'I didn't trust you. I thought you were in the pay of the Naylors. I've joined the long queue of people who've treated you badly. I'm sorry.'

She held out her hand. Benson took it, seeing the green cover of a Notice of Additional Evidence in her other hand.

'I'm glad we spoke this morning,' he said.

'Why's that?'

'Because I expect to depart my troubled life before you get to book yourself a decent lunch. Unless, of course, Ryan wants to see if his sister actually goes down, or gets off. Either way, dead today or dead tomorrow, we're reconciled. You're now invited.'

'To what?'

'My funeral.'

Shah didn't laugh. She was staring at the Notice of Additional Evidence.

'I've also come to warn you, Benson.'

'What about?'

'The rest of the trial. Understandably, you probably think Ryan's name is on the jury's lips. And you've made some strong points across the board. I thought they would be clinchers, to be honest. Even after Bucklow cracked, I was worried I couldn't get past them. I'm now confident I can use them against you. And I'm going to do so in a way that will make it look as if you've made a number of grave mistakes. That you are responsible for bringing home a conviction.'

Benson tried to read Shah's expression: she seemed to be worried for him.

'I'm sorry, Benson. I realise that if I win, this could put you in a precarious position with the Naylor family. But I have to put my case in the strongest possible terms. I have to frame my best points in the best way I can. It's my duty. I can't try and protect you.'

'Of course you can't. What are you on about?'

'My last witness. He's solved the problems you gave me. If you seek an adjournment, I'll object. You're the one who asked him to attend.'

Shah handed over the Notice of Additional Evidence along with a revised plan of the crime scene and an updated chronology. Then she left the room, with that quiet walk reserved for cemeteries. Benson scanned the attached deposition, hearing the soft crunch of gravel. Then he called Archie on his mobile. And together they went down to the cells.

'What he saw . . . it cuts both ways,' said Karmen finally. 'You can use this to my advantage.'

Benson gave a soft huff and accused himself. He ought to have spotted this before, when Karmen had immediately understood the tactical implications of seeking an adjournment after Bucklow's statement had been disclosed. Innocent people don't think clearly. They get flustered. They cry. They make stupid mistakes and say things they don't mean, to their lawyers, and in court, and it's the devil's own job to tidy up the mess. But Karmen had been cold, calculated, precise and sure. The drug dealer who'd planned the exploitation of children in care didn't so much have nerves of steel as no nerves at all. There'd been no emotional spillage in either situation. Of guilt for what she'd done or rage at being betrayed. Nothing. She'd just carried on with the performance. A flush of anger rose in Benson's throat.

'Stop treating me like a fool, will you?'

Karmen raised a trembling hand, her eyes widening with absolutely convincing anxiety.

'You've lost faith, haven't you, Mr Benson.'

'I said stop. Really. No more.'

'But I . . .'

'Karmen. You'll know that Ruth Mowbray killed herself yesterday afternoon.'

That development had been only briefly covered by the media. Along with her known connection to the Naylors. Without further explanation, it remained a tantalising detail.

'Why say this, Mr Benson? You know I've had nothing to—'

'What you won't know, Karmen, because we've been able to keep it out of the public domain – for now – is that Miss de Vere was with her at the time she blew her brains out. Mowbray told her everything. About you. And Ryan. And your father. My colleague Mr Congreve was with her. So let's just move forward with a very clear understanding between us.'

Benson couldn't work out if Karmen was holding back a smile, or whether she'd already turned a corner, without feeling, to deal with a new crisis. Perhaps like so many times before, she was appraising the odds, choosing her response. The naïve look had gone, though. A dull glimmer appeared deep within Karmen's unblinking eyes, and for a second Benson felt something very close to fear.

'I can still represent you in this murder trial,' he went on. 'But from here on in—'

'What makes you think I'd want you next time around?'

The question was uttered with icy calm, and quietly. It brought the conference to an end. Or almost. Karmen still had something to say.

'There may not even be a next time. Bucklow might find himself very much alone. And as for Ruth, and what she said to your friend here, and Tess – you call her Tess, don't you? – well, just forget it. She was deranged. About to kill herself. You can't rely on a word she said. And, if you hadn't noticed, it's irrelevant. You want to talk about a clear understanding? Get this: I didn't kill Billy Hudson. I'm innocent of the charge brought against me. You know it. I know you know it. And I expect to walk out of this court a free woman. If I were you, I wouldn't worry about anything else. Do you catch my drift, Will?'

43

'I think that was a threat, Rizla,' said Archie.

'You can't call me that, Archie. Not here. Not outside a bloody courtroom.'

'She's saying, if you don't—'

'I know what she's saying. Frankly, I've got other things on my mind. Like how I ever came to trust her.'

He'd lain awake in Tess's spare bedroom unable to think of anything else. Seduced by the story of a girl who couldn't escape her name, he'd ignored every warning, every signal, every hint that Karmen might not be as simple as she presented herself.

'Do you think she killed Hudson?'

'No, I don't. And I can fight for that.'

'And if you lose?'

'Archie, the threat means nothing. Win or lose, I'm finished. I'm caught between a brother and his sister, and they're both psychopaths.'

With that observation, Benson entered Number 4 Court, thinking of the essayist preoccupied with the subject of death. Michel Eyquem de Montaigne. And, of course, his student: the professor who'd followed his dog along a path, only to witness the aftermath of a murder.

Benson had forgotten all about Professor Cameron. But he'd now turned up, uninvited, to bite him on the backside. In a manner of speaking.

Only a few days ago, asking for him to be called had seemed a smart move. Leafing through the statements the prosecution didn't intend to rely on, Benson had come across an unsigned note, photocopied from the investigation team's phone log. He looked at it again:

Phone call. Keith Cameron. Re. Hudson murder.
18.5.2018
10.00 p.m.
Taking dog for a walk. Monty.
Saw man come through fence.
Path opposite Chiltonian Industrial Estate.
Call back.

No one had called the professor back. The reason was almost certainly because of one line: 'Path opposite Chiltonian Industrial Estate.' *That* path was on the other side of the railway line that ran behind HGT Ltd, some three hundred yards away. It was on the Ordnance Survey map of the area that had no doubt been consulted by the detective who'd evaluated the message. Anyone appearing through *that* fence wouldn't obviously be connected to a crime that had occurred a considerable distance away, and on the other side of the railway tracks. Hence the investigation team had decided not to follow up the call.

But when Benson had visited HGT Ltd, he'd seen another path. One that didn't appear on the prosecution plan or the Ordnance Survey map upon which it was based. *That* path ran directly behind the place where Hudson had been murdered. This side of the tracks. Twenty yards or so from the loading bay. Not knowing of its existence, whoever took the call had added what was intended to be a helpful note: 'opposite Chiltonian Industrial Estate'. Which was, of necessity, true. Only by making that reference, he or she had accidentally removed the man who'd appeared through the fence from the murder investigation.

Benson had hoped, first, that Professor Cameron had been referring to the unmarked path behind HGT Ltd. And second that he'd be able to shed more light on the man who'd escaped the attention of the police. Hence the request that he be called.

However, while the professor had left academia many years ago, he was far from inactive. Upon retirement he and his French wife, Marie-Edith, had founded Soutenons l'Enseigne-ment en Afrique, a charity that had built eleven classrooms in rural Senegal, supporting them with funds for books and equipment. Which is where they'd been at the time of the trial's opening, and until the weekend just gone. On returning home, the professor's wife had drawn his attention to coverage about the Hudson murder. Convinced there'd been some confusion about the two paths, he'd called DCI Panjabi and provided a statement, who'd then emailed it to Shah first thing in the morning.

And now Benson had it in his hands. His original hopes had been amply fulfilled. Unfortunately—

A loud knock broke Benson's rumination, and Mr Justice Garway came onto the bench. He'd read the statement. He'd seen the revised map. He'd studied the updated chronology. He'd been told the witness had been summoned at Benson's insistence.

'Why he wasn't contacted during the investigation, out of an abundance of caution, is a mystery to me. But there we are. Given what Professor Cameron has to say, I think the jury, and indeed myself, would be helped greatly if you could first review the sequence of events prior to the murder.'

'Such is my intention, my lord,' said Shah.

The jury were brought into court. Shah, having distributed the revised map and chronology, said the surprise arrival of a witness once thought to be inconsequential would bring everyone back to the heart of the case, the brutal killing of . . .

Benson barely heard her. He simply stared at the document before him, thinking hard:

R-v-Karmen Naylor
Agreed chronology

05.05.2017	First anonymous call to DAC Oakhurst: the Naylors are working outside of London.
09.05.2018	Second anonymous call to DAC Oakhurst: tip-off: seven days' notice: Bucklow will be transporting drug money on behalf of the Naylors to Heathrow airport.
16.05.2018	**Wednesday.** The defendant organises a meeting with Hudson for Friday evening at 9.00 p.m. Hudson then heads to Manchester to supervise Bucklow and others.
17.05.2018	**Thursday.** Operation Sparrowhawk. Bucklow arrested. £3,000,000 found in three suitcases.
18.05.2018	**Friday: the day of the meeting and the day of the murder:**
	8.14 p.m. Hudson arrives at HGT Ltd. Turns of CCTV cameras.
	8.58 p.m. The defendant arrives at HGT Ltd.
	9.17 p.m. The defendant leaves HGT Ltd. The defendant is with William Hudson for approximately 15 minutes.
	9.25 p.m. Professor Cameron enters the path between HGT Ltd and the railway tracks.
21.05.2018	**Monday.** Greg Kilgour discovers the crime scene.

'In short, ladies and gentlemen,' said Shah, 'the evidence you are about to hear relates to events taking place at HGT Ltd some five or so minutes after the defendant had left the premises. Minutes after we, the prosecution, say the murder had taken place. Minutes lost to your scrutiny, which, thankfully, have now been recovered. My lord, I call Professor K. C. Cameron.'

44

On the evening of Friday the 18th of May, Professor Cameron had taken his dog Monty out for a walk. These walks were habitual. He always left the house at the same time and he always took the same route. He'd done it for thirty years. He'd even counted the steps. Which is why he knew with precision that he'd reached the path behind HGT Ltd at roughly 9.25 p.m.

'I dropped Monty's lead and, being curious and disobedient, he went down the path to fool around among the trees.'

'You followed him?'

'I did.'

'How far along the path did you walk?'

'Twenty yards or so. I was directly behind HGT Ltd.'

'How would you describe the level of visibility?'

'Night had fallen. But I had a torch. Which I used.'

'And what did you see?'

'I was flashing the light into the trees on my right while walking, calling for Monty, but then I brought the beam in front of me to check where I was going, and there, in the middle of the path, was a motorbike, with the rider wearing a helmet with the visor down. Scared the living daylights out of me.'

'And then?'

'And then I heard sounds coming from the trees. A thud, a bark and a stumble. Immediately afterwards someone appeared moving quickly, chased by Monty. The motorbike fired up, this individual jumped on the back and, *whoof*, they were off. With Monty in hot pursuit.'

'Let's call the motorbike rider A and the person who appeared through the trees B. What can you tell us about A?'

'He was a man.'

'How do you know?'

'There was a whiff of aftershave. But that is by the by. As he pulled away, he swore at Monty in remarkably crude terms. It was a man's voice. Do you want to know what he said?'

'I don't think that will be necessary. How was he dressed?'

'He was wearing one of those tight black padded jackets that bike riders often wear, zipped or buttoned right up to the throat. Black trousers and boots. And, of course, the helmet. That, too, was black. And so was the bike. I saw his hands, and the skin was very dark. I'd say black, though that is not the most helpful of terms when it comes to a description of someone's complexion.'

'And now B?'

'I can't tell you if B was a man or a woman. He or she was wearing dark trousers and a dark jacket and a dark balaclava. Slung over their shoulder was a bag. I stumbled backwards, off the path, and the torchlight swung across his or her face, and I saw what I think was pale skin around an eye. I appreciate "pale" is no more helpful than black, or indeed white, but that's what I see in my mind's eye.'

'Can you help us with the direction B came from?'

'Certainly. HGT Ltd. My guess is that he or she jumped over the wall and landed on or near Monty.'

'Are you able to share any other impressions of what you witnessed?'

'Yes. Something difficult to pinpoint, but I am sure nonetheless. I sensed the whole interaction had been planned. And rehearsed. A was waiting for B, and B was relying on A; they were a team, and when A arrived, B knew what to do. They were off. No instructions. No hesitation. No fooling around. I suspect Monty almost foiled them. Hence the expletives.'

Blinded by the sudden glare of the motorbike headlight as it burst into life, the professor had turned aside, hands raised.

When he'd lowered them, he'd looked around, following the beam from his torch. He was alone. The silence left behind by the roar of the engine grew stronger. The sound of occasional traffic became noticeable. Moments later, Monty returned, trotting happily as if a job had been well done.

'Remain there, please, Professor Cameron,' said Shah. 'My learned friend Mr Benson will have some questions for you.'

45

Tess felt angry with Benson. He hadn't come to her bedroom. He hadn't pushed his way into her life demanding answers. He hadn't even been in the house when she'd woken up the next morning. She'd imagined coffee together, at least. A shared embarrassment over nothing, because nothing had happened. A stilted conversation. But no. He'd got up, stripped the bed and buggered off. She was angry at her own contradictory behaviour. She was angry she'd barely slept while he'd probably had a good night's sleep.

Thinking the Naylor trial was all but over, Tess went in to Coker & Dale and made herself that cup of coffee. But then, just as she brought it to her lips, her mobile rang. It was Archie:

'Get your arse down here.'

'Why?'

'Remember the bloke with a dog named after Field Marshal Montgomery?'

'No, Archie, it was—'

'Whatever. He's back from Senegal. He's about to give evidence. You need to hear it.'

Tess was seated beside Archie in Number 4 Court before the untouched coffee could have cooled down. And she listened

Fatal Proof

to Professor Cameron with something akin to astonishment, not so much at what was said as at her own entrenched gullibility. If she'd been taken for a ride by Karmen Naylor, the same could be said of Nina and Ekene Osabede. They, too, had played upon Tess's readiness to think that people who commit serious crimes tend to look like they're the sort of people who commit serious crimes. Nice people look nice. Villains have twisted faces. For a solicitor of her experience, it was lamentable. Her only consolation was that Benson had been fooled too. As Shah had sat down, Benson remained seated. There were no notes on his pad. No guidelines for his cross-examination. No anxious doodles. Just a blank page. Abruptly, he stood up, with a flap from his gown.

'In a way, you're a specialist in evidence?'

'In a way, yes.'

'Would you accept that documentary records made shortly after an event, and about that event, are more likely to be accurate – in terms of eyewitness detail – than those prepared much later?'

'Generally speaking, yes. Literature contemporaneous to an event is likely to contain details that might otherwise be lost with the passage of time.'

'Thank you. Colours.'

'Pardon?'

'Colours. I'm struck that your evidence is literally devoid of any colour. It is, of necessity, an account in black and white.'

'Because I saw no colours. That said, I made no mention of white.'

'We'll return to that, Professor Cameron. Your torch.'

'What about my torch?'

'Do you still have it?'

'No.'

'Why not?'

'It went the way it came. I found it . . . and then I lost it.'

'After finding it, did you ever replace the battery or batteries?'

'No.'

'Was the torch large or small?'

'Small.'

'How small?'

'The size of a Mars bar.'

'The beam. Was it wide or narrowly focused?'

'Wide.'

'How wide?'

'About a yard or so.'

'Sharp or diffused on the edges?'

'Diffused, but bright enough in the middle to illuminate what I saw.'

'Strong or weak, overall?'

'Weakish.'

Benson placed his hands behind his back. Tess watched the fingers lock and squeeze.

'You saw a black motorbike. On the black motorbike was a black man dressed in black: black trousers, black jacket and black boots . . . wearing a black helmet?'

'Yes.'

'Do you accept that the person who came running out of the trees – the person you describe as wearing dark clothing – might also have been dressed in black?'

'Given the tonal shades that meet the description, yes, I would.'

'So this person could have worn black trousers, black shoes, a black jacket and a black balaclava?'

'Yes. It's possible.'

'Do you accept that this person could have been a woman?'

'I do.'

'The black balaclava. How large were the holes around the eyes?'

'I'd say about four centimetres.'

'Circles or ovals?'

'I can't recall. But I grasp the direction of your questions, Mr Benson, and let me help you, and the court, immediately. Assuming an average eye is oval and three centimetres or so in length, I accept that the skin I saw was limited to a very small area indeed . . . perhaps no more than a centimetre between the eyelids and the edge of the material.'

'It was a fleeting glance?'

'Yes.'

'Using a weakish torch?'

'That was bright enough to illuminate what I saw.'

Benson's hands dropped to his sides. He was silent, gathering in his hopes. The cross-examination had reached that pivotal moment which can win or lose a case, for it is upon such banal questions, and their answers, that a murder conviction can turn. People had been executed in this very building on the strength of something seen in the half-light.

'We're agreed, Professor Cameron, about the importance of contemporaneous records?'

'We are.'

'When you got home that night, did you make a note of what you'd seen?'

'No. I called the police.'

'Did you make a note over the following days?'

'I saw no point.'

'May I ask why?'

'I was waiting for the police to get back in touch with me. When they didn't, I assumed what I'd seen was of no importance.'

'When did you prepare this witness statement?'

'Yesterday.'

'Eighteen months after the event in question?'

'That's right.'

'So everything you've said is drawn from what you see –
and I quote you – "in my mind's eye"?'

'It is. Which is a great pity.'

'Why?'

'If the police had interviewed me at the time, I might
have remembered more. I may have remembered differently.
Who knows?'

'This is my concern, Professor, because on almost every
particular you and I are agreed. I accept these two individuals had rehearsed what they were doing. I accept they were
both dressed in dark clothing. I accept the motorbike rider
was a black man. I will argue in due course that his associate
was undoubtedly a woman – something you are prepared
to accept. But this is where our unanimity ends. I will also
argue that this woman was black. Your evidence that you
thought you saw pale skin could lead the jury to conclude
that person was white. Do you think that would be pushing
your evidence too far?'

'I don't know. I saw what I think was pale skin.'

'Do you accept this woman could have been black?'

'I don't know. I saw what I think was pale skin.'

Tess's body had become tense. There was nothing more
Benson could ask. But this point was absolutely vital for
the argument Benson was constructing. Everyone in court
knew he was referring to the Osabedes. And they knew
that to bring home the identification, he needed not only
a man and woman, he needed both of them to be black,
for sure. Not just one of them. Professor Cameron cleared
his throat.

'I'm sorry, Mr Benson,' he said reflectively. 'I appreciate
your predicament. The mind's eye is all I have. I'm sure about
what I thought. I can only hope that what I thought is what
I saw.'

46

Shah closed her case, and since Benson didn't propose to call any witnesses, Mr Justice Garway invited Shah to address the jury. She closed a file on the wooden stand used by QCs to elevate their papers; she closed her blue notebook; she stepped slightly to one side, as if to leave behind any conflict between the witnesses, any confusion in what they'd said, any contest with Benson. Her expression was benign.

'Ladies and gentlemen, I've only ever told you what I was sure about. Do you recall my opening speech? I confessed that I had no idea why Karmen Naylor had killed William Hudson. I only told you that she must have done it. There was no other explanation. The forensic evidence alone condemned her. But, humanly speaking, that was an unsatisfactory state of affairs. The family of a murdered man, even if he was a criminal, need an explanation. An answer to the question "Why?" And so I told you it was my hope that the defendant would take this last opportunity to explain herself; to give some closure to Lisa Hudson, who'd warned her son many years ago that if he ever let down the Naylors, they'd kill him. I could only assume that he had let them down. Because a member of the Naylor family had killed him. What he'd done to deserve such a cruel fate was outside my knowledge. So I told you nothing.'

Shah was speaking quietly, which had brought a tense hush to the room. All eyes were upon her. She was in total command.

'I have tried to be fair to the defendant. I never tried to exploit the blood link she shares with her father. I made no reference to the murder of Jim "the Kite" Fitzgerald. I did not seek to have admitted the police intelligence report about the structure and activities of the Naylor Family Crime Group. You only know of these things because Mr Benson chose to bring them to your attention, believing that by so doing he was advancing the best interests of his client. Ultimately, I am grateful for his decision. But no one can say I tried to smear this defendant with the crimes of her family. I wanted you to judge her on the evidence, and nothing more.'

Benson might have begun to sweat with discomfort, but he had to hand it to Shah. She'd played her hand perfectly. This was a speech she'd prepared before the first witness had even entered the courtroom. She'd gambled on Bucklow cracking during the trial, and he had done. And she'd been gifted the evidence of Professor Cameron. This was going to be one of those cases where everything had come together.

'The evidence phase of the trial is now over,' Shah said. 'Karmen Naylor refused to speak to you. She refused to give an explanation to anyone – which is her right, as it is my duty to prove what I have alleged – which means that I could have been standing here still sharing your confusion as to why an itinerant waitress might have murdered a gangland enforcer. I am no longer confused. I imagine you aren't either. For this, I must express my gratitude to two people.'

The first, she said, was Mr Bucklow. Thanks to him, the jury now knew that Karmen Naylor was no waitress. She was no willing exile from the crime family into which she'd been born. She'd been the architect of a drug distribution scheme based on the abuse of children. Children with problems. Children in care. Children with drug habits of their own. The jury now knew that she was utterly ruthless. They knew – from the mouth of Mr Hudson himself, talking to Mr Bucklow – that if anything ever went wrong on the operational front, the penalty was death. It was a disclosure uncannily reminiscent of Lisa Hudson's warning to her son on his eighteenth birthday.

'I'm equally grateful to someone else, ladies and gentlemen. And that is my learned friend Mr Benson. I invite you to recall his skilful cross-examinations of three expert witnesses. He extracted three vital pieces of information. First, from Dr Sengupta: this was a killing that must have been carried out by a professional. Second, from Dr Merrin: that the chances of this defendant – understood to be a waitress without experience of violent confrontations – carrying out such a vicious attack and escaping in the short time available were virtually nil. And finally, Dr Tupton: that the killer, understood to be this defendant, probably needed help in moving Mr Hudson's body.'

From the corner of his eye, Benson could see the nods of the jurors. Shah was drawing them in, one by one.

'I'm grateful to Mr Benson for another reason,' continued Shah. 'Relying simply on a file note, he insisted on Professor Cameron being called as a witness. The police had failed to appreciate his significance. Those who instruct me had failed to appreciate his significance. I had failed to appreciate his significance. But he has answered all our remaining questions. I can now tell you what happened on the night of Friday the eighteenth of May 2018.'

William 'Billy' Hudson had returned to London from Manchester, trying to control his panic. He'd failed to manage a money-laundering operation. Three million pounds had been lost. A key player had been arrested. Everything Karmen Naylor had built during her eight-year absence from London was at risk of collapsing. Millions more would be lost. When Mr Hudson made his way to HGT Ltd he must have known that his days were numbered, as surely as his name was in the online calendar. The only question was which one had been chosen for the end of his life. Would it be that Friday evening? He seems to have thought so, because he rang his mother to say goodbye. He rang her to confess she'd been right all along.

'Karmen Naylor told the police she met Mr Hudson in the reception area. The troubled waitress with dreams of selling tyres through a business owned by her father had resolved to ask a thug to move aside. Give her some space. So that she and the terrified Kilgours could try and rival Kwik Fit. It is a laughable, desperate and unconvincing lie. Except for the fact that she was troubled. And resolved. Because shortly after eight fifty-eight p.m. she strode across the workshop, picked up a twenty-three-millimetre extending wrench and mounted the stairs that led to William Hudson's office. He came out to greet her. As he turned around, she struck him on the head with a glancing blow of such force that hair, flesh and blood became embedded in the wooden doorframe. He staggered across the room and collapsed. Being immobilised, he was powerless to resist what this defendant had planned for him. One can only hope that he'd lost consciousness.'

Shah took a long breath.

'This defendant didn't act alone. We know that now. Someone was there to help her. Someone who entered the building earlier in the evening, once the CCTV cameras had been turned off. Someone who waited until he was needed. This is the person Professor Cameron saw emerging through the trees. This is the individual – I'd say a man, not a woman – who helped the defendant move the body. A Naylor foot soldier, I suggest. And a protector, if things hadn't gone to plan. He left the premises by a different route to avoid any possible association with the defendant. In his shoulder bag was the wrench and the knife, which have never been found. Another accomplice was waiting on a motorbike. Together they made their escape. At much the same time, of course, the defendant drove off, like a bat out of hell . . . her mind not so much on the horror of what she'd just done, as on the sea.'

Shah took another ponderous breath; when she next addressed the jury, her tone rose fractionally.

'Mr Benson wants you to believe that this murder mimicked the execution of Jim "the Kite" Fitzgerald. He's pointed a finger at the aggrieved Ronsons, the bitter Kilgours, the abused Osabedes, and even his client's brother, the angry, side-lined Ryan. He can't make his mind up. He's going to tell you in a moment that he doesn't have to. He's simply indicating that these others wanted Billy Hudson dead. Well, I'll concede something to Mr Benson right now. I agree. Unfortunately, that won't help him. Because the first three had no reason to frame Karmen Naylor. And as for the fourth, her brother . . . why frame her? If he hated her that much, why not kill her? Why such a palaver? Isn't all a bit too . . . involved?'

Benson caught some more nods.

'I'll finish on what I believe is my best point,' said Shah. 'Mr Benson's argument rests upon a ludicrous premise. He wants you to believe that his client is nothing other than a humble waitress . . . with a first-class degree in business finance and management. I'm afraid it's another laughable, desperate and unconvincing proposition. You can forget all about the people he's named, ladies and gentlemen. And you can forget about "the Kite". The reason Karmen Naylor cut William Hudson's throat and dumped his body at sea is because that is how the Naylors deal with their enemies. We know that from paragraph seven of the police intelligence report, obtained at the request of my learned friend. It's a family tradition.'

Shah turned to face the dock; and then, after a moment of reflection, she sat down.

47

The court rose for lunch with Benson due to give his speech at 2 p.m. Tess's anger had been displaced by anxiety. There'd been a weight to Shah's phrases, a heaviness to her tone, a bulk to her arguments. Karmen Naylor was guilty. No other explanation was possible. How was Benson going to reply? Without a word, he went to the robing room. Shortly afterwards, she saw him leave the building, his hands patting his pockets, a cigarette in his mouth. Having no appetite, she watched Archie work his way through a line of pasties at Ye Olde London, and then returned to court at 1.30 p.m. hoping to catch Benson. But he was nowhere to be seen. Back on the solicitors' bench, she kept checking her watch. Archie turned up, eventually, but on his own. And then, at 1.59 p.m., her nerves raw with anticipation, he came through the door, just as Mr Justice Garway came onto the bench. There was something electric in his manner, a brusqueness to his movements.

'We've all made a mistake, ladies and gentlemen,' said Benson.

The surge of power had been brought under control. He was calm.

'I've made a mistake, Miss Shah has made a mistake, the police have made a mistake, the Crown Prosecution Service has made a mistake. We've all been concerned about how this defendant could have killed William Hudson and removed his body within fifteen minutes. I said, by character, she couldn't have done it; I said, physically, she'd have needed help. My learned friend, grateful to all and sundry, and especially to me, now rejoices. Because Mr Bucklow turns up and says she had the character, and Professor Cameron turns up and says he saw the help. What's more, we now know the why. Millions of Naylor pounds had slipped through Mr Hudson's fingers. Problem solved. Case closed. Off with her head. If you swallow all that, well, I'm afraid to say you, too, are making a mistake. Because that's not what happened. William Hudson wasn't killed between eight fifty-eight p.m. and nine sixteen p.m. He was alive and well. Probably laughing – like Miss Shah – at my client's hopeless dreams.'

The mistake, said Benson, was this: to think Mr Hudson was the victim of two attacks carried out by the same person.

'He wasn't. There were two attacks carried out by different people for different reasons at different times. We've been fooled by someone very clever into thinking this was a single event.'

Benson said he'd return to the identity of that individual in due course. For now, he wanted the jury to think of someone else. In May 2017 Billy Hudson didn't simply drop his girl-friend. He didn't simply deny being the father of her child. He hit her.

'We're talking about Nina Osabede, ladies and gentlemen. Who refused to speak to the police after the murder. A year earlier, her brother had gone to HGT Ltd on his motorbike and told Mr Hudson he was a dead man. Mr Hudson didn't take him seriously. He didn't take Nina seriously. He should have done.'

Call it imagination, but Tess felt the lights dim and she had the sense of an empty workshop and the heavy smell of grease and rubber and machinery.

'My guess is that Billy Hudson was taken aback when he saw Nina,' said Benson. 'He'd just left Karmen, he came out of the reception area, and there she was, the woman who claimed he was the father of her child. Standing by the tool cabinet, her hands behind her back. What did he say? I don't know. What did she say? I don't know. What did he do? He went up the stairs heading back to his office, hearing Nina's steps behind him. My guess is that he treated her with contempt. Maybe he offered her a few quid. Of this I'm convinced: he'd no idea what Nina had decided to do. When he reached the doorway, she hit him with all her strength, using that wheel wrench. Reeling from a depressed fracture to the skull, Billy Hudson stumbled and fell to the floor, vomiting . . . but with his heart still beating hard.'

This was a well-prepared attack, said Benson. He couldn't prove it, but there must have been some communication between Nina and the embittered Kilgours. Pete Kilgour in particular, who'd left the tool cabinet open. Pete Kilgour, who'd known that Billy Hudson planned to meet Karmen Naylor on that fateful evening. Pete Kilgour, who'd witnessed the rage of her brother and found an ally against the Naylors. Pete Kilgour, who decided to head off to Scotland at the opening of the trial.

'Nina didn't hang around,' resumed Benson. 'She put the wrench in a shoulder bag. She put on a black mask, because she couldn't risk being identified, and she left HGT Ltd. She clambered onto the bins – please look at photograph seventeen – and then dropped onto the other side of the wall, where, a few yards away, Ekene was waiting on his motorbike. Professor Cameron was right, this was a rehearsed manoeuvre. There was no fooling around. No need to talk. Except to ward off that dog who almost wrecked a plan hatched the day Billy Hudson had dared hit Nina Osabede. So ended the first attack, with Billy Hudson left lying defenceless on the floor.'

Benson took a sip of water. The imagined shadows remained in the courtroom. Tess was still there, at HGT Ltd, observing, it seemed, the arrival of someone else.

'Ladies and gentlemen, I am in the fortunate position of not having to decide whether Steven Bucklow can be trusted. That's your decision. My learned friend relies upon him entirely to explain why my client killed Mr Hudson. I intend to rely on him for two details reportedly coming from the mouth of Mr Hudson. First, Ryan Naylor hated his sister. And second, Ryan Naylor hated Billy Hudson. With respect, ladies and gentlemen, that's all you need to know. The northern operation of the Naylors? The money-laundering scheme? Who was the person behind it all . . . Ryan or

Karmen? I never thought I'd say this, but you can put all that to one side. All you need is this double hatred, hatched amongst children, and one other fact which you may have forgotten, until Miss Shah reminded you of it a few moments ago – and for that, I am very grateful.'

The online calendar, said Benson. A calendar that was consulted by members of the Naylor family.

'Ryan knew that his hated sister would be seeing the hated Billy Hudson at nine p.m. on Friday the eighteenth of May 2018. He knew they'd be alone. He knew this had never happened before and he knew it might never happen again. And so he, too, went to HGT Ltd. With a crew. And a knife. Because this was his chance to deal with Hudson and blame his sister. He knew the CCTV system would have been turned off. And he knew his name wasn't in the calendar. If he followed the usual protocols, no one would know he'd been on the premises. When he got there, of course, he found Billy Hudson lying on the floor. Injured. Alive. And helpless. Now began the second attack.'

Tess suppressed a smile; Benson had done it again.

'Miss Shah wants you to forget about the murder of the Kite. I want you to remember every detail. So I don't have to repeat myself. Because what then happened to Mr Hudson was central to Ryan Naylor's plan. He killed him, as my learned friend might say, in the manner reserved for enemies of the family.'

Assisted in all probably by the very people who'd got rid of the Kite, Ryan Naylor then got rid of Billy Hudson, leaving that trail of Smarties to make it look as though his sister had bungled the cover-up. She'd tried to make it look as though the Ronsons had got their own back, but she'd been caught by the science. Miss Shah thinks that's a palaver. Well, Benson would make an admission, too. He agreed. But if you're going to frame Tony Naylor's daughter, you'd better cover your tracks. And how better than to make it look as though the Ronsons might be involved?

'Like Miss Shah, I've saved my best point until last,' Benson said. 'With respect to the allegations made by Mr Bucklow against my client, they could hardly be more serious. I doubt if you can forget them. For my part, you can accept what you like. Credit everything he said as true, if that is where your conscience leads you. Condemn her as the architect of a scheme from hell. But be assured of this: convict my client for the murder of Billy Hudson and you'll be doing Ryan Naylor a favour.'

48

Mr Justice Mowbray began his summing up of the evidence the next morning. Throughout the scrupulously fair present-ation, Tess fought off a nagging question: why hadn't Benson given her a ring the night before, to discuss the impact, strong or weak, of his speech? It's what they'd always done. Emboldened by two gins, she'd gone to *The Wooden Doll*, but Benson hadn't been there. So she'd gone to Congreve's, only to find the door locked and lights out. She'd made her way home to finish the bottle. And now she was watching him dutifully taking notes, oblivious to her existence, simply alert for any judicial error that might give grounds for an appeal if Karmen was convicted. Towards 4 p.m. the judge moved on to giving directions as to the law, admonishing the jury to remember that Karmen Naylor was only charged with the murder of William Hudson. The evidence of Mr Bucklow was only relevant if it helped them with respect to motive, otherwise they were to remove what he'd said from their consideration. He then adjourned the case until the following morning.

Again, Tess waited throughout the evening for some kind of contact from Benson; and again, none was forthcoming. She tried calling Sally, but she didn't pick up, which led to more gin. All at once Tess thought of her mother. Of her confession. And she thought of her father. And his secret. And her own secret. And the ground between them that contained the dead.

The next day, Tess turned up at court with a ringing headache, hating the fleeting consolations of alcohol. Childishly, she'd intended to cold-shoulder Benson, but once the jury had been sent out to begin their deliberations he grabbed her arm:

'You really helped me, Tess.'

'How? What did I do?'

'That joke about Saint Joseph. And Eton. It's a good one.'

'You said you weren't listening.'

'Well, I was. And it was the key to finding Ryan's motivation. I thanked Shah, but I should have thanked you. Now let's go and see Karmen.'

'I didn't listen to your speech, Mr Benson,' she said quietly.

The conference room near the cells felt more cramped than usual. And Karmen seemed immense. Not physically, but in terms of presence. She filled the room with animal authority.

'I tried, don't get me wrong, but Miss Shah had me' – Karmen held out her open palm – 'right there. I couldn't stop listening. The jury was nodding . . . and, do you know what, I was, too. But thankfully no one was looking.'

'Karmen, the jury are now—'

'I know exactly what the jury are doing. Let me tell you what I am doing. I'm asking myself whether you planned all this: you showing the killer needed help, asking for the professor. You knew what he'd seen – you'd been to HGT Ltd, you knew there was a path that ran behind the back wall. And you knew that evidence of someone coming over that wall, at ten twentyish, would wreck your fifteen-minute argument. You see, Will, I'm weighing up whether you've tried to throw this trial. I'm wondering if you're Ryan's man.'

Tess had represented many professional criminals before. She'd sat in confined spaces and listened to their nonsense and lies. But Karmen was disturbingly different from them all. She had the supreme detachment of the insane. Expressionless, she was examining Benson as if he were a fly, one of his wings trapped between her delicate fingers.

'Karmen, there's something you need to know,' said Benson.

'Really?'

'Yes. I'm not scared of you. At all. I belong to that peculiar class of people who've died in this life and come back, not caring. So – to be honest with you – I wouldn't bother with the low voice and the staring. It has no effect. Now, I appreciate that's all part of the Naylor brand, and when this case is over—'

'I'd better walk free.'

'Or else? What? You'll cut my throat and dump me in the Thames Estuary?'

'The Thames Estuary is tidal. I can think of better places.'

'I've done my best for you, Karmen. Your brother is probably going to kill me. He'll probably go for Miss de Vere and my clerk, too. But we accept that as the price for defending you. For that reason, I've a favour to ask.'

Karmen had been transformed in Tess's eyes. The power and size had been burned away, like cellophane thrown on a fire. And while she remained dangerous, and mad, she was pinched and her skin was covered in blotches of humiliation. Her bloodless lips twitched.

'You want a favour from me?'

'Yes. You heard my speech. Every word of it. You know what I alleged against Ryan. In return, spare them.'

'Spare who?'

'The Kilgours. The Osabedes. Leave them alone. They had nothing to do with you being framed. That was Ryan's game, and Ryan's alone.'

Tess sat with Benson outside Number 4 Court, waiting for the jury to make a decision. They both stared straight ahead. Archie turned up and sat between them, working on a bumper book of puzzles. He kept asking for help but Benson and Tess ignored him. So he started doodling, like Ruth Mowbray, before she'd reached for Hudson's gun. With a huff and a groan, they went to the Crown and Thistle for lunch and talked about sea turtles. Then, having barely eaten, they went back to Number 4 Court, once more seated three in a row. Towards 5 p.m., after six hours of quite awful tension, an usher came onto the concourse just as a voice sounded from the speaker system. They shared the one announcement. The jury in *R-v-Naylor* had reached a verdict.

49

Benson hadn't noticed, but Ryan Naylor was in the public gallery. Whether he'd been there throughout his speech, he didn't know; what was for sure was that he was there when the jury came back into court. He was leaning on the brass rail, chin on his hands, staring at Benson. He'd come without the muscle. He'd come, presumably, to send Benson an early message: that he might be meeting the muscle shortly.

When Mr Justice Garway was settled on the bench the court clerk rose and turned to face the jury. Benson's mind was racing. The jurors must have seen Ryan, too. Do I stand now and get

Ryan thrown out on the grounds of potential intimidation or
do I leave him there, to hear the verdict? Benson didn't know
what to do . . . and then it was too late to act. The jury foreman
had stood up, ready to respond to the clerk's questions.

'Have you reached a verdict upon which you are all agreed?
Please answer "Yes" or "No".'

'Yes.'

'Do you find the defendant guilty or not guilty of the murder
of William Hudson?'

Benson focused on the woman he'd identified at the outset
of the trial: the middle-aged black woman wearing a chic
blue leather jacket. Benson had guessed, correctly, that she'd
be elected foreman. Today she was wearing a cream silk blouse
and a pair of brown trousers. She didn't look at the clerk.
She didn't look at the judge. She didn't look at Benson or
Shah. And she didn't look at the defendant. Her eyes were
raised with contempt towards the public gallery.

'Not guilty,' she said, separating each word to give it weight
and value.

There was an immediate stunned hush, followed by rustling
and muttering and the clatter of computer keyboards and then
a hum of voices, rising, with a rebuke from the judge and movement among the clerks, around the court and in the public
gallery, but Benson was concentrating on the jury foreman. She'd
shifted her attention to the dock and was looking at Karmen in
the same way she'd looked at her brother. Suddenly, she swung
a very different gaze onto Benson. Its purpose was unequivocal.
She was telling him she'd understood his ordeal; that she
respected him; and that . . . She turned to the judge, who was
addressing the jury, thanking them for their service. It was the
briefest of connections. The golden, unexpected moment of
solidarity – the first he'd ever received from a juror – was over.

* * *

When the court had cleared, Benson gathered his papers and pens. Turning to leave, he walked straight into Shah.

'An exceptional win, Benson. You persuaded me, never mind the jury. I hope never to face you in court again. Lunch, however, is a different matter. Might I call you? I'll be paying.'

'On that basis, I insist.'

Pushing open the courtroom door, with Tess at his side, Benson found DCI Panjabi waiting for him.

'I'd like to congratulate you, Mr Benson,' she said, extending her hand. 'And apologise. For the shortcomings of the investigation. We've all learned something these past few days. Especially me.'

Benson couldn't help but think of a sportsman who'd won a vitally important match on a technicality, shaking the hands of the great and good on his way to pick up some kind of trophy. A large silver cup, with shields around the base engraved with the names of Hudson's victims who'd never get justice. At least the harm he'd caused had ended, thank God. Benson just didn't like it ending in this way, with him raising up a prize for all to see, especially Karmen.

'Will you be going after the Osabedes?' he said to Panjabi.

'There's no evidence against them. Just your theory, which is surmise. We can't prove they went to HGT Ltd. We can't prove they were the couple on the motorcycle. We can't prove anything, except that one of them made a threat.'

'And so . . . will you be going after the Osabedes?'

'No. Case closed. There's no point.'

'Can I tell them that, off the record?'

'Tell them on the record.'

After more words of apology and praise, Benson made for the cells, ignoring Tess who was quietly singing 'Oh Mr Benson, Mr Benson, Mr Benson, aren't you wonderful'. She was still humming the annoying tune when they reached the tatty booth where Karmen stood, filling out the paperwork to collect her belongings. Tossing the pen through an opening in the reinforced glass panel, she turned around and said:

'I've thought about what you said.'

'Thank you.'

'Tell Kilgour it's Christmas. They can have their business back.'

'I thought that was Ryan's call. He's sold it. The place is earmarked for demolition.'

'Make some enquiries.'

'Okay. What about the Osabedes?'

'Tell them they're lucky.'

'I will.'

'And as for you' – there'd been no eye contact until now, but for a few seconds she looked directly at Benson; then she walked away and pushed open the door that led to freedom – 'I've done you a favour.'

A favour? *Done* a favour?

Karmen had only just been acquitted. She couldn't have done anything herself. She had to have given orders. Something was yet to happen. No longer performing, she'd spoken with a peculiarly unnerving flatness, the kind ordinary people use to observe a banality. Like rain in Manchester. Or the cost of a bus ticket. Benson and Tess sat in the Gutting Room describing her manner to Archie and Molly. And, together, they discussed the kind of favour Karmen Naylor might have done for Benson. A favour that would also serve her best interests – that much could be inferred from her graciousness to the Kilgours and the Osabedes, because going after either family would not have been a smart move, given the attention it would bring upon her, and when she had yet to face in court the allegations made by Bucklow. So what could she have done, or ordered to be done, for Benson that met her own needs? They all had a good idea. In fact, they all had the same idea. And in having it, they shared a sort of complicity in what they thought might unfold.

Consequently, there was no inclination to celebrate. There was no hooch from the jerrycan. No cake. They sat uncomfortably together, strangely expectant. Benson, feet up on his desk, hands knitted, couldn't expel an image from his mind: the fizz of a bomb, seen in one of those cartoons where the red and yellow and orange sparkle eats the long black fuse, heading ineluctably towards some ball of explosive beneath the wicker chair of someone reading a book or watching television or sipping a pina colada. Unsuspecting, they think they're in control of life. Sure, there are problems; but none they can't handle. And then, all of a sudden, BANG! All that's left is a pair of sunglasses and a bent straw.

At 10 p.m., after finishing off three of Archie's word puzzles, Tess turned on the news. The presenter didn't even begin with the outcome of the Hither Green Butcher trial. They cut to the chase: Ryan Naylor had been reported missing. A pool of blood, and a tongue, had been found on the floor of a gaming hall in Bermondsey understood to be the centre of his operations. Police had attended the premises after an anonymous tip-off to Deputy Assistant Commissioner Desmond Oakhurst, communicated through Crimestoppers. Facing the cameras, Karmen Naylor, in tears, had demanded swift action by the Metropolitan Police. She'd insisted they bring in divers to search the Thames Estuary.

'Yes, we had our differences,' she told an interviewer. 'But he was my big brother. No one will ever replace him.'

PART FIVE

freedom (n) **1** a memory worth living for. **2** a condition worth dying for. (You choose – *ed.*)

Saturday 20th March 2010

Ennismore Gardens Mews
Knightsbridge, London

Tess came downstairs thinking about Peter, who was still deeply asleep, and would remain asleep at least until lunchtime. Her uncertainty about their relationship had deepened. Still drawn to his brilliance and irreverence, she couldn't shake off the dismay she'd felt at his attitude to the Lomax Archive; his easy acceptance that victims must pay the price for peace. He didn't seem to experience rage, disillusionment or moral indignation. And now Tess was wondering if he had a moral code at all. She was fairly sure he was seeing other women. That she was one of many, and—

On the carpet by the front door was a large manila envelope. There was no stamp. No address. Just Tess's name. It had been hand-delivered. She opened it and drew out a letter:

19th March 2010

Dear Miss de Vere,
Brian died yesterday. We were married thirty-three years. Throughout most of that time he was traumatised by what he'd done in the army. I begged him to speak out.

I told him this was the only way he'd ever feel better again. Mr Jones, our solicitor, told us the case was too big for him. So we got in touch with Julia Hollington. Brian planned to tell you everything. When you came to our house, he changed his mind. When he went to get the files in the kitchen, he took one out of the box. The most important one. He didn't want you to see it. But I do. Here it is.

I'll respect Brian's wishes as far as I can. If you do nothing, I'll do nothing. Neither, of course, will Mr Jones.

Yours sincerely,

Brenda Lomax

Mrs Lomax had put the envelope through her door during the night. A day after her husband had died. Sick with apprehension, Tess sat at her kitchen table and took out the file.

Inside was a sheaf of papers. The first page was headed THE BLOOD BROTHERS. *Beneath the title were the names of three soldiers, giving their rank and serial number. The bottom of the page contained a sworn declaration, witnessed by Mr Jones, that the above-mentioned personnel had been members of a self-named secret death squad who'd operated in tandem with three members of the Information Management Detachment, calling themselves the Blind Eyes. The deponent was Sergeant Brian Lomax.*

The next page was entitled THE BLIND EYES. *Beneath the title were three names, each with a rank and serial number. Alongside, in capital letters, were the codenames. Towards the middle of the page was another sworn and witnessed declaration: that the above-mentioned personnel had been responsible for the targeting of individuals for assassination by the Blood Brothers. In this capacity, the said Blind Eyes had identified ten individuals who had all been subsequently shot. Their names were . . .*

Tess stopped reading. She flicked through the remaining pages, unable to process the minutiae. It was all there. Everything you'd need to set in motion the wheels of justice. In her hands was the key to the prosecutions and civil actions Julia Hollington had anticipated. The evidence required by DCI Flynn of the Historical Enquiries Team in Belfast. This file, the Lomax Archive and the video recording were all that was required to trigger an investigation that . . . All at once Tess heard a quiet voice from the past. She felt an itch in her ear and she tried to scratch it, but the discomfort was too deep. The feeling turned, like a maggot heading towards her brain.

'If there was ever a conflict between the requirements of the law and your own best interests, to which voice would you listen? The shout or the whisper?'

It was Julia. And Julia being Julia, she hadn't specified which voice came from where, but Tess had understood. She'd known what Julia was on about. She told her she'd obey the whisper of the law. She could hear the whispering now, mysteriously surviving the cacophony in her mind, the horrendous racket threatening to bust open her skull. She blinked, and out of the corner of her eye she seemed to see a spray of startled redwings.

Tess would like to have said she'd made no decision and was watching herself, devoid of any responsibility. But ignoring a whisper that can't be drowned out requires presence of mind, and effort. She went to a drawer, took out some matches and set light to the file over the sink. Mentally far off, she watched the burning black border advance towards the edges of the cardboard and paper until it burned her fingers. When there was only a scattering of charred confetti around the plughole, she rinsed the sink and wiped it clean. Then she opened a window and sat back down.

All the noise had gone. There was no whisper, no racket. Three hours later, a floorboard creaked in her bedroom. A plank groaned on the staircase. Peter appeared in the doorway, naked and proud.

'You were sensational,' he said, looking down.

Tess digested the judgement. He'd said something very similar about a spring roll from the White Swan Chinese takeaway.

'It's over, Peter,' she said.

'What is?'

'You and me. I'm not fast food. Get dressed and leave.'

He didn't show any surprise. He didn't seek further and better particulars. Or interrogatories. Abruptly limp, he simply turned around and sauntered off, scratching his right buttock. The plank groaned; the floorboard creaked. After a minute or so there was another creak followed by another groan, and then the front door opened and clicked shut. The silence in the mews and the silence within Tess joined together to create an immense inner weight. A lifeless weight, like a heap of dirty wet clothes pulled out of a broken washing machine.

'What have I done?' she said.

She meant the wanton elimination of evidence. But then it struck her: she'd just got rid of the one person who would have understood her actions, and approved.

50

The judgement of the press, from legal commentators to writers of no particular competence, was that Benson's defence of Karmen Naylor had been a tour de force. He'd not only secured the acquittal of his client, he'd identified the two-stage mechanism of the killing, and the parties involved, without the benefit of any direct evidence. There'd been no private investigators. No last-minute disclosure of material favourable to the defence. Nothing. He'd called no one to the stand. He'd simply extracted the truth about the last hours of Billy Hudson's life from witnesses whose testimony was meant to secure the conviction of his client.

'You can't read the papers, Will,' said Tess, changing gear to turn a corner.

They were en route to deliver messages to the Kilgours and the Osabedes. Messages from a gangland boss and the Metropolitan Police. Benson had never carried out such bizarre errands in his life.

'You can't surf the net either. You can't read this kind of nonsense without it going to your head.'

Benson had, in fact, already looked. More than looked. His disgust regarding Hudson and Karmen hadn't abated. But he couldn't remain insensible to the technical judgement of his peers. With Hudson dead and Karmen facing another trial, what did it matter if the technician allowed himself a peek . . . or two or three . . . at what they'd said? And so he'd bathed in the light coming off his computer screen. He'd basked in the warmth of inordinate adulation.

'You've already seen the lot, haven't you?'

'I intend to print them off. You're a very lucky woman.'

'Why?'

'To know me.'

'This is what I was worried about. That's odd.'

'I'm not odd. I'm just outright—'

'Not you. Snip-Snap. It's closed. Definitively.'

Tess had pulled up outside the hairdresser's. There was a CLOSED sign in the window. Attached to the building was an advertisement: PREMISES TO LET.

Benson gave Dawson's, the estate agents, a call and spoke

to Joe Featherston. Nina had returned the keys the morning before, breaching her notice period, losing her deposit and exposing herself to a civil claim for lost rent. She'd been in and out of the office within two minutes. There'd been no discussion. Agitated but focused, and pushing a pram, her child crying, she'd dropped the keys on the table and said, 'I'm off.'

Benson cut the call.

'She made a run for it, before the verdict came out.'

'We should have foreseen this, Will. After Professor Cameron gave evidence she knew you were going to say she'd been involved in the murder. Along with her brother. That made them a target for the Naylors. And it made them a target for the police, because if Karmen was acquitted the investigation into Hudson's murder might reopen. She was probably terrified of the Ronsons, too. No wonder she cleared off. Why didn't we think of this last night?'

'Because we knew she was going to be okay. She might still be at home.'

Benson called Archie and asked him to get Nina's address from her witness statement. They went there – Flat C, Block B on the Sandwell Estate in Peckham – and found the door unlocked. Inside, on the table, were the keys. Clothing was scattered over the floor, as if, said Tess, choices were being made. The essential stuff had been taken. The rest had been thrown to one side. With a presentiment of what they would learn, they drove to The Conifers half a mile away. This time Tess did the speaking, because she'd already met the warden, Mrs Chadwick. And Mrs Chadwick couldn't conceal her anxiety, because yesterday – at much the same time that Nina was at Dawson's – Ekene Osabede had come to collect his father. He'd thanked her for years of kindness and support, but said they'd decided, as a family, to return to Nigeria.

Almost all of Azuka's property had been left in his flat. Two suitcases and a box of oddments had been hastily packed and placed in the boot of a rented car – no, she couldn't remember the rental firm, because she'd been more concerned about Ekene's manner and Azuka's confusion – after which, without signing any of the necessary papers, they'd left with a screech of tyres. Back in Tess's Mini, Benson made a string of calls to Ekene's employer. He was eventually told that Ekene hadn't turned up for work. Hadn't turned up yesterday either. The London to Edinburgh service had been a man down. Twice in a row.

'We're too late,' said Benson. 'They've bolted. But they can't have gone to Nigeria, not that quickly.'

'Oh yes they can. They got paid, remember.'

'Well, they'll never know that Karmen let them go and that the Met aren't interested in starting fresh proceedings. They could have stayed here.'

'Azuka didn't want to,' recalled Tess. 'He didn't want his grandson to grown up struggling to be accepted. Maybe they made the right call.'

'Maybe. It's just a pity they left in fear. Wherever they are, they'll always be looking over their shoulders, wondering if the Naylors care enough to come after them. Same with the police.'

'We better go and see the Kilgours now,' said Tess, opening the car door. 'Before they bugger off to Scotland.'

Benson called Jack. Thankfully he replied; and thankfully, yes, he was still in London. He hadn't thought of leaving. They'd nowhere to go. Didn't have the money. Unfortunately. Well, Benson said, Fortune can still shine. He had some good news for the family. If they wanted to hear it, they should get themselves over to HGT Ltd in half an hour.

The descendants of Albert Kilgour, founder of the company,

were already there when Benson and Tess arrived. They were huddled together in the workshop, each of them smoking, with Jack shaking his inhaler. As soon as Jack saw Benson and Tess he nudged his sons. They turned, like a couple of suburban foxes, frightened but alert, ready to dart off if anyone came too close.

'Relax,' said Benson. 'As far as we're concerned you can swim around their graves. It must be a relief to know Hudson and Ryan are out of your lives.'

'It is, Mr Benson, it is,' coughed Jack. 'But you're forgetting Karmen. She's a Naylor, too. And she knows we kept quiet about that threat from Ekene Osabede, and we reckon—'

'Jack. Take a long, deep breath. Christmas comes twice this year.'

Tess took over:

'Karmen Naylor has cancelled the sale of the business. It's no longer being demolished. The money paid to the Naylors by the developers is in the process of being returned. The property is yours again. If you want to, you can try and rival Kwik Fit. The business founded by your grandfather is yours again.'

For a man with serious respiration problems, Jack was shockingly silent. Benson thought his heart had given out. But then the low wheeze came, along with a high whistle. He tossed his cigarette away. His face went a livid purple, and then a rasping sob broke out of his lungs. Tears began streaming down his face. His sons grabbed him, like rugby players in a scrum. All three were pulling at each other, trying to get their hands on ten years of shared suffering so they could fling it away. Benson had never heard anything like the noise . . . save, early in his sentence, from his own mouth, after he'd been told his mother was dead.

Benson and Tess headed for the car park. They'd just reached the forecourt when a step sounded behind them. Benson turned. It was Pete.

'Don't leave,' he said. 'Not yet. There's something you ought to know.'

51

So this was Pete Kilgour, who'd fled to Scotland. If his father had put on weight through comfort eating, Pete had lost it through anxiety. At least that was Tess's guess. He looked undernourished. Even now, after freedom had been delivered to him on a plate, he was ill at ease, chewing a lip and bending an old business card back and forth.

'Tell him,' said Greg.

'Go on, Pete, tell him what happened,' added his father.

They were back in the workshop, the Kilgours bonded by eagerness and the self-importance that comes with secret knowledge.

'You got it all right, Mr Benson,' panted Jack, nudging Pete with a heavy elbow. 'It's incredible, but you got it spot on. Pete, c'mon, tell him.'

After some more folding, until the card split, Pete began his story.

He'd come back to HGT Ltd on the Friday night, the night of the murder, because, like Benson had said, the tool cabinet had been left open. It was the kind of thing Mr Hudson didn't like. The kind of thing he got angry about, though God knows why, because he had nothing to do with the business. Pete had parked on Southbrook Road, not far from the front entrance. Just as he'd got out of his car, he'd seen Karmen leaving the premises. She'd turned right, heading to the junction with Burnt Ash Road. After she'd gone, Pete had gone inside, hoping Mr Hudson was out of view; hoping he could lock the cabinet and get out without being seen.

'I came through there,' he said, pointing at the door that led from the reception area to the workshop. 'And I looked over to Mr Hudson's office. The door was open, the light was on, but I couldn't see him. So I walked real slow towards the cabinet, getting my keys out, trying not to make a noise . . . and just as I got to the cabinet, I heard a voice. Someone was speaking. I listened . . . and I thought, that's not Mr Hudson. Then I heard a sort of gurgling sound and I thought I better take a look. I wish I hadn't, Mr Benson. I wish I'd cleared off, got out that building and gone home.'

But he hadn't done. He'd slowly walked up the stairs that led to Mr Hudson's office, again, as quietly as possible, hearing that voice, a familiar voice now. When he got to the doorway, he'd frozen.

'Mr Hudson was lying on the ground, and Ryan was sitting on a chair, leaning over him, talking to him. Telling him he was dead. Laughing. Saying he'd always hated him. In his hand was a knife. No, not a knife, a sort of razor. The kind you see in the films when a mafia boss is having a shave. And he leans forward and starts wiping the blade on Mr Hudson's clothes, his shirt or cardigan, or whatever, and he says, "Rot in hell, Billy," and then he stands up. He just stood there, looking down, this small knife-razor thing in his hand. He folds the blade and puts it his pocket, and he turns around and sees me. I couldn't move. I couldn't speak. I thought he was going to kill me. I thought he was going to get that knife thing out, but then he smiles and says, "You're just in time, dickhead."'

Ryan had gone out and brought his car round to the loading bay. Then he'd told Pete to grab a leg. He'd taken one, and Ryan had taken the other, and they'd dragged the body across the floor. When they'd reached the roll-over shutter, Ryan had opened it and pushed Mr Hudson into the boot.

'He then says, "Get in." And I says, "Get in where?" And he says, "Not the boot, you prick. The car." So I get in the front seat and he drives off . . .'

Turning left to avoid the CCTV camera on Southbrook Road.

Ryan had been elated, tapping the steering wheel with a thumb. Using his mobile phone, he'd put on Oasis. He'd joined in the singing. 'Don't look back in anger.' He'd asked Pete if he liked Oasis. He said Oasis were the thing. He'd kept shifting songs, but coming back to that one track, and then he'd put on Dean Martin, and he'd asked Pete if he'd liked Dean Martin.

'He went on like that, the whole time. Coldplay. Foo Fighters. Frank Sinatra. Back to Oasis. I'd no idea where we were going. What he was going to do to me. He just kept driving, one hand on the steering wheel, the other holding his phone, listening to music and asking me questions.'

They'd been heading along the A20, through Sidcup and then Swanley, and then Ryan had taken a turn off into the Kent Downs.

'Eventually, he drives into this wood. I can take you there if you want. And he takes a path, a wide path through these trees, and then he stops and reverses and angles the headlights so they shine into the trees bit, if you see what I mean, and then he gets out and tells me to get out. He calls me dickhead all the time and I'm thinking, this is it, he's going to kill me. He's going to get that knife thing out.'

Instead, Ryan had got a spade out, not from his pocket, obviously, but the back of the car, and he'd told Pete to start digging. And while he'd been digging, Ryan had pulled Mr Hudson's body out of the boot. Pete had vomited and Ryan had told him to stop being a dickhead and keep digging, and when he'd got down a few feet Ryan had told him to grab a leg again, and together they'd dragged the body to the edge of the hole. 'I'll do this bit,' Ryan had said, and he'd kicked the body until it rolled over into the grave.

'He says to me, "Do you want a slash?" and I says no, and then he gets his thing out and pees on the body and then he tells me to pick up the spade and get to work and then I was sick again and he called me a total dickhead. But before I start filling in the hole, he leans in with a handkerchief or something and dabs it on Mr Hudson's neck and puts it in a plastic bag, the kind you put leftovers in, for the freezer, and then he says, "What are you waiting for, dickhead?"'

After Pete had finishing burying the body, Ryan told him to get back in the car. He'd driven to Swanley and given him money to buy a train ticket back to London. As Pete had got out of the car, Ryan had said:

'Speak to anyone, and your dad's dead. Got it? I'll put him in another hole.'

Then he'd driven off.

Tess had listened to the entire nightmarish tale with her eyes fixed on a large oil stain on the concrete. When she looked up, she saw Pete had torn the business card into tiny fragments. His father was patting him on the back and Greg was nodding, as if he, too, had been there and was confirming the shared ordeal.

'Okay,' said Benson. 'I now know why you went to Scotland.'

'Look, I'm not doing no digging or anything. But if you want, I can take you to his grave.'

'I'll get back to you on that one, Pete.'

Tess and Benson didn't speak. They just sat in the parked Mini staring ahead, onto the forecourt. But Tess knew what Benson was thinking. Pete Kilgour had just confessed to various serious criminal offences. Along with his father and brother, they'd committed a few conspiracies, too. They'd probably have a good defence of duress, but that didn't change the obligation that now presented itself to both of them. This was not a conversation they could forget. They ought to contact DCI Panjabi immediately. Tess glanced to the side. Benson had taken out his mobile phone. The screen lit up. His thumb hovered. And then he looked out of the window. Clouds were slowly passing over HGT Ltd. Together they watched them form shapes and dissolve and form again, with hints of misty blue appearing through the gaps.

'He's lucky to be alive,' said Tess. 'The only reason Ryan didn't kill him is because if Pete had disappeared, that would have made him a suspect in the Hudson murder. And Ryan wanted to frame his sister.'

Benson nodded. Tess continued:

'Killing Hudson was unauthorised. That's why Ryan acted without the team. Even if he hadn't tried to frame his sister, he'd have been put down for this.'

Benson was still nodding. Tess spoke again, reaching over and touching his arm.

'Let it go, Will. What's the point of recovering Hudson's body? For Lisa, sure, I agree. But look at the cost. Is it worth putting the Kilgours in the dock, all three of them, just when they've got their lives back? And if the Kilgours have to face the music, so do the Osabedes. They're all of a piece.'

The hazy patches of cobalt were growing stronger. It was going to be a nice day. Crisp and clean. A good day, regardless of the messiness of people's lives. When it became obvious that Benson wasn't going to speak, Tess took back her hand and turned the key in the ignition. The Mini coughed and pulled away from the kerb, with Tess twiddling a knob, trying to find some decent music on the radio. In the end, she settled for country and western. The usual stuff. Pining and loss. Promises of loyalty. They began to hum, and Benson turned off his mobile. There was an entirely new bond between them, one they'd never speak of. They were partners in crime.

52

Throughout the trial, Orla's disclosure to Tess that she'd had a species of encounter with an Australian had lain at the back of her mind. Now that the trial was over, the memory of that conversation came to the forefront, demanding attention. There was more to be said, somehow. But Tess didn't know what, and she didn't know how. And she certainly didn't know when, because time had run out. Her parents were going back to Ireland on Sunday, tomorrow; and today, Saturday, was her father's seventieth birthday. This was the day Orla had prepared for night and day, trawling her husband's professional and personal history, after he'd left the merchant navy, sending out invitations to anyone of significance who'd known or worked with him. There was going to be a surprise party. She was hoping her husband would see her differently, afterwards, and forgive her.

'I'd like to go home leaving all the poison behind,' said Orla in Gaelic. 'I know we can't go back to where we were – I mean as a couple – because I accept that's been changed. By me. There's this difference now, and it won't go away. But we can have something new, and good, can't we?'

'You can have something better.'

Orla's fine-boned hand gripped Tess's wrist.

'Really? Do you think that's possible?'

'I do, Mum. Because you've put your faith and trust in the truth. You've hidden nothing. Something good is going to happen. I know it.'

Tess's father had been lured out for the day by one of the guests, a former college provost. In their absence the caterers had arrived. So had the other guests. By eight in the evening the flat was crowded and hushed, with thirty-four people waiting for the front door to open. The quiet was agonising for Tess, because she could almost hear her mother's heart beating with expectation and hope. Expectation and hope that she'd put there. Voices sounded on the pavement, and then, even as the handle turned, Orla jumped in the air and shouted:

'Surprise! . . . Happy birthday, darling.'

Tess shuddered at the fragility. The words had cracked. Laurence's mouth dropped open and then the music began. Some crap by Mozart. Crap, thought Tess, because she could never tell the difference between one symphony and another. She'd often said so to her father, and he'd replied just as often, 'That's because you don't listen.'

I hope you're listening now, Dad. I hope you can hear what Mum is saying to you.

Gradually, the guests broke into small groups and Laurence, lamenting that he was underdressed, and without a tie, began moving around the room, squeezing tweedy elbows and kissing powdered cheeks. Tess, feeling her stomach turn, watched her mother follow him as if she were on a lead, reaching out, at intervals, for his hand, only to be subtly rebuffed as he pulled away or folded his arms or touched someone else; and throughout she smiled winningly, never flagging in enthusiasm, talking cheerily, before moving on to wherever he'd gone next.

While tracking this inobtrusive humiliation, Tess, too, was on the move. There were people from Dublin, Galway, London, Edinburgh, you name it. Anywhere and everywhere, except a cluster of places no one would associate with a retired historian. And everywhere she went the guests dropped talk of alumni or vice-chancellors' salaries or recent publications, wanting to know about the trial.

'Do you know what I call it?' said a bespectacled wag from Preston.

'Go on,' chimed a cluster of invitees.

'The Hither Green Clusterf—'

'Not here, Norman. We're in polite company.'

'Forgive me, but that's hardly original.'

'There's nothing wrong with being derivative.'

'Quite right. There was a time when men of letters showed their learning by such referencing.'

'And what about women?'

'There weren't any.'

'Really? Then why do you exist?'

'I meant of letters.'

'Are you sure about that?'

'I'm sure I said what I meant to say.'

'Tell us about the trial, Tess.'

She tried. But she couldn't get a word in edgeways. One question folded into another before she could reply. Had Benson been given inside information? Had someone told him that Ryan was Hudson's killer? Had he been scared to blame Ryan in open court? Was he aware that as a result of exposing Ryan as the killer, Ryan had been executed, and that without Ryan the Naylor network might well collapse? That's what the papers were saying. And what about Bucklow? It was easy to condemn him, but he'd stepped out of his grubby secret world. It's only when lowlifes like him owned up to what they've done that the police can actually do anything. And that's not all. Others follow suit . . . and that's what was happening. A couple of Naylor players had turned themselves in. Offering to give evidence in return for a deal like Bucklow's. Same thing in Dubai. And to think, Benson began the whole—

Dubai.

All at once Tess saw the gaudy splatter of jelly and bruised fruit on newsprint, with a head thrown back in rapture. Archie's arms were around her, his thick jumper pressed hard against her mouth and nose.

Don't look, Tess. Just don't look.

She couldn't breathe. Her ears were ringing and purple spots burst across her mind.

'Are you all right? You've lit up.'

'It's the Hither Green Lustre.'

Tess pushed between Norman and this other joker, dropping her champagne. The sound of shattering glass brought a sudden lull, as between waves crashing on a shore, followed by a whoop and schoolboy applause. She hit the door handle of the French windows and, stumbling outside into the small back garden, her lungs opened.

Tess was sitting on a wooden bench. To one side was a lemon tree wrapped in a white protective covering. A sort of shroud paying homage to winter, though it was a trick, because the tree was very much alive. On the other side was a terracotta pot with a very dead camellia. Facing was a brick wall. Old, pitted brick. Altogether charming. Maybe fired in the same kilns that had serviced HMP Kensal Green.

'Are you feeling better?'

Tess's father had come out several times and been sent back in. So had her mother. Tess had wanted to be alone. The two of them had looked at her through different panels of the French windows, misting the glass, each of them framed by the lattice. Now that she'd calmed down, she'd allowed her father to stay.

'You've been through an incredibly difficult time,' he said gently. 'And I'm incredibly proud of you. Not many people could—'

'I know everything, Dad.'

'You'll forget it all soon enough. Once you start another case.'

'Everything.'

'And everything will recede and then disappear. You're strong. You're—'

'It won't. I know you were in the army, Dad. I know you never weathered a storm off the Cape of Good Hope or met a one-toothed pirate. I know you were one of the Blind Eyes. I know Ruffcut conspired with Bluebell and Flywheel and the Blood Brothers to murder ten men, understood to be members of the PIRA. I know four of the victims were innocent. I've met the family of one of them. I've shielded you from the law. I've crossed a line and there's no way back.'

Tess had to face her father. She had to see him. She couldn't let the sound of her words just bounce off that wall.

'Dad, I understand your position. I really do. Bluebell told me you were an idealist. That you joined up to do something good, to make things better. Only you didn't. You made things worse. And then, after leaving the army, you met Mum, and rather than tell her the truth, you made up a wonderful past, in which no one had been targeted and no one had been killed . . . only I came along, and you looked at this new life, and you remembered how you'd messed up your own. You withdrew, and you only returned once you'd built up the strength to carry on with the lie. As I say, Dad, I understand your position; it's awful, and as far as I'm concerned, you can carry on hiding the truth about yourself – in many ways, that suits us both. If you were to speak out, now, like Bucklow, that would put moral pressure on me – but please, please, please, please, please, never accuse my mother of betrayal again.'

Laurence did not look at Tess. He was staring ahead like a trooper on parade, still, in part, the youth who'd signed up for a few years' service. There was no turning back, even now. Tess tried to guess which brick his eyes had settled upon, and having chosen one, she stared at it hard. This was their inviolable connection, at this moment of unwanted but unavoidable honesty, the joint perception of a brick in a wall. Tess didn't hear her father move. She simply saw a blurred shape rise . . . and return, dutifully, to the hell he'd made for himself. A spear seemed to prise open her ribs and enter her heart. He'd learned how to mimic joy. And gratitude and well-being. He'd learned to fake attentiveness to others. He'd mastered the dark arts, so as to live in the light. But he must have suffered terribly. He must be suffering now. And – worst of all – Tess knew he would always suffer. For the rest of his life, he would perform the humdrum and burn, as he'd always burned. Like me, she thought. For this had become her own story. She turned to look the way he'd gone, along a path of stepping stones through grass and moss, tears welling up; tears for him, for her mother and for herself.

Laurence was standing beside Orla, their backs to the French windows. He was giving a punchy speech. His friends were laughing. They were raising their glasses. And Laurence had his arm around his wife, not casually, as a man might after decades of marriage – or even like he'd done when Tess had been a child, taking her for granted, as lovers eventually must – but hungrily, possessively, squeezing hard; too hard; hurting her.

53

Benson met Sally in Hammersmith as agreed, at 8 p.m. on the Broadway, and together they walked along Fulham Palace Road. They were both very much aware that Tess was nearby, with her parents, celebrating her father's birthday. They were also aware that they'd both avoided her calls earlier in the week, during the evening after speeches had been given and after the judge had begun his summing up. On both occasions they'd been together, in the Edward Rayne pub, near Raynes Park station. A part of London they'd never been to before and where Tess couldn't possibly amble around the corner.

They'd met to share information about Tess, yes. But also to discuss Sally's findings.

While Benson had been preoccupied with the trial, Sally had got to work.

She'd found the article in the *Belfast Telegraph* mentioned by Benson, and that had been her starting point. While the HET had been wound up in 2014 following budget cuts, the investigators had returned to ordinary duties within the PSNI. Sally had traced a certain DCI Patrick Flynn. And he'd been happy to talk, since Sally was enquiring about a matter that was on the public record, and because he was still angry. Very angry. About the closure of the HET. Anyway, he'd remembered Tess and Peter, the duo from London. He'd met them in February 2010. They'd handed over some old intelligence paperwork that had been forensically useless. No, he wouldn't let her see it. What he would do was give her the name of the person who'd given it to Hollingtons. Sergeant Brian Lomax of the Lancashire Fusiliers. DOB 26.08.1933. Sally had then investigated the said Lomax. He'd died of skin cancer on the 18th of March 2010. His wife, Brenda, aged eighty-one, was still alive. Like DCI Flynn, she'd been angry. And ready to talk.

'We've a meeting on Saturday night,' Sally had said, finishing a second pint of Guinness.

Benson had been impressed. At her findings.

And now they were pushing open an iron gate to a sombre terraced house facing Bishop's Park in Fulham.

'That policeman in Belfast shouldn't have given you Brian's name. That was naughty. But I understand. When they shut down the HET, they shut down investigations into three thousand two hundred and sixty-nine murders. All committed between 1968 and 1998. Brian had wanted to do his bit. He was involved in ten of them. But at the last minute he changed his mind. What am I doing? Come in. Go in there, to the sitting room. I'll make tea. You'd like some tea? Good. Yes, in there, on the right.'

Brenda hobbled down a dark corridor towards a well-lit kitchen and Benson and Sally did as they were told. The furnishings were tired, the walls dull and the pictures and lampshades faded. Years of sunlight had taken away the colour from everything. The vibrancy of a life shared with Brian had gradually disappeared. Benson felt he was in an antechamber. Brenda was waiting to enter the Greater Room Upstairs. Or was it Downstairs?

'My husband did dreadful things,' she said, putting a tray on a low table. 'It's why he got cancer. That's what I think. He felt bad for what he'd done, but then he did nothing about it. So he got ill. Then he told me and then he told Hollingtons. But it was too late. The cancer had a hold of him.'

'What did he tell them?' asked Benson.

'That he'd helped a death squad pick off terrorists.'

'Ten of them?'

'Not quite, Mr Benson. Brian found out four of them were innocent. That's when he decided he couldn't go on.'

Brian and two others had formed a secret group, calling themselves the Blind Eyes. And they'd chosen the targets, handing the information to three soldiers, the Blood Brothers, who'd pulled the triggers. Brian had been as guilty as any of them, but part of him had always known it was wrong. That's why he'd kept files on everything they'd done. He'd hidden them in the loft. Even Brenda hadn't known they were there. Until the cancer diagnosis.

'And this is the paperwork that your husband gave to Miss de Vere and Mr Farsely from Hollingtons?'

'Yes.'

'You know that they were unable to use it? Same with the police in Belfast?'

'I do, yes.'

'This is lovely tea.'

'Thank you. Do you want a biscuit?'

'No, I'm fine. After Brian left the army he worked as a process server for Jones and Co., a firm of solicitors, up the road in Walham Green?'

'Yes, Brian had known Mr Jones at school.'

'Mr Jones specialises in crime?'

'Yes.'

'Why didn't Brian turn to Mr Jones for help?'

'He did. And he sent him to Hollingtons. A big firm, with experience of taking on the government. Mr Benson, you're cross-examining me.'

'Sorry, I can't help it. How is it Mr Jones didn't tell Brian that the evidence he'd saved for thirty-eight years was missing something absolutely vital: a sort of fuse . . . something that would make those files explosive?'

Benson watched Mrs Lomax carefully. She'd begun to run a finger beneath the cuff of her blouse. One shiny shoe was tapping the other. Benson took a mental step back. She'd dressed up for this meeting. Her hair had been nicely done. She'd put on lipstick. This was a very important moment for her. She didn't mind being cross-examined in the least. She was loving it. But she was also being unnaturally careful.

'Brenda, if I may—'

'I'm not prepared to answer any more questions on this, Mr Benson,' she said. 'Because I've made a promise to someone.'

'Tess de Vere?'

Mrs Lomax suddenly looked exultant. But she wouldn't confirm Benson's supposition. She ignored it.

'I will tell you something that has nothing to do with my promise. It's why I agreed to see you. I got a visit from a young man last week. During your trial. He'd come all the way from Belfast. He wasn't as fast as you, or as cheeky, but he came with similar questions. He wanted to know about Brian and his papers.'

'What was his name?'

'This man told me his uncle had been shot by the British army in March 1972. He couldn't prove it. But the family were convinced he'd been targeted by a death squad, and they'd made a mistake and would never admit it. And he told me something else.'

Benson's intuition ignited. But he just sipped his tea.

'This man, and his family, had tried to find out the truth once before. Two years ago. They'd contacted Miss de Vere, who was now at Coker and Dale. There'd been a meeting. With his dad and his granddad. They'd all come over from Belfast.'

'This is 2017?'

'Yes. February. They'd wanted to know if Brian had said anything to her and Mr Farsely about the killing – something that wasn't in the papers that had gone to the HET. And she said he hadn't, which is true. I was there. He'd only told them what they'd done and then he'd handed over the files.'

'Why did he come to see you?'

'Because he's wondering if the family had been lied to.'

'Why would he think that?'

'Going over the meeting, again and again, he thought Miss de Vere looked very uncomfortable. He thought she might be hiding something . . .'

'Like you?'

'Yes, Mr Benson. Just like me.'

'So what did you tell him?'

Mrs Lomax's attention flickered.

'That Miss de Vere had told him the truth,' she intoned. 'Brian had said nothing about the killing of his uncle.'

Benson savoured the arrangement of words. It had the poise of a response crafted by a lawyer. Possibly Mr Jones. The sentence was no doubt true. But it didn't mean Tess hadn't been hiding anything. Brian had said nothing. But had someone else?

'This man won't be deflected,' said Mrs Lomax.

For the first time she sipped her tea.

'He's resolved to find out what happened. You see, he's young and angry. In his twenties. He wasn't even alive when his uncle was murdered. But it's often the young who won't ignore the past – they've a knack of chasing after things their parents would rather forget.'

'Does he intend to contact Miss de Vere again?'

'I don't know. You might ask him yourself.'

'What's his name?'

'Merrigan. Dominic Merrigan. Would you like a biscuit now?'

Benson and Sally kept well away from Hammersmith. They walked, slowly, to Fulham Broadway, where they'd go their different ways on the Underground. Streetlights cast shadows while headlights drove them away. The shapes swung like dizzy figures on a merry-go-round.

'We've found the reason for Tess leaving Hollingtons in 2010,' said Sally.

'And why she dropped us both in 2017,' added Benson.

He couldn't conceive why bad stuff on the part of the army in the early seventies would provoke a personal crisis for Tess. She had no military connections. And like Merrigan, she hadn't yet been born. Yet it had done. And he felt for her. Because the crisis wasn't over. Unlike Benson's, it wasn't restricted to something that had happened in the past. It was unfolding, even as he and Sally were advancing along the pavement.

'I've a very bad feeling about this,' he said after yards of moving in silence, their feet falling into step; the kind of thing that used to happen with Tess.

'Me too,' said Sally. 'Me too.'

54

That Dominic Merrigan was possibly still in London and might yet approach Tess once more had the feel of a threat. But there was nothing Benson or Sally could do to protect her. They couldn't warn her without revealing their investigation. For the same reason, they couldn't approach Merrigan – who would, no doubt, be very interested to know that Tess had suffered a breakdown shortly after the Lomax case had floundered. Nothing could be done to prevent or slow down whatever was unfolding. All Benson and Sally could do was continue inching forward.

'I'll look into the Merrigan family,' Sally had said. 'And you?'

'The de Vere family. Let's see if their paths ever crossed.'

The gradual disintegration of the Naylor Family Crime Group continued. To the surprise of everyone the Ronsons began to fall apart, too. With each arrest there was a squeal in some interview room. With every squeal further arrests followed, either among the Naylors or the Ronsons. Karmen's expectation that Bucklow might find himself alone had proved to be unfounded. That she'd been so confident demonstrated the scale of her arrogance, an arrogance born of power. A power that was draining away with every new desertion. Within weeks Karmen was alone, but still living with her father in his mansion near Dulwich Park. Photographers who wouldn't have dared approach her, or anyone in the Naylor set-up, now followed her to Costcutter, or into the park when, struggling with a wheelchair, she took her father out for a breather. The resulting images ended up in the tabloids. The byline writers had a field day. The more serious commentators focused on what might be called the final pending arrests, because – said sources close to the investigation – the scale of evidence against Karmen and her father was monumental.

Upon conviction, it was observed, asset-recovery personnel would kick down the front door of their entire material existence. It was goodbye to *Allhallows Rest* and *Little Winner* and an awful lot more. Father and daughter were going to lose everything except the clothes they stood up in – and even those, in Karmen's case, would belong to Her Majesty's Government, because she'd be in prison. Tony would probably escape that fate because he was too sick to defend himself. But he'd still end up on benefits, in a state-run care home – to any other pauper a privilege, but to him a nightmare. That the police hadn't yet moved in showed how careful they were being in the management of the anticipated prosecutions. Meanwhile, Karmen could only wait. Unable to abandon her father, she was like a rat in a bag with a brick, waiting to be thrown into the Thames.

And then the call came.

Karmen had contacted Tess. Her tone had changed. She didn't even cite the cab-rank rule. Anticipating the arrival of armed officers at five in the morning, ten of them smashing their way into the family home, she wanted to plan for the inevitable. She was begging Tess and Benson to represent her.

'I've arranged a conference for Monday morning. Ten a.m.'

'I thought I'd be seeing her again,' said Benson. 'Somehow her story didn't feel complete.'

Tess arrived half an hour early. They were both ill at ease. Karmen would be coming through the door, as many defeated criminals do, wanting pity; claiming they'd changed; oozing remorse; seeking the camaraderie decent people extend to the penitent. Wanting a heart-rending mitigation before the judge considers sentence. But neither Benson nor Tess could put to one side their knowledge of what Karmen had done. The county lines scheme she'd devised, which had so pleased her father, revealed a heart-stopping disregard for the children at the centre of the operation. No sentence could fit the crime. Because once those kids had been pulled into Karmen's world, it was very difficult to draw them out. Some would be rescued. But others would be lost.

'She's late,' said Tess.

Benson checked his watch.

'We'll give her until half-past.'

But Karmen didn't arrive at half-past. So Tess gave her a call. A man's voice she didn't know answered.

'Yeah?'

'Can I speak to Karmen, please?'

'I'll just put you on speaker.'

The man was walking somewhere. There was laughter in the background. A door opened and closed. Then the man spoke again:

'Where's Karmen? C'mon . . . where is she?'

After a sound of clanging, a dog barked and growled. Then the line cut.

Benson and Tess looked at each other, their disquiet at what Karmen had done transformed into apprehension at what had been done to her. Benson began pacing the room, while Tess called Coker & Dale, checking if any message had been left by Karmen or anyone else about the planned conference, explaining her absence. Tube delays. A fall at home. A damaged water pipe. That kind of thing. She called Karmen's home number, expecting Tony to pick up, but there was no response. Meanwhile, all Benson could hear was the rabid barking in his mind; the vicious snarl and the rattle of a heavy chain.

'What do we do?' said Tess.

'How the hell would I know?'

'There's someone here for you.'

Archie was standing at the Gutting Room door, bemused. Beside him was a boy aged about eleven or twelve. He was dressed in what appeared to be a brand-new tracksuit with brand-new white trainers. He looked like a mannequin from a sports shop window come to life. Except . . . he was wearing gloves and holding a plastic bag. Seeing Benson's gaze drop, he threw the bag across the room.

'This is for yous,' he said, cocky and self-important. 'The job's been finished.'

Then he turned around and left. Absolutely calmly, as if he'd just handed over a receipt.

Archie hitched up his trousers.

'Shouldn't he be in school? Why hasn't someone grabbed him by the collar?'

'What's in the bag, Will?' said Tess.

Benson took out a mobile phone. He knew it was a burner. He knew there'd be no prints on it. He knew the geolocation would have been disabled. He knew it could never be traced to whoever had given it to the boy. A victim. A child who needed someone like Archie in his life. There was no call history, no messages, no photographs . . . nothing except a video. Dated yesterday evening at 6.43 p.m. Stepping well away from Archie and Tess, he pressed the play triangle.

The film showed *Little Winner* bobbing alongside the jetty at Allhallows. It was a blustery evening, with a pink sky and gouges of purple and blue among the waves. Benson recognised it from the prosecution photographs. But that was mere background detail. Karmen was centre stage, stumbling backwards on a path, hands raised.

'No, please, no . . . please, no.'

There was whining off camera, a high, choking sound only interrupted by gusts of wind overwhelming the microphone. Suddenly, a huge brute of a dog, flat-coated and copper-brown, with muscular white thighs, appeared, bounding forward, leaping high, bringing Karmen to the ground, not even barking, just ferociously busy—

Benson dropped the phone. The noise carried on, of screaming and eating and laughter, until Archie had grabbed it and ran out of the room, swearing, fiddling with buttons and stabbing the screen, trying to turn the thing off. But he was too agitated. So the mayhem of gorging continued, as if it was happening on the clerk's room floor. Benson banged his hands against his ears, and closed his eyes, crying out, to drown any sound that might get through. He stayed like that until his shouting ran out of air. And then Archie touched his arm.

'It's over,' he said. 'I've called the police.'

Responding officers found a mauled body believed to be that of Karmen Naylor on open ground, twenty yards from the jetty. The identification was presumptive, because the individual in question was unrecognisable. Tony Naylor was found in the adjoining cottage. He'd been locked inside, gagged and tied to a chair by a window. He was in such a state of distress that he'd been sectioned under the Mental Health Act, sedated and taken to hospital. DCI Panjabi went through the details, expressing her disgust at this sickening crime. No stone would be left—

Benson tapped the remote, turning off the television.

'So ends the Naylor Family Crime Group,' he said quietly. 'All that's left is a madman.'

As evening had turned to night, the sitting room on *The Wooden Doll* had gradually darkened. And just as gradually Tess had merged into her surroundings, into the books, the clutter of ornaments and the round brass windows; Benson's surroundings. Traddles, heard but not seen, was moving around, his paws tugging at the carpet. Desultory conversation had dwindled and then died, replaced by a tingling atmosphere, identical to the night Benson had insisted on remaining with Tess after the suicide of Ruth Mowbray. This time, she'd stayed with Benson. And Benson was wondering what part of his boat might pass for a spare room.

'You okay, Will?' she said.

'Never felt better.'

'I'm off, then.'

She'd spoken, feeling her way through the darkness. When she was an outline against the night sky, breathing unevenly, Benson replied.

'If the Ronsons finished the job, who started it?'

55

The press had already addressed the question. While Benson was innocent of any wrongdoing, the murders of Ryan and Karmen seemed to be nothing other than the natural consequence of a process he'd begun in Number 4 Court of the Old Bailey. He'd uncovered biblical sibling hatred on the one hand, in effect provoking Tony Naylor, and on the other he'd shown the murder of the Kite was yet to be avenged, offending the pride of Stuart Ronson. He'd set the members of a family against each other, and he'd set one gang upon another. No wonder mass desertions had ensued. You'd have thought, wrote the crime correspondent for *The Times*, that such a Shakespearean outcome had been Benson's plan from the outset. Indeed—

'You're not as clever as you think you are,' came a voice from the trees that shielded Seymour Basin from the main road. 'Shah's right. Why the palaver?'

Benson, legs crossed on his bench, had just lit his morning roll-up. He looked over at the figure descending quickly along the path.

'Grab your coat. We're off to visit the real crime scene.'

Tess emerged onto the landing stage, dressed in the same black court gear she'd been wearing the night before. She stamped a foot.

'C'mon. I haven't slept. I'm not in the mood for messing around. I said grab your coat. Now.'

Tess couldn't slow down.

She sped towards south London, speaking in riddles and ignoring all Benson's questions. You'll see, she said. Just let me get there first. Why the palaver? It was a good question. Worst thing is, my father was right. Keep things simple. And if you keep things simple – no offence – there was no two-stage attack. Several speed camera flashes later, she pulled up alongside Peckham Rye Park.

'Is this it?' said Benson.

'No. This isn't where it happened. This is where it began. Over there . . . somewhere. August 2016. A bunch of youths attacked Nina and Hudson intervened. That, Will, was the moment that changed everything.'

Tess revved the engine and pulled away. Five minutes later she swung off Forest Hill Road and pointed out of the window.

'We're here.'

They were in front of the Be All and End All café. Tess walked ahead and almost kicked open the door, making straight for the counter.

'Benson, this is Buster; Buster, this is Benson. I'll have a coffee, milk, no sugar. I won't be paying.'

She then went straight to a booth away from the window and sat with her back to the wall, facing the door.

'This is the spot, Will.'

'What the hell are you on about? No offence, but have you taken something?'

'This is the crime scene. This table. This is where the details were thrashed out.'

Benson had refused a coffee, leaving Buster open-mouthed to fiddle with his espresso machine. Tess was off even before Benson had sat down:

'The woman who came here in sunglasses. If it wasn't Mowbray, who was it? That's where I began. Well, actually, I began with your question. Just as I was leaving last night. Who started the job to wipe out the Naylors? And I thought of that woman. When I got home, I was still thinking of her. Who was she? You'd made sense of everything in your completely brilliant but wrong speech . . . except for her. She was planning things with the Osabedes. She handed over the envelopes, remember? But what was her interest in what they were going to do? Don't bother answering, I haven't finished. So I did what you always do. I drew up a chronology. I took the chronology from the trial and I joined it to the chronology of the Osabedes. And it's more than interesting. Oi, Buster, you racist slug – where's my coffee? Concentrate, Will, or you'll miss what happened. It's not obvious.'

Benson couldn't imagine Tess snorting speed. Or coke. But she had all the signs. Flushed. Detached from her surroundings. Talking fast. The lot. Except dilated pupils. Tess's were sharp with absolute concentration.

'Okay, back to August 2016. Hudson meets Nina. She's under no illusions as to who this guy is. She knows. He's a serious criminal. And he's blown away by Nina. He stuffs his face at the family table. Azuka puts his hands over that face, trying to get at the inner man, and he likes what he sees. Sort of, because he's blind, but he's found something. And it fits. Because this hammer-wielding hard man is seen holding hands and whispering right here, at this table. For months. A café he'd never been to before . . . because he didn't want to be recognised. This is a relationship he was hiding. Mowbray knew nothing about it until the trial. Okay?'

'Okay.'

'Right, Nina gets pregnant in January 2017. She says she didn't tell Hudson. I don't believe her. You'll see why in a minute. In April Tony has a stroke. Karmen comes home. The next month, May, the besotted Billy smacks Nina in the gob and their relationship is over. Same month, according to Mowbray, Hudson wants out of the game. Same month, all in May, the Osabedes and this woman in sunglasses start planning something in the very café where Hudson used to meet up with Nina. Then, in June, Karmen takes over. The very same day – in the afternoon – someone calls DAC Oakhurst with a tip-off. A year in advance. Giving him plenty of time to prepare.'

'What are you saying, Tess?'

'I'm saying Hudson and Nina's break was a sham. I'm saying it was Hudson who called Oakhurst, not Ryan. Just keep listening. We now jump forward to May 2018. Up north, Kershaw is busy stuffing four million quid's worth of drug money into old cement sacks, ready to be laundered by Bucklow. Oakhurst has been given the date, time and travel route. Thank you, slug. Now slide back to where you came from. Hudson prepares to head north. There's going to be a meeting with Karmen when he returns on the Friday. What does he do? For no reason whatsoever, he puts it in the online calendar. Just in case Karmen takes it out, he tells Greg Kilgour. Again, for no reason whatsoever. Unless, of course, it was all part of a plan. Covering the eventuality that Karmen avoids the CCTV cameras. He wants proof that Karmen arranged to meet him. He's tense. On his way out of London, he tells Mowbray something bad's going to happen. He can feel it. And he gives her his gun. Which is outright weird. Are you with me so far?'

'Sort of. Oi, racist slug, I'll have a coffee. No milk, no sugar. And I won't be paying either.'

56

Buster did as he was told. When he'd brought the coffee and slid back behind the counter, Tess seemed to slam into another gear, opening up the engine.

'Hudson meets up with Bucklow on the Thursday, south of Manchester. But for the first time ever Kershaw's been and gone, along with the empty sacks. Why the change in routine? Hudson has already put the money in the suitcases. Three are put into the van. But we know from Mowbray that there was enough money for four, not three. Yes, Will, I'm saying Hudson removed the fourth before Bucklow arrived. Someone else took it away. My guess is they were en route to Rotterdam, but we'll come to that shortly. Anyway, Hudson feeds his lines to Bucklow, about how the Naylors are falling apart, how he'll end up dead and that he should cut and run, blah, blah, blah, and off Bucklow goes . . . heading straight for the open arms of DAC Oakhurst. Meanwhile, Hudson gets back to London late that night. My next guess is that he got up early the next morning and drove to Allhallows to plant evidence on the jetty and the boat – though it's possible he'd done it some other day, when he'd put some blood on Karmen's Golf. Whatever, whichever, come Friday he's as nervous as hell. Super-tense. Because the big one is yet to come. That evening, he heads off to the Four Ravens dressed in a conspicuous green cardigan and shirt with bright red buttons – one of which was missing, of course, because he'd chucked it onto *Little Winner* – the sort of kit that anyone would remember, and which would easily shed if dragged across the floor, leaving transfer material ready to be found by the forensic people. You know what I mean. Smarties. After downing a beer and a sandwich, he leaves the pub and goes to HGT Ltd, half an hour before Karmen is due to arrive. Why?

Because he's got things to do. First, he calls his mother, who won't be answering, and he delivers more lines: a cryptic message that only she would understand – a reference to her being right about the risk of the Naylors eventually killing him. Which, of course, is about to happen. He takes the wrench and some of his hair, skin and blood – collected the day before, weeks ago, months ago, I don't know . . . but it was discussed right here – and he batters them into the door-frame. Next, he tips over some furniture and – here's another guess, but it's good one – he takes out a large-volume syringe, fills it with his blood, stored in one of those plastic bags you get in hospitals, and he gets on his knees, pressing it and waving it around to simulate an arterial bleed from a low-level assault, with columns on the wall . . . creating what Dr Merrin called a textbook example of a catastrophic injury. Next, a couple of fingers go down his throat and out pops the sandwich. Off comes the cardigan and he drags it over the floor towards the loading bay. Are you with me now?'

'Very much so.'

'When Karmen arrives, he goes downstairs. Well away from the made-up crime scene. They must have spoken about Bucklow, the missing million and who the hell could have tipped off the police. My guess – and it's another good one – is that Billy said it had to be Ryan. Karmen would have swallowed the accusation hook, line and sinker. She leaves in a rage, planning, I suspect, a probe into her brother. She's barely left Southbrook Road when Hudson, masked and carrying a bag containing the wrench, syringe and empty blood bag, clambers over those bins, clears the wall and lands on Monty.'

'Has anything really upset you recently?' said Benson.

'Actually, yes. My parents are drowning in shit and there's nothing I can do except wave from the shore. Are you suggesting I've lost it?'

'Well, that would explain why—'

'You've really annoyed me now.'

'Tess, this story doesn't work. If the Osabedes had planned all this with Hudson, intending to frame Karmen, Ekene wouldn't have threatened to kill him. That threat, witnessed by the Kilgours, would have ruined the plan. Not only did it draw attention to the Osabedes, it gave the police a future suspect. They were just lucky the Kilgours said nothing.'

'I cracked that nut at five this morning. At first, Hudson and Nina were working alone. Secretly. They were going to pull this off together and, at the right moment, Nina would explain to her family what they'd done. And then she'd quietly slip away to join Hudson. No one would be any the wiser. But Ekene nearly wrecked everything when he went and threatened Hudson – a threat he might have carried out – so they brought him in on the plan. Which meant Nina could stay at home with Obi.'

'But why would Hudson hit Nina?'

'To make it look like they really were no longer a couple. Look, if Hudson dies one month, and his body vanishes, and then his girlfriend and child vanish another, it could nudge the police and the Naylors into thinking that something dodgy might have happened. Remember, both Karmen and Ryan knew they hadn't killed him. And if it wasn't the Ronsons or the Osabedes, then who the hell was it? So Hudson and Nina had to make the break look convincing. And they certainly convinced Ekene.'

Benson shook his head, his mind a blur.

'No. Sorry. What about the blood, the syringe and the know-how and—'

'Lisa's partner is a nurse, Will. A theatre nurse. Neil Ashford knows all about blood. He deals with the stuff every day. Transfusions. Storage. You name it. Blood is his thing. He taught Hudson all he needed to know, and he stored Hudson's samples . . . which his mother then brought north when she came to collect the fourth suitcase. She took the money abroad.

It's money for Hudson and Nina and their child – Linda's grandson. She'd organised her little trip to Rotterdam at the very time the money was being transferred, the day before her son would be murdered. Then came the really bad luck. The one time he decides to call her in twelve years, she happens to have left her phone behind. Can't you see what happened? Hudson wanted out, because he'd met the extra-ordinary Nina. And now he was about to become a father, and he knew Karmen would never let him go. So what did he do? After years of silence, he rang his mother. And the two of them cooked up a scam that would allow Billy to start over while removing the people who stood in his way and might come after him if they ever found out. It's genius. The pundits have got it all wrong, Will. By all means keep the cuttings, but the person who brought down the Naylors wasn't you. It was Hudson and his mother.'

'But why give Mowbray a gun?'

'For God's sake, get a grip. Hudson knew Bucklow would crack. He knew the trial would set Karmen onto Ryan and Ryan onto Karmen and the Ronsons onto the Naylors . . . that there'd be a bloodbath. He suspected Ryan would come for Mowbray. Call it mercy, call it covering all options, but he wanted her out of the picture, too. By Ryan's hands or her own. He literally got rid of everyone. Except Tony, of course, who's already finished.'

Benson was shaking his head. Tess could read his mind: he really thought he'd cracked it.

'Truth is, Will, the jury might have believed you, but your double attack theory isn't that convincing. Not really. Not if you want to make sense of all the evidence. And you haven't dealt with the woman in the sunglasses.'

Benson finished his coffee and shrugged on his duffel coat.

'What are we going to do?' said Tess, calm now.

'We're going to dig up Billy Hudson's remains.'

57

Benson looked out of the car window at the passing buildings, the lampposts, the traffic, the pedestrians. The bits and pieces of ordinary life, into which – according to Tess – Billy Hudson had made his escape. Could he have pulled it off? Fooling the police, forensic experts, the prosecution – and Benson himself, who'd eviscerated the facts, trying to discover what had really happened. Was Hudson out there now, with his partner and child? Browsing the net and laughing?

We'll soon find out.

Leaving Tess in her car, Benson strode onto the forecourt of HGT Ltd, where he came to a sudden halt.

'What the hell?'

The exterior of the building had been completely repainted. The front door and all the window frames had been replaced. There was a brand-new yellow sign with black lettering above the entrance:

HITHER GREEN TYRES
A family business since 1946

Benson marched into the brightly lit workshop. The interior, too, had been repainted. The smell of fresh opportunity hung in the air. Three vehicles were raised up on gleaming red hydraulic lifts. Jack and Greg, dressed in matching racing green overalls, were joking with a customer, shoulder-punching and laughing. Personnel had been taken on. Two women and a man, all busy and smiling, like counter staff at McDonald's. Being employees and not family – Benson thought – they'd been given different kit: navy blue overalls. The whole team looked classy and modern and prosperous.

Working hard beneath the HGT Ltd logo suspended from the ceiling.

'What the hell?' repeated Benson, whispering this time.

Another large sign, covered in glossy blobs and spatter, hung above the door to Hudson's former office:

LONDON CRIME TOURS (VISIT 7)
See the room where Naylor hard man
Billy Hudson bled to death.
LCT passholders: Free
Adults: £5
Children: £2

Benson gave a wolf-whistle.

'Things are looking good, Jack.'

That remark rather killed off the fun, at least for the two Kilgours. Jack waddled over, while Greg, in sympathetic motion, retreated backwards, stumbling into a new tyre lying on the ground. Back on his feet, he nodded a hello, and then, businesslike, he went through a doorway, presumably on his way to warn Pete.

'I never thought you'd be into murder tourism, Jack. Are you on TripAdvisor?'

'Not yet. We've only just started. But we're hopeful. Blimey, is that an old Mini Cooper over there?'

'It is.'

'Let me change the tyres. For free. We do brakes now. I'll take a look. Personally. If they're spongy it's—'

'Another time. We were wondering if we might borrow one of your tools.'

'A spanner?'

'No, Jack, a spade.'

'A spade?'

'Yes. Where's Pete?'

Jack patted his pockets, looking for his inhaler, sweat returning to his brow like in the old days, when Billy Hudson had made unreasonable demands. He began to wheeze. It was Pavlov's dog all over again.

'He's not in today. He's . . .'

'Don't tell me. He's gone back to Scotland?'

'You make it sound odd, Mr Benson. But there's a lot to see in Scotland. Have you never been to Windermere?'

'Windermere's in England, Jack.'

Benson couldn't be bothered to thrash out the truth. To hear him say that Pete had pumped out the story for a hefty wedge. Which is how they'd managed to give HGT Ltd a makeover. Benson already had a good idea who'd paid up, and where they'd got the money from. Leaving Jack damp and panting, he went back outside sure that Pete was behind a toilet door, not daring to breathe.

'The bastard's alive,' muttered Benson, drawing in the cool morning air.

And then he recalled the glint of humour and intelligence in Billy's eyes, caught in the photograph obtained by the police and used in the trial to give the jury some idea of the man who'd been murdered and whose body had never been found.

'They probably planned a quieter exit,' he said. 'A few months after the trial had ended. Instead, they were forced to bolt before the verdict.'

'Because the trial didn't go according to plan,' said Tess. 'Because you'd found out about Ekene.'

Benson dropped into the passenger seat. He couldn't help but admire the sheer breadth and scope of the scam. Its audacity. But he was disturbed, too. Hudson hadn't only escaped the Naylors. He'd escaped the claims of the court. He'd avoided the years in prison that were now being dished out to his former comrades.

'What do we do now?' said Tess.

Benson clipped on his seatbelt.

'We find them.'

'But they've vanished, Will. How can we possibly work out where they've gone?'

'That's easy, Tess. We just ask a travel agent.'

58

Oyster Travel Associates was perhaps the smallest business premises Tess had ever entered. To create a sense of space, large posters of distant lands covered the walls. There were glorious mountains and rich vines to the left and tropical islands and azure oceans to the right and straight ahead broad rivers and golden plains, and a door leading to an uncomfortably voluble toilet. A woman in her late teens, early twenties, stepped out to the sound of water rushing to fill up the cistern. In high heels and a tight yellow dress, she made her way towards a desk as if she was on stilts for the first time.

'Good morning,' she sang, red and smiling. 'Thinking of a weekend break?'

'Now there's a good idea,' said Benson.

'Well, I'm Sam. And the first thing we always say at Oyster is be careful with private homes advertised as holiday lets. Yes, they're convenient, but—'

'They sometimes get used in county lines operations.'

'That's not what I was going to say. What are "county lines" anyway? We don't offer them.'

'It's a way of distributing drugs, Sam. Using children. Not a nice thing to do.'

Benson walked over to the only other desk in the room.

Leaning over a closed pad and neatly arranged pens and a sleeping desktop computer, he said:

'We'd like to speak to Lisa.'

Sam swallowed uncertainly, gawking at Benson and then at Tess. The cistern, filled now, went abruptly silent.

'She's not here. She's taking a break. She takes lots of breaks, actually. Honest.'

'I see.'

Benson went to the door and with a flick of his wrist switched the sign from OPEN to CLOSED.

'You're not going to hurt me, are you?'

'Do we look like the sort of people who hurt travel agents?'

'It's not that, it's just . . . well, Ms Hudson's got a bit of a complicated family background, if you see what I mean.'

'Oh we do. We do.'

'And a few people have been . . . sort of killed and that, and Lisa, Ms Hudson, even got worried for herself at one point – that's how she ended up with me, because other people are too frightened to work here – but you need to know I just take bookings and warn people off the easy options. I don't know nothing.'

'Don't worry, Sam. All we're after is what you do know.'

Tess sat at Lisa's computer and tapped the keyboard. The screen lit up. The password box and a blinking cursor appeared against an image of a huge open oyster shell, holding the world as its pearl.

'We're officers of the court, Sam,' she said. 'We need to speak to Lisa. We've a message for her. A message that will make her family situation far less complicated. Are you going to help us deliver it?'

Sam didn't know what to do. She was probably remembering some film scene where well-dressed strangers come looking for information. They seem to be really kind but in fact they're really violent. They say they're one thing but they're another. Tess said:

'What's the password, Sam? That's all we want to know.'

Sam bit a lip, glancing at Tess's handbag, her eyes saying, 'Anything could be in there. Absolutely anything.'

'Capital O, small b, small i, then two, zero, one, seven in numbers.'

Tess gave a sigh.

'Damn, I should have known.'

She tapped in Obi2017 and, with a flicker, she was into Lisa's private world. Her diary. Her booking history. Her emails. After half an hour's browsing and note-taking, and a few quick searches on Google, Tess had found out all they needed to know.

'Say nothing, Sam,' Benson said at the door. 'Especially not to Lisa. Her life depends on it.'

Tess brought Benson to a bench in Ruskin Park, five minutes from Oyster Travel Associates and in the shadow of King's College Hospital, where Neil Ashford did his best to help save lives. Neil Ashford, who loved Lisa so much he'd risked his career to help save her son. In a fancy, she imagined them meeting here for lunch, to sit on this bench, discussing the finer points of arterial blood flow, diagnostic patterning and the removal and storage of body samples. For such a daring and intricate plan, the elements of the logistics had been very easy to find. It couldn't have been otherwise. Like Benson had said on the way to Camberwell, a man can vanish under one name, but if he wants to travel he'll need another.

'I'll leave out the dates,' said Tess. 'Lisa and Neil go to Rotterdam from Thursday to Sunday. They cross over at half-eight in the evening on a ferry from Hull, having exchanged the blood and stuff for the suitcase. They stay at the Westvoorne Hotel. Oyster Travel Associates only sold one other ticket to Rotterdam for that weekend. And it's one-way. To a foot passenger leaving from Hull on Saturday morning.'

'The day after Hudson was "murdered".'

'Yes. Oddly enough, he also stays at the Westvoorne Hotel. Hudson has become Michael Washburn. I imagine he got totally plastered that night, along with his mother and Neil. The next day, Lisa and Neil head back to London and Washburn takes a train north to Groningen. Then all they had to do was to hang on in there and hope the police took the bait. Which they did.'

'Meanwhile, Washburn gets on with his life.'

'Preparing for the arrival of the others . . . which they do eight months later, just before the trial ended.'

'Exactly. Pushed by you. And it's the same story. Oyster Travel Associates only sold four tickets to Groningen for that time, and all to the same family. They went by rail from St Pancras. Three adults and a child. One-way. Nina has become Kesandu Asinobi. I forget the other names. That's what Lisa was handing over in the Be All and End All, Will. New IDs. Birth certificates and passports. Obtained by Hudson before he disappeared. For Nina, Obi, Ekene and Azuka. All they required for a new life. What an irony. It's exactly what Buster would have wanted.'

'Did they book any accommodation?'

'No.'

'Have they gone to Nigeria?

'No. Lisa would have bought the tickets and she hasn't done.'

'Then they're still in Groningen.'

'Where Lisa visits frequently. She's there now. They can't keep Grandma away.'

'Have you got a home address?'

'No. But if you Google "Kesandu Asinobi hair salon Groningen" guess what comes up?'

'Snip-Snap?'

'Almost. She went for "Knip-Knap". Hasn't been open long, but she's got her own place in Oosterpoort, not far from the Verbindingskanaal. It's a great area, I understand, for students and young couples. There are lots of old buildings to see. Fishermen's houses too.'

'Miss de Vere . . . you're brilliant.'

'I am. You're lucky to know me. But there are a couple of wrinkles I can't work out. First, what are we doing, Will? I've no message. That was all bollocks. What's the point of the chase?'

'We misled a court. They need to know that we know.'

'Okay, agreed. I'm on board. The other wrinkle: Lisa went to Groningen during the trial. On her own. By car. A quick trip. Eight hours there and eight hours back. I'm wondering why.'

'Oh, that's easy.'

'Are you going to tell me?'

'Having worked everything out so far, I'm going to leave you to finish the job. Are you free tomorrow?'

'I can arrange it.'

'Fancy a trip to Groningen? I'm interested in those fishermen's houses.'

59

Getting there was going to be a total nightmare. No doubt that was partly why Hudson had chosen the place. There were no direct flights. The best route was by train from London to Rotterdam and then another train to Groningen. The route taken by Nina et al. Which, added together, would take all bloody day. Assuming they found Hudson the next morning, they'd still have to remain in Groningen. And that meant two nights in a hotel. At least.

Such was Benson's heated complaint to Tess.

In fact, he was thrilled. That was three days with Tess. Most of it in a confined space.

But he was soon disappointed. Rather than settle into an increasingly intimate discussion – very gently, very naturally – Tess gave her attention to a heap of files. Even before the train pulled out of St Pancras she was murmuring into a Dictaphone. Of course, he wasn't entirely surprised. He'd just hoped that his expectations would be quickly defeated. Ultimately, they were crushed. Tess worked methodically, glancing up to smile between tasks, closing one file and opening another. So Benson's thoughts settled on the man they intended to confront.

In preparing Karmen's defence, Benson had researched as minutely as possible the life of William Hudson. By the time he'd turned up in court, he felt like he'd met him once, and run off. He'd read the report produced by the Tuesday Club. He'd scoured newspaper reports. He'd spoken to a retired police officer he trusted. Unknown to everyone, he'd spoken to Lewis Derby, the person who'd schooled Hudson, aged eleven, in working for the Naylors. Benson had met him in a pub where, drunk on handouts, Derby had slurred his tales like a broken tourist attraction. Asked to describe Hudson, Derby had said, 'There are cold villains, who feel nothin', nothin' at all, and just do the business. And then there's the likes of Hudson. A very, very angry man. Even as a kid. Very angry. Unstable. Look what he did to me, for Chrissake.' A judgement entirely consistent with Benson's previous research. There was no question about it. William Hudson had been a very dangerous man. The same could be said for Michael Washburn. And he was living in Groningen, and no one realised it.

Which was why Benson wasn't entirely happy with simply confronting Hudson. With knowledge came responsibility. It was a question he wanted to explore with Tess, only she was otherwise engaged. It was only when they met to eat later that evening, in the hotel dining room, that Benson felt he could approach the question.

'Tomorrow, Hudson and the Osabedes will know we share their secret. What happens then?'

Tess pushed her food around, thinking.

'We go home and leave them to it.'

'Go home? Don't we have a responsibility to his victims and his neighbours?'

'He could have stayed with the Naylors, but he didn't. To do what he did requires more than ingenuity. Maybe he's changed. And if he has, what's the point of blowing things apart?'

Tess thought some more and wiped her mouth with a starched napkin.

'It doesn't happen often, Will . . . but sometimes it might be better for everyone if we turn a blind eye.'

That, thought Benson, is the Farsely doctrine that Tess had resisted. Hearing it from her mouth surprised him.

'I can't follow you on this one, Tess. Letting the Kilgours go is one thing; staying silent because Hudson turned from a frog into a prince is another.'

'Whatever happened to the More than One Chance Fund?'

'Foundation, Tess.'

'Foundation, then. Look, Will, I can't follow you either. I'll come along, just to see him sweat, and then it's over to you. But you better call the police now, so he can't—'

'No. First I need to be sure he's alive. Then I'll give him a second chance.'

'Which is?'

'To turn himself in. That's what's on offer, Tess. Not a free pass. If he accepts, I'll give him a bottle of champagne.'

'And if he refuses?'

'Then I'll call Panjabi.'

'I can't quite see the choice.'

'It's between accepting responsibility for what he's done and leaving the police to prove it. Either way he faces a court.'

'Okay, sounds straightforward enough. What's the plan?'

The plan was straightforward enough, too. And it unfolded the next day without a hitch. Except they hired a car for no good purpose, because it transpired Nina lived within walking distance of where she worked. Having purchased a bottle of champagne, Benson and Tess stationed themselves in a café down the street from Knip-Knap. They watched Nina arrive on foot to open her business. They then went for a drive – they had to do something with the car – visiting those fishing houses. *Schipperswoning*, they were called. Late afternoon, they returned to the café and waited again. Towards 6 p.m., high on caffeine and tension, they saw Nina close the salon and set off, on foot once more, presumably for home. At a discreet distance, they followed her, turning this way and that until she reached a row of shops. Passing through a gap in the buildings, they came to a narrow tree-lined lane running directly parallel to the Verbindingskanaal. To their left were old houses leaning into each other. To their right the glittering water, and a thread of colourful barges moored beneath the overhang of branches, weighted with spring. Nina came to a small bay that had perhaps once been a lock, and a set of steps descending to a landing stage. Beside the landing stage was a boat. An old thing, in blue and white, with brass windows and gleaming varnished wood and heavy black mooring ropes, and laundered bedsheets flapping in the breeze.

Benson felt he'd arrived at Seymour Basin. Taken aback – he'd imagined an ordinary house – he watched Nina negotiate the steps and slip out of view.

They gave her fifteen minutes to get her coat off, pour herself a drink and find out how Obi had fared at nursery. Then Benson went on board, followed by Tess.

60

There were three armchairs neatly positioned at the rear of the boat. Seated in the middle, regally, was Azuka. To his right was Nina, open-mouthed. To his left, clutching a sleeping Obi, was Billy Hudson. But Hudson wasn't like the man in the photograph. He'd lost weight. He'd grown a beard and his head was shaved. He looked scared. Benson heard himself say:

'Where's Ekene?'

'You mean Chinaka,' said Nina. 'He moved.'

'Why?'

'He got a job with Philips.'

'Great.'

'Yes, it is. It's a good job, with a future. Why the champagne?'

Benson, unsettled, looked at the bottle as if it were a high-end cosh.

'It's for you. Maybe.'

'You're joking.'

'I'm not. Where's Lisa?'

'I'm here.'

Lisa, wearing an apron, came into the room and went to Billy's side, remaining standing, a hand on his chair. She was staring at Benson and Tess, harder, insofar as that was possible, than anyone else. In a sudden flash of imagination, Benson saw himself as Lewis Derby, the day he'd come to take Billy out for a drink on his eighteenth birthday; the day Lisa had told her son to never come home, not until he'd finished with the Naylors. She'd watched him go as if he was setting off

on a long voyage. It had been a crucifying moment; a moment
that turned into an eleven-year separation. Lisa had refused
to soften. She'd drawn a line in the sand. And in the end Billy
had somehow made it home, through quite a storm. He was
there, at her side. Only he wasn't. The more Benson looked,
the more he couldn't make a connection between the bearded
figure and the man in the photo.

'Who is this?' said Azuka, smiling; though he wasn't Azuka
now. But it had been Azuka who'd once run his gnarled fingers
over Hudson's face and found a trace of kindness. 'A friend
of the family?'

'No,' said Lisa. 'It's a man who's come to take Michael
away.'

They actually use the new names, thought Benson,
nonplussed. This is no game. They actually live out this home-
made reinvention. It would have been bizarre if there wasn't
something alarmingly real about the chemistry between them.

'Why?' said Azuka, or whoever he was now. 'What has
Michael done?'

'Nothing, Dad. Absolutely nothing.'

They were all waiting for Benson, or Tess, to say something.
But Benson couldn't find the words. Everything he'd planned
to say had evaporated. He couldn't even remember what he'd
said to Tess the night before. And Tess was leaving Benson
to take the initiative. After all, she was only for provoking a
sweat and then heading home.

'I'll come with you,' said Billy, or was it Michael? 'I get
why you're here.'

He placed Obi tenderly in Azuka's arms and came towards
Benson, and Benson looked over Michael's shoulder and saw
Lisa aged thirty-five, appalled, when Billy had walked towards
Lewis Derby.

'Just hear me out first, will you?'

61

They sat on deck on white plastic chairs among plastic plant pots, screened from the lane above by a couple of white bed sheets that had been hung out to dry on the washing line. They flapped gently with each breath of wind. The sun had begun to fall.

'The same day that Karmen took over, she called the Ronsons. I was there. She arranged a meet.'

There was something about the way Hudson sat forward, arms resting on his thighs, that banished Washburn to the sitting room.

'She knew she was at risk,' he said. 'She didn't trust Ryan. She knew her father was out of the game. And she knew that if ever the Ronsons wanted to hit back, for what Tony had done, now was the time. She wasn't just going to apologise. She was going to do something her father would never have done. Build a partnership across the UK, starting with a cut of the northern gig. Making it a joint venture. The first of many. She'd already made connections in Holland, Portugal, Spain, Italy. She had a business model . . . That's when I decided to call Oakhurst. And I told him that if he helped me, I'd deliver not just the northern business but the two families. The Naylors for sure and maybe the Ronsons. But it would have to be on my terms.'

Benson glanced at Tess.

'Your terms?'

'My terms. I wasn't interested in a deal. I didn't want immunity. I didn't want a new name and a crap house in South Shields. They'd get me. Somehow or other. The Naylors or the Naylors' partners. Finding me and Nina and Obi would be easy. Even if we'd gone to New Zealand or Australia. And what about Azuka? And Ekene? You can't leave anyone behind, because they all become vulnerable. So I said no. Forget established policy. Forget witness protection. Forget anything official. If you want my help, it's on my terms. I'll give you more than you could possibly want, but I need to die. They need to think I'm dead. And if my plan worked . . . these people would end up killing each other. Everyone needed to be dead. It's the only way to bring what they're doing to an end. Prison doesn't work.'

'Oakhurst knows you're alive?' asked Benson.

Hudson nodded.

'He's the only one. Apart from you two . . . and whoever you've told.'

'We've told no one.'

'Oakhurst?' stressed Benson, astonished.

'Yeah. Don't ask him. Just trust me. Unless you're going to blow the whistle.'

Benson now understood the dilemma facing the Deputy Assistant Commissioner when he'd taken that call routed through Crimestoppers. He'd probably been eating a bacon sandwich while dealing with some tedious HR problems. And then, still chewing, he'd picked up the receiver, only to be offered the kind of spectacular result he'd worked for night and day all his professional life and which, in quiet moments in the evening, he knew he'd never achieve; quiet moments in which he'd told himself all he could do was keep plugging away, year on year, taking out people on the edges, hoping, one day, to lift someone from the inner circle. And then, with a measure of pride, draw his pension. But now this caller from within was offering him the works, and more. But at a price. Oakhurst would have to put his uniform to one side. He'd have to break the law himself. His profile would support his co-conspirators in breaking the law. And then he'd have to mislead a jury. That had been quite a predicament.

'All I needed was ID that could never be cracked open,' said

Hudson. 'I couldn't trust the people used by the Naylors. Couldn't trust anyone out there, because everyone can be bought.'

'Except a decent police officer,' added Benson.

'Yeah. Someone who cared about what I wanted to do as much as me. Someone prepared to match me, risk for risk.'

'That's why you called a year in advance, to give him time to work out how to source what you needed?'

'Yeah. He told me it hadn't been easy.'

Benson could imagine the rest. Oakhurst couldn't have used the usual channels. He'd have had to call in a few favours, probably from a department without a connection to law enforcement. Benson wasn't especially interested. The fact is, Oakhurst had delivered. He'd produced the down payment, as it were, with the balance falling due in the trial, when he'd paid up in full . . . with Benson as the unwitting cashier. And now the Naylors were finished and the Ronsons were weakened, maybe enough to fall apart.

'What made you turn, Mr Hudson?' said Tess. 'Meeting Nina? Meeting Azuka? Finding out you were about to become a father?'

'No. I'd already decided I wanted out.'

'Why?'

Hudson, still leaning forward, averted his gaze.

'It was after Karmen came home and told Tony what she'd been up to. I was made Karmen's representative. And I'd go up there, to Newcastle or Manchester or Leeds, and I'd meet these guys, all like Bucklow, who were working these kids . . . we'd always used kids, as runners or watchers, but this was different, at least I thought it was different. It wasn't just one or two, it was hundreds . . . and they were all taking the risks and getting rapped and Bucklow just laughed and found some more, and I thought there's no future in this, not for them, not for us, they didn't have a chance, they weren't reliable, they needed help, and then I thought, the kids we used didn't have a chance either, and . . . and . . .'

'You'd never had a chance?' said Tess.

Hudson's foot was tapping the deck as if it was a hammer and he was still looking to one side.

'I don't want no pity. I did what I did.'

'From the age of eleven.'

'Yeah.'

'We did our research on you, Mr Hudson. Everyone says you were a very angry—'

'And I don't want no therapy neither, right? I killed off Billy. And I killed off the people who took him. Okay? I set one onto the other and now they're dead. If you want to bring me back, get on with it. I'm not running nowhere. There's nowhere I can go. My only chance for something different is here, as Michael Washburn.'

And it was at that point, thought Benson, picturing Hudson back in London, confused by disgust, too involved in wrongdoing to see beyond the emotion, which would die, as feelings do, or be smothered by a few pints in the Four Ravens – and it was at that point Hudson had looked out of a car window and seen Nina Osabede surrounded by a group of youths. He'd gone to bed that night with the unforgettable memory of an old man running his fingers over every scar on his face.

Benson felt Tess lightly touch his arm.

Without a word they stood up and made their way off the boat, onto the landing stage and back up the steps to the tree-lined lane. The evening sun lit the tight buds of folded leaves with that strangely bright light that only comes at the end of the day. Long shadows stretched behind them and long shadows came towards them and they were compelled to shade their eyes. Turning into a darkening street, Benson lowered his hands and realised they were empty. He'd left the champagne behind, on the table in front of Michael Washburn.

62

'What are you going to do, Will?' said Tess that evening, after Benson had ordered another bottle of wine. A rather cheeky Saint-Estèphe. 'Make the call or let them go?'

She was expecting him, in the first instance, to outline the consequences of a call to Panjabi. Inevitably, all those involved in the conspiracy would be arrested: Hudson, Lisa, Neil Ashford, Nina, Ekene, Oakhurst and even – depending on what he knew – Azuka. And to cap it all, Obi would go into care. The Kilgours would be arrested, for taking a million quid's worth of drugs money. (Tess had eventually worked that one out. Once Benson had learned about Ekene's altercation with Hudson, he was on to the Osabedes. He could easily recall Greg or subpoena Pete. He could easily turn his attention to the missing body – always the weakest part of the entire plan. So Lisa had driven to Groningen and brought back the price of a good story, which good old Pete had rehearsed to perfection, probably after watching *Goodfellas* for days on end.) What else might influence Benson's thinking? Well, she thought, it had to be the epic nature of Hudson's project. For want of a better expression, its moral vision. He'd prevented a link-up between the Naylors and the Ronsons. He'd stopped them going international. There was a bid for atonement in all that. Reasons to give a man a second chance.

'What am I going to do?' he repeated. 'I'm going to prevaricate, dither, put off and quibble.'

'Let him go?'

'I didn't say that.'

'It amounts to the same thing.'

'It depends why I'm prevaricating, dithering, putting off and quibbling.'

'Well, why are you?'

'Not because of the fallout, bad though it would be. I've never represented anyone where the fallout for the family hasn't been catastrophic. If that was the test, most charges would have to be dropped as soon as the evidence has been collected.'

'So why the hedging, evading, fudging and stalling? Because you no longer think he's dangerous?'

'Not really, no, though I think that is true.'

'Why, then?'

'Because my own history crashed into me this evening. I walked onto a boat just like mine, and I'd seen a man just like me. I might have been innocent of any crime, while Hudson was guilty of many, but I'd become someone else, too. Who I'd once been had disappeared, just like him, and there, right in front of me, was this . . . other man. I didn't recognise him. I couldn't tie him to the criminal in the photograph or the thug described by Lewis Derby. It was as though whatever had happened to me, after eleven years inside, had already happened to him. He'd been to hell and back. And he was in exactly the place I'd once been – beginning all over again.'

'And?'

'I thought of a lad I'd known called Doyle. A man now. With a B tattooed on each buttock. Bob – his sphincter doubled for an O, and—'

'Are you serious?'

'Okay, forget Doyle. But it's linked. He did something when he was young that was plain crazy. So he went to prison. But then he changed. Only he's still banged up. So the man serving the sentence isn't the lad who committed the crime. He shouldn't be there . . . not any more.'

'And so?'

'I looked at Washburn and his family, and I thought of me and Doyle and so many others, the deserving and the undeserving, all of them with devastated relationships, and . . . I just couldn't be the one who took him away. I still can't, even if I should. Especially if he's no longer the brute who terrorised south London.'

Tess filled Benson's glass right up to the rim.

'Sounds to me like a case for the More than One Chance Fund.'

'Foundation, Tess. It was going to be a foundation. Not a fund and not a trust. A foundation.'

Tess went to bed exhausted. She'd had no proper rest since she'd stayed up all night, driven to make sense of the woman in the sunglasses. On the train to Groningen, she'd done her best to work, but most of it would probably have to be redone. Not because she'd been tired and had probably made mistakes but because she'd been acutely aware of Benson's presence on the other side of the table. His sheer physicality. The energy he put into anguish. His smell. She'd felt the same disorientating awareness visiting the *schipperswoning*. And while sitting in the café, spying on Nina. In every exchange, joining every pause between every word, was the purr of this vibrant engine, originating from his whole body, from his tousled hair to his trimmed fingernails. It tuned his voice and drove his every movement, however slight. She'd felt it humming throughout dinner as he frowned, grappling with his inclination to show mercy. She'd felt it when he'd said goodnight, only half an hour ago.

While she was tired, she couldn't sleep. If Benson had confronted something of his own story, so had Tess. She lay in the absolute darkness thinking of her own escape from the claims of justice. The victims left behind. And the need to create something new in order to survive. But she'd failed there. Something had died, for sure. But unlike Hudson she couldn't become someone else, like an actor in a play. And unlike Benson she'd never been—

The door to her room opened and closed, the connecting door between her room and Benson's. She sat upright, wide awake, no longer tired. That generator of non-stop existential distress was over there, somewhere in the darkness.

63

Benson stood in the dark as if he was on the edge of an abyss. He couldn't see a thing. There wasn't the barest contour of a single object. The curtains, like those in his own room, were ridiculously heavy and they'd blocked out any light from the streetlamps below. Having opened the door, he wanted to turn around and head back to the other darkness, but he couldn't. He couldn't resist the weight that was in him, a weight that was moving forward like a train carrying all his unhappiness and hope, a sleeper that had lurched out of the Old Bailey on the day of his conviction. Where it would take him, he'd never known, but the thing had finally run out of fuel and was now slowly coming to halt. His chest grew tight. He knew she was over there, sitting up, staring, unseeing.

'I haven't finished what I was saying, Tess. About the humming and hawing.'

His voice was dry with thirst and panic.

'When I walked onto Hudson's boat I remembered when I first walked onto mine. I looked at the Aga and the brass windows and beams, and the ropes outside, keeping me moored, so I couldn't float off. I looked at my boxes full of books. And my pictures leaning on the sofa. And I thought this is it. My new life begins. I put the books on the shelves and I put the pictures on the walls and then I wondered what now? Day after day, I moved things around. And then moved them back again. I was trying to get things just right.

But something didn't quite work. And I realised it would never quite work. How could it? I was a convicted murderer. And then you walked on board, someone I'd last seen when I'd been sentenced.'

Benson felt the abyss shift. It grew deeper and longer and wider. But there was no sound. It was astonishing. This upheaval was taking place in utter silence.

'I didn't want you to leave, Tess,' he said. 'I've never wanted you to leave. And every time you went away, I was left adrift and lost and lonely.'

Do I tell her, thought Benson. Do I tell her that her belief in me kept me sane? Even though I never heard from her, year after year? Do I tell her that nothing in my world matters except for her? Do I tell her that I don't want a life of constantly rearranging furniture? Do I tell her that I don't care about whatever happened at Hollingtons? Or whatever happened with the Merrigan family? How do I express all that, simply, without having to write a book longer than *War and Peace*? What do I say?

'Tess, I love you,' he said. 'I've always loved you. I'll always love you.'

Benson thought of all the chip-nets hung between all the landings in all the prisons he'd known. They'd all been cut away. There was nothing to break his fall. Nothing to save him. But he couldn't stop himself. The weight, the awful weight he'd been carrying for so long, was still on the move. He was walking in the dark, inching towards the chasm, arms extended.

'Tess, please say something. Don't leave me like this.'

He reached the edge of the bed and then, out there in the blackness, his hands found two others. Tess had been reaching out, too. For a long moment their fingers were locked, at arm's length. Then he let go and his heart stopped, because she let him go; she didn't resist, but her arms were still there, extended, and his hands were moving along her wrists, onto her elbow, up to her shoulders, along her neck and into her soft, short hair. His heart began to pump blood again, and she rose up, supernaturally warm, and his past and present came to a shuddering halt.

'Tess, please speak. I'm one of those men who needs to hear words.'

Benson clung to her, losing any sense of where he ended and where Tess began, the two of them transformed into this single emanation of otherworldly heat. Her voice was very quiet and trembling; he could feel a beat against his chest:

'I want no dodging, eluding, skirting and shirking. Does that suffice?'

'Perfectly.'

'Not from me and not from you.'

'Agreed. Do we have a formal understanding? I'm prepared to put the terms into writing.'

'Will?'

'Yes?'

'Stop talking.'

64

Before going to Groningen, Tess had planned to visit Abasiama on her return. Their conversation had felt incomplete. That's why she'd gone back for a second round. And it was the same urge to pursue unfinished business that had prompted her to consider another appointment. But when she got back to London she abandoned the idea. Abasiama's consulting room seemed a far-off place, and the strangely masochistic impulse to continue with a process that only wounded her had disappeared. She was simply happy in the moment.

Benson made her laugh. He wasn't even trying. Constantly serious, he could find the dark cloud to every silver lining. And when he got going, he really got going. Particularly first thing in the morning. If Tess was to comment on the flap of a butterfly's wing on *The Wooden Doll,* unless restrained Benson's mind followed the potential consequences through to a tornado in Haiti. He was the only person she'd ever met who read Schopenhauer for fun. In fact, he was the only person she'd ever met who read Schopenhauer at all. Who else could find light in German pessimism? What Benson didn't seem to realise was that for all his problems, resulting from his incarceration, his outlook on life was obscurely positive. The last word always went to the breeze that followed the storm.

Or maybe he was simply happy, too.

Tess told Sally about the development. She'd expected the elation that can only come from a close friend. And anyone watching Sally would say that was exactly what happened. She said everything she was expected to say. But Tess detected the slightest of hesitations.

'I'm thrilled for you, Tess,' she said, rubbing her hands.

And then she'd run to check the pasta.

As a couple they kept their separate lives, Tess at Ennismore Gardens Mews and Benson on his boat, each with their own commitments and interests. A routine began to take shape, of random meetings during the week and a fixture every Friday night, running, often, into the weekend. And when they weren't together, they exchanged WhatsApp messages like teenagers.

The spring sunshine blinded Tess. It bounced off a round brass window making her shift position. She edged along the into the shade. Legs astride, Benson was standing in front of the Aga like a captain at the wheel. He'd been talking to

Traddles about how to cook a halibut, but had suddenly begun addressing Tess:

'Why don't you leave C and D, Tess? We could set up De Vere and Benson. Or Benson and de Vere. Or Bevere's. I quite like that . . . Anyway, you'd handle the investigating and I'd do the court stuff. It's effectively what we do already. The only difference is that you'd take no other cases. We'd be working together and—'

While Benson had been talking to Traddles, Tess had been scrolling through her homepage, thumbing her way down the various articles suggested, it seemed, by an algorithm that tracked her myriad interests. An algorithm with a very long memory. Because one of the articles that had been proposed came from the *Belfast Telegraph*. The headline seized her attention like the shout of her name from a stranger in a crowd:

Victims campaigner Joe Merrigan dies aged 90

Tess acted before she could make the decision. She tapped the title. The article was up and she was reading it hungrily.

His heart has finally stopped. Mr Merrigan, 90, whose 19-year-old son Robert died in a hail of gunfire in November 1972, was a tireless campaigner for justice. His determination to—

'We'd be offering a unique service,' said Benson, tapping a wooden spoon on the rim of the pan. 'We could do what the hell we liked, too. Taking on people who can't get legal aid. People who—'

Tess stared ahead at the bright shapes thrown on the wall. Only two years ago Joe had leaned over her desk with his nails practically digging into the wood. Beside him, sitting so far back in his chair it seemed he didn't want to be in the room, was his son Andrew. And beside Andrew sat his own son, Dominic. Dominic . . . he'd watched Tess like her father had watched redwings, with an intensity impossible to describe. Joe had seen the archive handed over to the HET.

'Did Mr Lomax say anything, Miss de Vere? Can you give me any hope? Anything at all?'

And Tess had remembered the look on Lomax's face when she'd told him her surname. He'd recognised it. And in recognising it, he'd abandoned a decision ground out by thirty years of hard-edged remorse; he'd decided to forgo justice for some at the expense of compassion for one, someone he'd never met before. Why? Because Tess seemed to be a nice girl. Because Lomax thought she and Peter Farsely had been an item. Because he'd thought, oh Christ, let her go. Why should she suffer? Why should her life be wrecked? She obviously has no idea what we did back then.

Any more than Obi would ever know what his father had done . . . back then.

'There might be issues with getting a contract to provide legal aid services,' said Benson. 'But so what? The whole system is wrecked anyway. Now, if we—'

And Tess had looked Joe in the eye and told him straight, without a quiver or a quibble, that she knew absolutely nothing that might bring them some peace of mind. Even as she was speaking, using her best, carefully articulated legal voice, Dominic had been drilling into her temple, silent and irrationally determined, because he couldn't know anything – there was nothing to know – but he was watching her, not out of fascination, like her father watched birds, but like Benson with a witness, when he knew he'd found another damned liar.

'Tess? What do you think?'

Benson was standing in front of her, wooden spoon in hand, made ridiculous by a flowery apron. Smoke seemed to rise from the sink behind him.

'You're on your bloody phone, aren't you? You haven't listened to a word I've been saying.'

Tess shifted out of the shadow and the light hit her again.

'I know it's a Saturday, and I know we had plans, but I really should work . . . right into tomorrow.'

'Work?'

'Yes. You'll find out. It's what Archie calls a humdinger.'

What would happen to the halibut? Benson, in his graciousness, joked about a change in dining companion. Traddles, he observed, was partial to righteye flounders. Did you know, he said, that most species lie on the ocean bed on their left side, with both eyes on their right. They were blind to a predator coming from leftfield, and—

Tess threw her arms around him, saying 'I love you, I love you, I love you.' And Benson said he'd buy halibut every week. Maybe every day. What did she think of halibut for breakfast? And lunch? And dinner? And . . . she ran off, stumbling onto the landing stage and heading through the trees, up the incline towards the gate in the iron railings that Benson never locked because he was all screwed up. He couldn't lock a single door. The doors on the boat were always open. He was always exposed. He was completely vulnerable to all manner of attack and intrusion. He just didn't care.

She reached Seymour Place and, head thrown back, walked to her Mini, parked in exactly the same spot she'd found when she'd come looking for Benson all those years ago. She leaned on the brilliant cherry red bodywork, lined with chrome, and she sobbed, with tears rising from a place in her soul she didn't even know existed, a dark place of sand and wreckage, accumulated and then forgotten about.

And then she went to work. She'd told the truth. A big case was in the pipeline.

The plans to which Tess had referred involved going to Congreve's in the morning, Ennismore Gardens Mews in the afternoon and Sally's in the evening. The middle component was postponed to another day, to be coupled with a visit to Molly's. Why the plans? Marie-Edith Cameron, wife of the professor, had rung up Congreve's not seeking legal help but to enquire if there were any furnishings or objects they'd didn't use any more. Anything they could sell to support the school project in Senegal. As it happened, after Benson had taken over Congreve's, everything connected with the day-to-day running of a fishmonger's had been stored in the basement and the attic. More than that, over time, the Congreve family had used both places to dump all manner of things they couldn't bring themselves to throw away. Benson had taken advantage of the space, too. A similar kind of stockpiling had taken place in the homes of Tess, Sally and Molly. So arrangements had been made.

Benson had never witnessed such industry.

The whole lot, every knife, lamp, drill bit, postcard, extension lead, suit, skirt, shoe, table, chair, electric razor, book, garden fork, necklace, cup, not to mention the weighing scales and cash till purchased by Archie's grandfather – whatever could be accumulated by a business and a family over the years – was carefully brought downstairs, or upstairs, and placed in the back of a van borrowed from someone who'd been encouraged to join the great push. After reconvening at Sally's a few hours later, the same process occurred. Whatever could be recycled was taken. Afterwards, windows were thrown open, upstairs and downstairs.

'Education is so important,' said Marie-Edith. 'I can guarantee, everything will be turned into books, pens, paper and computers. Teachers. A schoolroom. A better future.'

After an *au revoir*, husband and wife drove off, leaving Benson and Sally strangely humbled. They watched the van turn the corner, heading towards Turnham Green. There'd been no admonishment or preaching. Just lifting and carrying.

'My mind turns to other stuff that needs clearing out,' said Sally, closing the cellar door. 'I've done my homework.'

Sally was referring to their investigation into Tess. When they'd left the Lomax home in Fulham, they'd agreed a division of labour. Benson was to look into the de Vere family. Sally was to investigate the Merrigans. A glass of wine in hand, they went outside to her small garden overlooking the river.

'Dominic Merrigan is the son of Andrew,' said Sally.

Benson gazed upon the grey flats. The tide was out and the silt and debris were in view. A can, a few smoothed bricks, a plastic bottle, a length of rusted pipe.

'And Andrew's brother, Robert, was shot dead in 1972 coming out of a fish and chip shop. It was a drive-by shooting. The thinking at the time was that Robert had been targeted because it was believed he was in the IRA, something his family have always denied, and which has been confirmed by the IRA itself. Now—'

'Sally, stop.'

'You mean shut up?'

'Not quite, but I can't do this. Maybe I should, but I can't. Not since Tess and I became . . . a thing.'

'A *thing*?'

She'd spoken like Lady Bracknell on hearing the infant Jack Worthing had been found in a handbag. The aristocratic tone didn't quite match her appearance. Sally was wearing a blue-striped Breton top and dark blue trousers, made formal by a pearl necklace and matching earrings. Even though they'd been grubbing around in a vaulted room more like a crypt, Benson sensed she'd dressed up. She'd looked forward to this meeting. She was bristling with energy.

'I see.'

She flicked her hair to one side.

'So what?'

It was a bloody good question.

'Are you telling me you're not interested in the Merrigan family?' she said. 'You don't want to know what happened to them? The campaign they've led? The dead ends they've faced? The lies and deceit they've had to battle against? The story of a family that is somehow linked to Tess? This doesn't concern you?'

Benson didn't respond, so Sally continued:

'So you know what happened in Strasbourg? And why she became homeless? And what happened when she met Dominic Merrigan, who won't be stopped? She's told you everything?'

Benson turned away from the shining mudflats.

'No, Sally, she hasn't. I still don't have any of the answers to any of the questions. We're in the same place. What I do know is this: I'd rather be with Tess and have unanswered questions than answer the questions without having Tess. I'm sorry.'

Sally pondered this, then she smiled with a certain sadness.

'I understand, Will. Totally. I've done it for years. It works, in a way.'

Benson wasn't in court on Monday morning, so he went to chambers intending to work on a slew of pending cases. A mixed bag of burglary, theft, fraud and violent disorder. Only he found himself reading *Benson's Guide to the Underworld*.

happy (adj) **1** feeling contentment (best forgotten about). **2** *colloq.* slightly drunk (all the happiness you're going to get. See **hooch**).

He'd written those definitions with bitterness. Twenty years ago. A part of him still wondered if they might be true. Happiness. For Schopenhauer it was simply a moment of relief between guaranteed disappointments. Because every fulfilled desire leads to new anxieties. Best forget it, then . . . but happiness had come upon Benson. It wasn't a feeling to ignore, or a memory to be suppressed or revived. It had risen with the sun in Groningen and it wouldn't go away. Even at night. His life had become non-stop daytime.

The point is, he thought, I don't want happiness, as such. I don't care if it disappears tomorrow. I just want Tess.

Sally's acquiescence had contained a rebuke. But she was yet to recognise the full implications of Benson and Tess becoming a *thing*: all the answers to all the questions would now come to Benson without him having to investigate anything. Insofar as the seeds of any disappointment were quietly germinating, if and when they opened, they'd share the consequences together. It was this realisation that had enabled him to pass through that connecting door and risk rejection. Happiness had been the furthest thing from his mind. He'd only known that if he could cross the abyss and reach Tess's side, then it didn't matter what might happen afterwards. He'd be there, with her.

'Rizla?'

'Yes, Archie.'

He stood filling the doorway with worn-out corduroy and Shetland wool. Molly was crouching to look through a gap.

'We've been thinking,' he said, holding out his healed thumb horizontally, like an emperor at the games. 'Why doesn't Tess join us here? Permanently. We'd make a hell of a team.'

'I have to say – Mr Congreve and Miss Robson – that is an irresistible submission. Mention it to her within seven days or face the wrath of the court.'

Archie gave a thumbs-up and Molly gave a hip, hip hooray and Archie called for silence.

'You'll be interested to know she's just instructed you in a humdinger. The Vauxhall Murder.'

He pointed a finger at Benson's duffel coat.

'I never thought I'd say this, Rizla. I'm happy for you. For once, everything's looking good. Real good. We're heading straight to the Chip-net. And I'm paying.'

Acknowledgements

I warmly thank: Clare Smith and Zoe Gullen at Little, Brown; Victoria Hobbs at A.M. Heath; Jo Millington, forensic scientist, at Millington Hingley; Mr Marcos Katchburian, Consultant in Trauma and Orthopaedics; Ursula Mackenzie, Françoise Koetschet, Sabine Guyard and, as always, Anne.

Any errors with respect to the law, criminal procedure, the prison system and forensic science are my responsibility.